Dirty Red

Also by Vickie M. Stringer

Imagine This
Let That Be the Reason

Dirty Red

A NOVEL

VICKIE M. STRINGER

ATRIA BOOKS

New York London Toronto Sydney

A Division of Simon & Schuster, Inc.
1230 Avenue of the Americas
New York, NY 10020

First Atria Books trade paperback edition July 2007

ATRIA BOOKS and colophon are trademarks of Simon & Schuster, Inc.

For information about special discounts for bulk purchases,
please contact Simon & Schuster Special Sales at
1-800-456-6798 or business@simonandschuster.com

Manufactured in the United States of America

10   9   8   7   6   5   4   3   2   1

The Library of Congress has cataloged the hardcover edition as follows:

Stringer, Vickie M.
Dirty Red : a novel / Vickie M. Stringer—1st Atria Books hardcover ed.
   p. cm.
1. African American Women—Fiction. I. Title
PS 3569.T69586D57 2006
813'.6—dc22   2006042993

ISBN-13: 978-0-7434-9348-2
ISBN-10:   0-7434-9348-6
ISBN-13: 978-0-7434-9363-5 (pbk)
ISBN-10:   0-7434-9363-X (pbk)

This book is dedicated to the three jewels in my crown:
Mia McPherson, Kaori Fujita and Lisa Woodward.
Ladies, this one's for you!

God, protect me from my friends.
I can handle my enemies . . .

Dirty Red

CHAPTER 1

Wifey

A little privacy, please?" Red lifted her right eyebrow as she studied Q, who was leaning against the granite-topped vanity in the oversized bathroom. She noticed how his hands were balled into fists—fists which could easily pummel her to death. Q's knuckles blanched as he gripped the counter's edge. It was easy to imagine him slipping on a pair of brass knuckles at any moment. She didn't want to think of what he might do to her—that is, if things didn't work out.

"Pee, bitch! Knock it off and drop them pants!" Q screamed.

Red slowly began to slip her True Religion jeans down to just above her knees. The more Q screamed at her to hurry, the more she began to calculate her next move. "Fuck you, nigga! Can a bitch piss in peace, goddamn it?"

"As many times I done ran up in that pussy, I know you ain't worried about me seeing it now." Q refused to take his eyes off Red for even a second. Detroit, Michigan, niggas were clever and calculating. They didn't trust anyone, including females. It was a dog-eat-dog world on the streets of Detroit and females weren't immune to getting a beat-down by a nigga in the game.

Q stood an even six feet with dark brown eyes and dark hair that he kept cut in a low faded Caesar. With Shemar Moore looks, his outward appearance hid a dark past. Q hustled with a vengeance and felt that life owed him something. At first, his future included a career as a professional football player, but a knee injury changed all of that. So, the streets gave him the fame and power that a professional sports career would have. He reaped all the benefits and recognition of a celebrity.

Red, trying to gain control over the situation, used another tactic in her huge arsenal to calm Q down a notch. Getting up off of the toilet and pulling her pants back up, she walked over to him and touched his arm. "Q, would it be so bad if—"

"How would I know it's mine? Y'all some trick-ass bitches and this is y'all's number one game!" he interrupted.

Her tactic failed. *Damn! It didn't work,* she thought.

"Nigga, ain't nobody tryin' to trick yo' ass. What the fuck make you think I *wanna* be carrying your seed?"

"See, your whole tone changed just like that." Q snapped his fingers. "Y'all bitches is scandalous, always tryin' to fuck wit' a nigga." He folded his arms and got comfortable, as if he had all the time in the world to wait.

"Scandalous?" Red shouted. She rolled her hazel eyes and sat back on the toilet as Q glared at her.

"Did I stutter? You heard what I said . . . scandalous! Shit, in my twenty-four years, I done seen some bullshit from y'all hos." Q stared Red dead in her eyes and pointed. "Now piss in that cup so I can dip this stick to see if the line turns pink."

"Nigga, this is ridiculous. After all this time, this is what I'm reduced to? A pregnancy test?" Red was intentionally stalling. "It's gon' turn pink, and then what, nigga?"

Q shook his head, tired of Red talkin' shit. "Just piss already. Damn."

In the "D," niggas had to maintain their manhood by not allowing shiesty-ass women to fuck over their dicks. But Q had a weakness for a woman carrying his baby, and Red knew this. Like most other men in his line of work, Q wanted some part of his own flesh and blood to carry on his legacy in the event of his demise. Q was no stranger to responsibility and doing the right thing, and felt guilty denying a child and mother when he knew damn well he had enough money to take care of them. He held resentment in his heart for his own daddy for abandoning him, his mother and four siblings when he was young, and vowed to never be like him.

This made Q an attractive and lucrative target. He had already been tricked on a couple of occasions when he was a youngster. And to make matters worse, neither of the two children even looked like him.

Then one day he spotted one of his kids at the mall with some guy who was rumored to be the "real" father. Q had been taking care of the little bastard for two years. Come to find out, the baby's mother, Rochelle, had both Q and the dude pushing a stroller loaded with shopping bags thinking they were the father. She was playing both of them niggas for their cheese. All she cared about was their money and how much they were spending on her. From that moment in the mall, Q got hip to the bitch. He waited several days, giving her just enough time to snooze, and caught her out at a club and put his "act right" on her ass.

Always a man of his word, and not one to waste time barking about shit he couldn't make good on, Q gave her a thorough ass-whipping till she begged for mercy. His wrath curtailed any other woman from trying that shit again, at least on him. Ho-checking was simple—do it in front of other hos, and they all got the picture. After teaching Rochelle not to mess with a nigga from the streets, Q did what most men do—he bounced, leaving her with no dick, no money, and a screamin'-ass kid.

Now hip to most of the games played by the sack-chasers, Q had gotten to the point where he packed his own jimmys and placed them on his nine-inch dick himself. When he was done handling his business, he disposed of them in a napkin and placed the napkin in his pocket to be discarded later. Hell, for all he knew, bitches would open the used condoms and try to get some sperm to inseminate themselves, in the hopes of getting knocked up. Whatever the case, he wasn't having it.

Red and Q had known each other in passing, spotting each other at the hot spots and concerts. He peeped her when she was with her girls, and he holla'd at her. They even went as far as exchanging numbers and talking a time or two on the phone. They just kept it cool. Red didn't give him too much play because she was "with" Bacon and didn't want to mess that up. And there was no reason for her to leave her green grass for unknown pastures. But once Bacon went away, she needed to have a man around, and Q was willing.

For some reason, Q felt Red was different. He gave her credit for being above the chickenhead games that most girls played. But he was soon regretting his judgment, and found she was a wolf in sheep's clothing.

Red was the street E. F. Hutton; when she spoke, everybody listened. On this particular day, she found herself hemmed up in a bathroom at the Renaissance Hotel. Out of all the things she could've been doing on such a pleasant afternoon, she was in a plush hotel bathroom, running game, as usual.

Red wasn't your average bitch, though. Don't get it fucked up; she was a cold showstopper and she knew it. She had an average build; nothing was too big or too small. Her complexion was her star attraction. It was toffee-colored with a reddish hue, flawless, not a pimple in sight. Her mom's Puerto Rican genes gave her long, curly red hair with just the right luster. Her hazel eyes were courtesy of her father.

She could put a halt to rush-hour traffic with her Puerto Rican beauty complemented by African-American features. Her angelic smile and heavenly white teeth were the perfect cover for being as foul as she wanted to be. Always rockin' her game face, she knew how to bat her Cover Girl lashes and mesmerize even the hardest nigga into being an unwitting victim.

Oddly, Red had a rough edge about her that she combined with a powerful sex appeal. Her malicious ways were masked by her million-dollar smile. Always dressed to perfection, Red expressed her femininity by the length of her heels, whether they were sandals, boots or slides. This automatically gave her five feet, five inches of height the presence of a giant and she carried herself as such.

Red was definitely a dime, no doubt, but her ways made her ugly. Nobody and nothing could keep her from doing her dirt. Not only was Red a vindictive person, she also was a master dissembler. Living life in a New York state of mind, her goal was to get rich at all costs, regardless of who was hurt in the process. Red believed that there was no Lady Luck. Every opportunity meant preparation. She was convinced that success was not all that mysterious, and life was a game that needed to be played. And when it came to her, there were no rules—and it was always her turn.

"Okay, can you get me a glass of water from the bar?" Red asked in a meek whisper.

"No, bitch, we gon' stay up in dis piece until you pee. I don't give a damn if it takes all day or all night." Q was getting more vexed by the moment. He couldn't believe that Red was wasting his time. He didn't know why she had picked a hotel to tell him this. As far as he was concerned a corner gas station would have been just fine. Not only had she picked a hotel, she picked the most expensive one in Detroit.

She sat on the toilet and rested her face in both of her hands. Q couldn't tell if she was crying or not. He didn't give a damn, either.

Looking at his diamond-studded Chopard watch, and then back at Red, Q noticed the room had gone silent. He prayed that she was not pregnant and vowed that although the pussy was some of the best, he wouldn't be caught dead fucking her again.

One question kept coming to mind: *How did this happen?* Q was the most careful with Red. Despite her complaints, he used protection every time. *But, there was that one time . . .* His rational mind couldn't determine how she had gotten the slip on him. Q often thought if she wasn't so scandalous, he would wife Red in a heartbeat, but she couldn't be trusted. It made no damn sense why someone so fine kept shit going all the damn time.

Over and over Q began to regret the decision to fuck her raw. People say that a man thinks with the wrong head, and now Q realized that the old saying was true. He sucked his teeth in disgust.

The next thing he knew, Red had diverted his attention from the matter at hand. He looked on as she slowly leaned back against the rear of the toilet. She spread her legs and began to rub her clit. She looked up at Q and began to lick her lips in a suggestive manner.

"We gon' waste this room and our time on this shit when I could be breakin' you off a little somethin' somethin'." Red flashed her most irresistible smile.

"Look, Red, piss in the cup in two minutes or I'm leaving." The longer he waited, the more irritated he became.

Without saying a word, Red spread the lips of her pussy and fingered her clit a little more. She took the same two fingers and sucked them. *Damn! She don't fight fair*, he thought. Red knew he had a thing for watching her masturbate. He couldn't help the bulge that began to rise in his jeans, and he watched Red stare at his erection, licking her lips with appreciation.

Q walked over to Red and cupped the back of her head. Red leaned forward, lifted his T-shirt and blew on his stomach. She reached down to her pussy again, and then lifted her hand to Q's lips for a taste. He sucked on her fingers, sliding his tongue up and down them as he closed his eyes and relaxed into the rhythm of the foreplay.

Meanwhile, Red pushed her other hand into her pussy.

"Wait! I got to pee!" Red pushed Q back. The force caused him to open his eyes and stumble just a bit. Red grabbed the cup and spread her legs wider. She only filled the cup up halfway. She quickly handed Q the partially filled cup.

"Here, nigga." Red continued to pee into the toilet. The trickling sound of the stream was music to both of them.

Red tore off the toilet paper, wiped herself and pulled up her hip-hugger jeans. Q leaned on the sink again with his jeans slightly undone. Red teasingly brushed up against him while she washed her hands and smoothed out her ponytail. She grabbed her Louis Vuitton handbag and searched inside for her lip gloss. As she applied it, she watched Q study her every move in the mirror. She seductively licked her lips.

"Well? Do your fuckin' test," she demanded.

Q hesitated. Maybe he shouldn't have put Red through all of this. *But it's impossible for her to be pregnant. The bitch has to be lying*, he thought.

Red stepped into the other side of the suite and lay on the bed, flipping TV channels.

Q nervously placed the dipper into the tiny cup of urine. He put the stick on the counter and gazed into the mirror as he waited for the verdict.

The stick stayed white for a long time and he wondered how he would kick Red's ass in the ritzy hotel without going to jail.

He buttoned and zipped his jeans. As he buckled his belt he paused. Suddenly, the white stick turned a strong pink. Q grabbed the box and reread the instructions.

Clear indicates a negative result. Pink indicates the presence of the hormone that indicates pregnancy.

"Pink for *YES*!" he whispered to himself. "Damn, she sho' *IS* pregnant!"

Q walked into the suite and saw Red curled into a fetal position, with her hand resting on her stomach. He lay down beside her and moved her ponytail to one side to kiss the back of her neck. Q used his index finger to trace the hidden Chinese tattoo that ran down her back and across her shoulders.

Red opened her eyes, which were hidden from his view, and a wicked smile spread across her face.

Got him!

Q began to undress Red and she put up no resistance.

"Wait, I got to pee again." Red slipped off the bed and into the bathroom. "I'll be right back," she whispered.

Inside the bathroom, Red removed the tiny tube that she had

inserted into her vagina earlier that day. While Q's eyes were closed, she'd loosened the stopper on the vial that contained the dummy piss; then she'd pushed her fingers inside her vagina and released the liquid into the cup. She now wrapped it in tissue paper and placed it in her purse. Red gazed into the mirror to admire her work. She winked at her reflection and thought, *Here's looking at you, bitch!*

Red returned to the room to sex Q down for the last time. She slowly walked toward the bed and stopped at the foot of it. She slid her T-shirt over her head to reveal her supple breasts. As she crawled onto the bed, Q spread his legs and exhaled deeply. Red was determined to be as tender and gentle as she could be. She smiled at Q and his once stressed expression began to soften.

When Red lay on top of him, she felt his muscles relax. She trailed small kisses up his midsection until she reached his navel. She circled his navel, dipping her tongue in and out. Q began to moan aloud, increasing Red's arousal. Giving pleasure was as easy to her as breathing. Red's goal was to put into Q's mind that this was love and not just another time around the track. As Red licked upward, she found his erect nipples. She began to suck on them, discovering a pleasure point on his body that even he didn't know was there.

"Umm, baby," Q moaned as Red nibbled harder on his puckered right nipple. She flicked her tongue over his sensitive spot and sucked harder and harder. She heard the faint rhythm of his heartbeat grow louder and stronger. Red moved to the left nipple and shifted to the right side of his body.

Q began to roam her body with his hands. As he grabbed her ass cheeks with his hands, they began a rhythmic winding. Q gave it his best shot as well. He had never given Red, or any woman for that matter, some head, but when it came to sex, Red was top-shelf and she never failed to bring the freak out in him. Q pulled Red up to where his mouth could meet hers. As his tongue slid in and out of her mouth, he circled her lips with the tip of his tongue and made sucking motions that took her breath away.

Q rolled Red over onto her back and spread her legs. Diligently, he began to move his head downward to suck her clit. With his forefinger and thumb, he penetrated her a bit and then slurped her clit until it became harder and harder. Even as she neared climax, Red refused to allow the pleasure to cloud her mind. No matter how good it felt, she couldn't dare allow some bomb-ass head to interfere with her plan. With the money she was about to gas Q for, Red knew that another climax like the one she was about to have was just a vibrator away.

Without a doubt, Red knew that with a baby on the way, Q would try to wife her. However, she didn't want to be his wifey. She wanted to be his beneficiary and that was just what she planned to be. She wanted to have her cake and be able to eat it, too.

"Don't stop! Yeah, suck it right there, daddy," Red said, moaning. She grabbed the back of his head to make certain he didn't move. In many respects Red was like a man; wasn't nothing like getting that clit licked. Shit, Red understood men and why they always wanted their dicks sucked. The fact was, that shit felt good.

"Ooh . . . oh . . . um," Red groaned, pulling Q's head deeper into her legs as she exploded. Q emerged with cum dripping down his cheeks, his goatee filled with the slimy remnants of what shot from between her thighs.

Q rose to his feet, wearing a pleased look because he'd satisfied Red. He kissed her and, without wasting time, forcefully penetrated her pussy. The way he humped like a dog in heat, Red realized that eating the na-na was a turn-on for a man as well as for a woman. And the fact that she screamed his name made the beast in Q's sex game come out. Q fucked Red like he wanted to tear her a brand-new pussy.

After a simultaneous climax, the two collapsed into a panting, sweating heap. When her breathing slowed down and her heart stopped trotting, Red noticed that the air smelled like boodussy. She crept over to the window and opened it to air out the room. Next, she led Q to the shower, where the afterplay continued.

Spent, Q and Red lay intertwined in each other's arms all afternoon, thinking of baby names and making plans.

"QJ. I like that one if it's a boy," Q suggested.

"QJ?" Red asked, circling her finger on his chest.

"Yeah, Quentin Junior, or Q Junior."

Red didn't give a damn if the baby was named Duck Sauce. "Oh, yeah that is nice. QJ." She nodded.

"Or if it's a girl, we could name her after my mother, Patricia," Q continued.

"Oh, your mom. That would be nice," Red said. "Don't you think it's kind of early to be discussing names, though? I mean, I'm only about four weeks pregnant." She figured that would give her a few months before she was supposed to start showing.

Q shook his head. "Names are hard, you know. They stay with the child forever. Yeah, I want something my child will be proud of."

"Yep," Red agreed. "Whatever you want, Daddy, you got it."

"You just take care of yourself. Stop that bullshit, Red. Seriously, I want a healthy baby. No more blunts. No more clubs, and no more muthafuckin' trickin'. I swear, Red, I catch you at a club, it's over. And if I catch you on that shit, then we gon' have problems."

Nigga knock you up, he think he own you. "True dat, baby, I hear you." Red kissed him on the chin.

Q put his plan down with promises and assurances. He even added an apology for his skepticism. "Yo, Red. Baby, I'm sorry for doubting you. You know how it is. Women out here doing some foul shit for that cheddar, you know?" Red listened in silence and Q even saw the feistiness leave her demeanor. "I'm not wit' bitches baby hustling. I'm gon' work with you, though," Q promised as he rubbed her shoulder. "You ain't gon' go through this alone."

Q placed a phone call from his cell to his boy Ezekial and told him to deliver a package to the hotel. When the package arrived, Q gave Red detailed instructions. "Don't open this bag until I leave. You'll know that I'm 'bout it," he said, then kissed Red on her forehead.

"Okay, Daddy," Red replied.

Once Q left the suite and she heard the hotel door latch click,

Red opened the package and removed a Crown Royal bag. Inside the bag was the most beautiful sight she had ever seen. There were three big knots of folded and rubber-banded $100 bills. Popping the first two bands loose, Red spread the money all over the bed, licking her thumb as she began to count.

When she got to $20,000 and had one more band to go, Red stopped counting. It didn't even matter. She was hoping for ten grand and Q had already doubled her expectations.

Crime paid, but being "pregnant" paid better when you had skills. Satisfied with herself, Red quickly rubbed her hands together in an up and down motion. Overall, she hadn't done bad for herself today. First, she had gotten a physical orgasm, and now she had reached a mental climax and that was the best of all. Power was Red's motivation.

Many thoughts flooded Q's mind as he walked through the lobby, trying to get out of what he thought was a bad dream. As he headed toward the exit, his best friend, Ezekial, who was waiting for him in the bar, ran after him. Ezekial was short and kinda stubby. He was that guy that was round about the middle, clean shaven with a bald head. Because Zeke had caught a cab, it was easy for the two men to jump into Q's black Range Rover. Q turned the disc changer to his favorite, #5; the sounds of 50 Cent filled the car. Q drove down I-75 and moved into traffic before starting light conversation. Zeke could tell something was on his mind, so he tried to lighten the mood. Zeke's voice came through with his favorite saying: "Every day is payday."

"What's up, Zeke?" Q asked.

"You got it, what's good, Q. I didn't think you was ever gon' come downstairs. Was that pussy or business?" Ezekial asked.

"Nothin', man, thanks for coming through," Q responded.

A couple minutes later, Q took a deep breath, sighed and asked, "Do you remember that honey name Red?"

"Yeah, who could forget that scandalous bitch!" Zeke said, cracking the window.

"I was upstairs with her and man, she pregnant."

"You ain't fallen for that bullshit, nigga? Tell me it ain't so?"

"Yeah, I thought the same thing, but I made her take a pregnancy test and well, it turned pink."

"Pink! Nigga, fuck that schemin' bitch. I told you not to fuck with her. No you didn't run up in that hot-ass pussy raw?"

"Man, you know how it goes."

"I told you about that bitch and the time when I fucked her in the hotel room, I woke up clipped of about five thousand. Damn pickpocket," Zeke fussed, squirming in his seat. "Red swore on everything she loved that she was innocent. Then you turn around and bareback her and get caught out there."

"Man, I can't even remember fuckin' her like that. That's why I wanted a pregnancy test. What could I do but find out? Next I want a paternity test."

"If you want me to make you feel better, you can forget it. That's what the fuck you get," Zeke said, moving his nine millimeter from his uncomfortable backside to his lap.

"Don't do me like that, dog. I don't even know what I'm gon' do."

"So you asking me for advice?" Zeke paused, then continued. " 'Cause if I was you—I would get ghost on that whore in a minute. Tell her to lose your fuckin' phone number."

"Nah, you right. I can say fuck her, but I can't go out like the average stereotype. I can't turn my back on my seed. That's about me and my character. But what I will do is make her have a paternity. I need to be sure the baby is mine."

The two came off exit 71, East Grand Boulevard, in silence.

CHAPTER 2

The Letter

Two and a half weeks later . . .

Red,

    I hope this scribe finds you in the best of health and spirits. I'm writing you to find out what in the hell is going on. I called the house and I heard you answer, but you didn't accept my phone call. It's been over three months since your last visit.

    At mail call, I don't get any letters, nothing. A nigga threw bricks at the penitentiary to take care of you and this is how you gonna do me? You just gonna turn your back on me and walk away like I wasn't nothin' to you? I moved you out of the projects. I took damn good care of yo' ass.

    Dre said he saw you riding around, flossing in my ride wit' another nigga. When I see you, I'm gonna kick your muthafuckin' ass. You a foul-ass, trifling, cutthroat, ungrateful whore.

    These walls can't hold me forever and when I hit them bricks, my size 12 is going straight up your ass. Bitch!! See me when they free me!

Bacon

Two-and-a-half weeks after pulling her scheme on Q, Red couldn't believe that Bacon's muthafuckin' ass would have the audacity to write her some bullshit letter. Red was trying to hustle her way and here this nigga was trying to get emotional and bold on her ass.

She tossed the letter next to the stack of hundred-dollar bills that sat on the glass Pavori end table, which probably cost more than the average person's entire living room set. She had seen it in a magazine at the spot where she got her massages and facials. She knew that nobody's crib would be rockin' anything like it, so she just had to have it. She had to have it so bad that she had it shipped all the way from Italy.

"Fuck dat mark-ass nigga," Red said, huffing. In one smooth move, she took a pull from a blunt, let the smoke rush out the corner of her mouth, then passed it to her girlfriend Terry. Red was a realist. This was the real world and she needed cash given to her on a daily basis. Bacon's money was yesterday's money. After all, a fly bitch like Red never looked back. Old money was old news.

Red leaned over and picked up the bottle of orange OPI nail polish and started to polish her toes. "I don't know what done crawled up in his ass. He must have dropped the soap again." The girls burst out laughing. Their cackles floated throughout the house and echoed off the twenty-foot ceilings. When their raucous laughs subsided, Red's tone turned serious. "It's getting harder and harder to eat off of these niggas. Muthafuckas keep going to jail. Dumb asses can't stay free. Don't these niggas know that a rest, dress and impress type bitch like me needs a sponsor?" Though Red held a decent-paying job at one of the city's most prestigious real estate firms, she had no intention of working hard for the rest of her life.

"Girl, you ig'nant," Terry said as she finished off the blunt. She stood up from the butter-soft, cream-colored leather sectional sofa and stomped the butt out in the ashtray. She stumbled over to the full wet bar and helped herself to a glass of Rémy on the rocks.

"No, really. If I hadda saved a G for every money-getting, club-hanging, trick nigga that I met, then I would be rich. But now, if I had a G for every nigga asking me, *'You gon' ride wit' me? Do this time with me?'* " Red wiggled her toenails to dry them. "Nigga, please."

"Girl, ain't that the truth? My phone damn near got turned off due to collect calls from niggas in jail." Terry lit up another blunt and blew smoke rings over Red's head.

"Girl, they should know by now that I ain't about to do it!" Red said, reaching for the blunt.

"Nope," Terry chimed in.

"I mean, Bacon done went and got himself a life sentence damn near, talking that 'are you gon' wait?' shit. Seems like all the niggas from da block on lock. Big Daddy from 120th called me C-O-L-L-E-C-T and I said 'Hell no' in the phone as loud as I could. 'Cause before he even thought about asking, he already knew the answer: *I ain't about to do it!* Shit, I need to get that on a T-shirt so when we meet these law-breakin' niggas, they know from the gate . . ."

"I ain't about to do it!" both girls screamed in unison, laughing.

"I was that bitch on the side, the ride or die chick, the out-of-town babe and often the freak of the week," Red explained. "But shit, what the hell is fair exchange gon' do for me? Not a damned thing! Hell, a bitch gotta eat, too."

Terry nodded. Red didn't expect her to argue the point. It didn't matter what Red said, Terry was going to grin and agree.

"I mean, wasn't I a victim? Bacon was my main source of income." Red didn't wait for an answer. Instead she sashayed over to the bar, her stilettos clicking on the hardwood floor, and plopped three ice cubes into her glass before pouring herself a drink. Terry knew that when Red was on a rampage, it was best to just sit back and chill the fuck out.

"Terry, with all my sponsors in prison, what in the hell am I supposed to do?" Exasperated, Red continued to ask questions. "Can you believe this muthafucka talkin' all that rah-rah shit?" Red paused for Terry to answer.

"Hell, yeah, I can believe it," Terry said right on cue. "What did you think Bacon was gon' say when he found out how you was out here livin'?"

"I ain't tryna hear that shit. Bitch, you crazy," Red chuckled softly.

"No, bitch, you da one crazy. He ain't get life, you know. That nigga coming home one day, in case you forgot." Terry plopped back down on the couch and waved the letter in the air as if it was a red flag intended to cause a bull to come charging any minute.

"Why muthafuckas want you to be in jail with them? Help them do they time and shit! I didn't help them do the crime."

"But you helped them spend the dime," Terry replied. She looked at Red, then fanned her hand around the room, indicating Red's lavish lifestyle.

Red wasn't studdin' Terry's comments. She applied her last coat of polish, tightly closed the bottle and blew on her toes. Terry was like all the rest of her so-called friends. They wanted to be her and have the money, power and respect. Bitches were always looking at her sideways.

"How much time he got left anyway?" Terry asked.

Red twisted her mouth to the side and clucked her tongue. "Muthafucka got twenty years before he sees the parole board. He done did six months on a twenty piece, talking about 'when I get home.' Don't think so. Just because he a prisoner of the feds, don't make me a hostage of love." She rolled her eyes. "Talking about kicking my ass when he get out. Yeah, right." Red tossed her ponytail and scrunched her face into a scowl. "If he can lift his old-ass leg when he get out."

"Oooh, you wrong for that," Terry cautioned.

"Get me a glass of orange juice," Red ordered Terry, who immediately filled the request.

"Damn! Bacon got twenty years?" Terry heaved a sigh as she walked into the kitchen and opened the fridge. "That's like forever. No wonder you sittin' around like a Teflon Diva, never scared and shit. He ain't gon' be kickin' yo' ass doing twenty years. I know dat nigga's mind is all fucked up."

"Yeah. I'm sure it is." Red flashed a devilish grin. "Hand me that notepad in the kitchen by the phone. Bring me the pen, too."

"Damn, bitch," Terry said, huffing. "Do I look like Florence the maid?" She walked back over to the couch with the pad, the pen and the glass of orange juice.

Ignoring Terry's joke, Red's expression changed. She was thinking about something and her face put Terry on edge. "Why you lookin' all serious?" Terry appeared frightened for a moment, and then put on her tough face. "Girl, you know I was just playing." She handed Red her drink and took a seat across from her.

"Good." Red took the pad and pen from Terry's hands.

"What are you 'bout to write?" Terry inquired as she sipped on her drink.

"I'm going to write that nigga back. When I get finished with him, he gon' be on suicide watch." Red shot off an evil grin; Terry shook her head in awe.

"Don't do that, Red." Terry sounded frightened, reaching out as if she was going to grab the pen out of Red's hand. "Girl, just ignore him."

"No, fuck dat," Red snapped, hating the fact that Terry was trying to piss on her parade. She held onto her pen, a resolute look on her face. "Remember all the times he played me and I sucked that shit up 'cause he was P-A-I-D?"

Terry stared at Red like she didn't remember anything.

"Girl, look, don't even feel sorry for his ass. Do you remember the time I had the apartment on East Jefferson Avenue? The Shoreline East apartment?"

Terry rolled her eyes up in her head like she was going through a mental file cabinet.

"When I lived downtown?" Red's patience was running out and she was almost shouting. Her arms were flailing in the air with frustration. "Whatever. If you can't remember, then I do. Girl, this nigga was so tight with his money that he made me beg for every dime, and when I wasn't beggin', trust and believe, he made me fuck for the buck. Well, the lights got turned off and I kept calling this nigga, telling him I needed the light bill money.

"Honey, listen. He stayed out of town playing his game, until they turned off the lights. A bitch was in the dark with candles and shit. Bacon came home like wasn't nothing new. I kept asking him, nicely, of course, if he noticed anything. Like the fact it was dark in the house. And he then replied, 'Suck my dick by candlelight and I got you.'

"Girl, I was so heated, I sucked that nigga's dick by candlelight and all sorts of other shit for the promise of bill cash. He came through, but that was the low point in my trick days. Trust and believe. I vowed that I would be caught dead before I let another nigga have that much power over me—doing for me what I can't do for myself.

"Girl, it is ridiculous! So I ain't even tryna hear you take up for this so-called helpless muthafucka. He getting what his hand called for." Red held the pen and pad firmly in her hands. "It's my turn to floss on his ass. How about that?"

As Red started writing, Terry shrugged. Fuck it. What did she care if Red pissed that nigga off? If that bitch didn't know that niggas with Bacon's status could reach out and touch someone even from behind bars, then that was her own stupidity.

Bacon was a die-hard, thugged-out, murderous hustler. He got the name Bacon from having so much bread that he used the old slogan, *"I can bring home the bacon, fry it up in a pan,"* as his personal motto. His rep preceded him everywhere he went. From city to city, from jail to jail, Bacon had a name that carried him. And he always paid like he weighed. Bacon was big and stocky; at six feet, six inches, he towered over everyone. There was no doubt that Red wasn't the only one holding him down during his bid, but it was important that Red treat him right.

However, after the sentencing, it seemed like Red just didn't give a fuck. It was hard for her to even pretend to be concerned. During their previous talks, Bacon told Red that what was in the stash she'd have to make last. What in the world did he tell her that for? It wasn't enough for her to remain true-blue. In fact, no amount of money really was enough for her to stay committed. When the judge lowered the gavel after announcing: "You are sentenced to twenty years," while everyone else sobbed, Red silently cheered as she sat on the cold mahogany bench.

Red knew that Terry didn't really give a fuck about any letter hurtin' Bacon's feelings. Terry just didn't want to see Red cut off the coattail on which Terry'd been able to ride. Red had been quite friendly with the stash Bacon had left behind.

Red and Terry went as far back as way back could go, in the schoolyard of Chrysler Elementary School. They both were in second grade and damn near toothless. Terry was teased by all the kids because she peed on herself from time to time. Everyone called her "Pissy." Terry was used to not having anyone to play with, but when Red befriended her, her entire world changed. Terry was a dark-skinned, knobby-kneed girl. Her greatest asset was her hair. She was one of a few black girls to have naturally long hair that fell to the bottom of her shoulder blades. Terry made it a point to doll herself up, but it was really no use due to her pissy smell.

Terry and Red met on the playground and right away became cool. Red would defend *"Pissy"* when the other kids wanted to break on her. Red even hipped Terry to Depend, which she stole from her own grandmother. Even at that young age, Red also had the common sense to put Terry on a schedule. Every time Red would go to the bathroom, she would take Terry with her.

"See how this works, T?" Red would ask. "You drink something. A little while later, it comes out."

Even so, Terry was so lazy that she wouldn't even want to go to the bathroom. She would just sit on the ground somewhere and piss on herself. Over time, though, Red was able to help Terry control her weak bladder. As they grew older, her enuresis only got out of control when she drank too much liquor and either passed out or couldn't walk to the bathroom.

During middle school, Terry moved to the other side of town. Although this separated the girls for several years, in their senior year of high school they saw each other again. When Red met up with Terry the second time, Terry was driving a beat-the-fuck-up

Toyota Corolla. The car looked so bad you would have sworn that Mike Tyson had gone twelve rounds with it. They had developed into young women with breasts and asses. Still, Terry was nothing more than a project for Red, who was at it again, trying to clean up the mess she had found in her friend.

Terry had spit out three bastard kids from one nigga to the next by the time she and Red finished high school. She couldn't spit too much game 'cause she was too busy spitting out kids. She was living in a shack across town and her petty hustles were elementary to Red.

Terry did have some redeeming qualities, though, and was not above a scheme or two. Besides being in Red's pocket, she was reliable as ever. Red cleaned Terry up and kept her close. One thing for certain, two things for sure: Red kept all of her enemies close. Any and everything Red did for Terry was something that Terry could not do for herself. Red always profited from someone, one way or another. She inspired envy and imitation and her friends not only wanted to look like her, they wanted to be her. Like many great conquerers before her, Red recognized the power of the ignorant, loyal follower.

Terry lusted for money, power and respect. She didn't want to see her extravagant shopping sprees, trips to the spa and designer bags paid for by somebody else's dime come to an end. She had just gotten a new Cadillac Escalade, thanks to Red's auction hustle, and was in the process of buying a new home. Who could blame Terry for wanting to leave a matchbox with filthy carpets? Terry was playing everything—from whores to horseshoes—to get her house money. What did she care how Red handled her business?

CHAPTER 3

With Friends Like These

*E*ven Oprah said it so it had to be true: Detroit was the poorest big city in the country. Littered with abandoned buildings, trashy casinos and with a sky-high unemployment rate, you'd never believe it was once called the "Paris of the Midwest." After the closing of the many automobile factories that gave Detroit its livelihood and the subsequent rise of drug and gang activity, the gap between the "haves" of the suburbs and the "have-nots" of the city was gaping.

Red despised Detroit and everything in it. In Red's crazy-ass mind, she planned to make the city her bitch and strike it rich by exploiting as many of its residents as she could reach. She figured, hell, Detroit should be used to it by now.

Red had been exploiting Q for three weeks already with the pregnancy scheme, but still couldn't come up with a plausible way to make her belly protrude. How could she make herself appear to be showing?

Pondering her scheme for another moment, Red quickly

turned her attention back to her closet. She rummaged through racks and racks of designer clothes, reminiscing over the thousands of dollars' worth of the trendy threads she no longer wore. To be out of fashion was like trying to run out of breath. It just couldn't happen.

Summer was right around the corner, so Red decided that she would fake a miscarriage just as it started to get hot. That way, she could still look fly and buy herself a new wardrobe to jump things off.

Terry finally woke up and stumbled down the hall from the guest bedroom into Red's room.

"You awfully chipper this morning, Red." You could smell the morning liquor breath. She looked like something awful.

"Hell, yeah." Red caught a whiff of Terry's breath. "Ho, you look fucking terrible. Go brush yo' funky mouth before stepping to me in the morning."

When Terry returned, Red was excited to tell her what had been going on in her mind.

"Terry, shit, a girl been thinking about all we talked about regarding Bacon. I'm gon' let that sleepin' dog lie. I'm not gonna seek revenge. I'm just gon' do me and focus on myself."

"A bitch gotta do what a bitch gotta do," Terry said with a grin, hoping she would benefit from the next scheme up Red's sleeve.

"I'm in my closet cleaning this shit out. You wanna look through these clothes?"

"Hell, yeah," Terry said as she sorted through the pile Red placed in the center of the floor.

After a couple of hours, Terry had showered, dressed and left with a Hefty bag full of hand-me-downs. It was almost one o'clock and Red continued to clean out the rest of her closet.

Having cleared out a considerable amount of space, Red planned to head straight to Fairlane Town Center and buy more for her already exclusive closet. She went through her garbage pile, one item at a time, holding dresses and shirts up to her body, double-checking her selections.

She confirmed what was official and discarded the dated apparel into a pile that would be donated to the local women's shelter. If she had to look at the homeless, she figured they could at least look good. The chimes from her doorbell startled her. Who could it be? She hadn't invited anyone over.

Red exited her bedroom and turned left at the banister that overlooked the foyer of her grand entrance. The marble floors that flowed through the house sparkled when the morning sun, which beamed through the skylights, hit it just right. Suddenly she could see her friend Kera as she peered through the smoked glass doors and waved at Red.

"Just a minute," Red yelled over the customized wrought-iron banisters of her winding staircase. "Wad up, ho?" Red said after answering the door. Kera stood in the doorway, her five-months'-pregnant stomach protruding before her. She was dressed in a straight, knee-length denim skirt with a short-sleeved shirt.

"You got it, beyotch!" Kera replied. She hugged Red and stepped into the marble foyer. "Girl, no wonder you don't let muthafuckas come over. This place is off the chain! Every time I'm here it's spotless." Kera gave herself a tour as she waddled from room to room, appraising the furniture and admiring the décor of the English Tudor.

"Wait, wait! Before I forget, good looking the fuck out," Red said as they walked back up the stairs to her bedroom.

"What's up?" Puzzled, Kera stared at Red quizzically.

"For the piss." Red tilted her head to the side and gave Kera a "don't you remember?" look.

"Oh, my bad. Did it work?" Kera asked.

"You pregnant, ain't you? Or is that a pillow underneath there?" Red caressed Kera's bulging belly.

"I wish it was. But at five months what can I do?"

"We ain't going there," Red replied. "You decided to fuck for free, and bareback. Guess you was in love." Red playfully rubbed Kera's shoulders.

Kera switched from the sensitive subject of her pregnancy. "So who did you use the pee trick on?" She was dying to know.

Red knew better than to tell all of her dirt. The minute a bitch got mad, she would be up in Q's face, crossing her, so she replied, "Carlos."

"No way!" Kera said in disbelief. "You fucked Carlos?"

Red picked the clothes up from the floor and placed them on the bed.

"Sure did . . . only once, though."

Red knew what Kera was thinking but didn't want to say: *How in the hell, or why in the hell, would you fuck Carlos?* That was exactly what Red wanted her to think so that no one would care who her "supposed" baby daddy was. That way they couldn't fuck up her scheme.

"But Red, he's in a wheelchair." Kera perched on Red's four-poster, down-covered bed.

"True dat, but his dick works betta than the niggas who ain't in a wheelchair and his tongue definitely ain't broke." Red gave Kera a high five.

"Girl, you nasty." Kera searched through the pile of clothes and held them up to her body for size.

"Whateva . . . he gets a twelve-hundred-dollar-a-month disability check." Red snatched the clothes out of Kera's hand and smashed them into garbage bags.

"Word?" Kera confirmed.

"Word." Red gave her the "don't act like you don't know" look. "And he gave me a grand to eat my pussy and sit on his dick." Red tied a knot in the bag and opened the left side of her oversized shoe closet. Once inside, Red opened the cherry-wood hamper she kept there, which revealed a bag of dirty clothes for the laundry. "The head was so good, I should have paid him."

"You sick, girl. Hold on, wait a minute. Don't even think about giving your shoes away. Wait until my feet go back to normal size and I'll help you go through them." Kera walked over to the shoe closet and admired the contents. It was packed. All the boxes had a photo on the outside of what was inside.

"Girl, you got that. I'll save them for you, but you know I wear an eight."

"I know I can wear an eight. Not a problem, baby." Kera blew Red a kiss.

The girls headed back to the living room and Red filled Kera in about the letter from Bacon and how she and Terry had just missed each other.

"You know I don't like Terry's ass," Kera explained. "Glad I missed that ho. I mighta had to swing on that bitch."

"Girl, y'all still beefing over that nigga?" Red asked, knowing damn well that Kera wasn't pleased with the fact that her soon-to-be baby daddy was Terry's man.

"And if—" Kera was just about to get started when Red cut her off, lifting her hand.

"Don't even try that 'and if I was your friend' shit. You already know we don't beef over no niggas, and he was with *her* when your ass tried to steal him. Didn't nobody tell you to fuck him bareback and end up with the consequences of bun-in-the-oven-and-nigga-back-with-his-bitch syndrome."

Although Kera felt wounded, there was nothing she could say or do in her own defense. Red was absolutely right. She drew first blood on Terry, and it turned out that Terry got the man and had the last laugh.

"I gotta put these clothes in the washer. Make yaself at home. I'll be back in a sec." Red headed down to the lower level, where the laundry room was located.

At first, Kera was too speechless and stunned to move from her seat in the great room. One thing for sure, Red could never be accused of sugarcoating the truth. Red was a connoisseur of the comeback—always ready with a hurtful, yet truthful, comment to stop the madness before it even got started.

Kera wanted to get even with Red for being so cold-blooded. Couldn't she show some sympathy for her situation? Didn't she know pregnant women were sensitive and could cry at the drop of a hat?

To kill time, Kera walked around the great room, admiring Red's exquisite taste. She walked over to the sound system and

pressed Play on the CD changer; Mariah Carey's "We Belong Together" floated through the house. Walking past the center table,
she noticed a notepad and a letter addressed to Bacon next to it.
Kera listened diligently to make sure she heard no signs of Red returning. Next to the letter was an envelope. Kera ripped half a
sheet from the pad and quickly copied the address onto it. Again,
she listened for any sounds of Red returning and placed the piece
of paper in her bra. Kera's heart pounded loudly, her adrenaline
pumping. She wanted to cut Red deep. She wanted so badly to read
the letter. Before she knew it, she was sitting on the edge of the
couch with the notepad in hand; her eyes bulged. As she took in
every word, Kera couldn't believe what she read.

Dear Bacon,

*Or, in your case, should I call you John? This is the letter
you been beggin' for.*

*Well, let's see. It would be virtually impossible for you to
kick my ass, seeing as how you will be an old and gray bastard when you come home. Your dick is so little that I can't
believe you even wear a size 12 shoe. There goes that myth.
When I first met you I sized you up real good and I knew the
dick was going to be swinging. Boy, was I wrong. I guess that
teaches me not to judge a book by its cover, or a dick by its
shoe size.*

*I hope with all the free time on your hands you now realize
that I never loved you. As quiet as it was kept, I didn't even
like you. Before you got locked up I couldn't even stand the
sight of your face, and let's not discuss the sound of your
voice. Why do you think I haven't been accepting your calls
lately? Yeah, your boys saw me flossing in your shit. I was
flossing their shit too.*

*Your dude Chris eats pussy better than you ever could,
and your partner Stan's cum tastes like ice cream in my
mouth. You hear my voice when you call your phone? After
today, you'll hear "I got a block" on all my phones. Don't try*

that three-way shit either, 'cause I got Call Intercept. Fucker, just turn homo and die. I got your loot, you took the case, now press that bunk and do that muthafuckin' time.

You the man, remember? You that nigga, right? This pussy is yours, right? Wrong! You a has-been and I ain't got time for no shoulda, woulda, coulda stories. You should have stayed free. Certainly, nobody told you to fall in love with me.

You snooze, you lose. You did all the work, but now my new man and I reap all the benefits. The best thing you could have ever done for me was to get locked up. The pimp game got flipped on your ass. Now do the best thing for yourself, get you a boyfriend, let him suck your dick and leave me the fuck alone.

Wake up! You played yourself. Charge it to da game.

Red

Kera quickly placed the notepad back in what she hoped was the same exact spot it had been in. She slid the pen next to the pad, hoping to make it look legit.

Without warning, Red came back into the room and startled Kera. Trying to look calm, Kera acted like her heavy breathing from being surprised was due to a contraction. She played it up too, rubbing her stomach and panting.

As soon as she came into the great room, Red's antennae went up. It wasn't like Kera to be found in the same spot Red left her. The television wasn't turned to BET for videos. She wasn't on the phone paging someone or trying to making long-distance calls to her family in Virginia. She wasn't in the kitchen raiding the fridge. Although music was playing, the bitch was up to something.

Not letting on that she knew something was up, Red sauntered over and joined her friend on the couch. "I know you hungry. There's some snacks in the kitchen."

"Now, that's what I'm talking 'bout." Kera got up to raid the kitchen.

"Get us some drinks while you're in there, girl. Those stairs are about to kill me." She wanted her to walk away so she could figure out what was going on.

When Kera exited the great room, Red noticed the pad and remembered that she'd left the letter to Bacon on the table. Red looked at the notepad and didn't notice anything suspicious. She looked at the letter; it was right next to the envelope, just as she had left it. Still, something didn't feel quite right.

Red picked up the notepad and flipped past the two pages on which she had written. She then noticed the top half of a torn sheet of paper still attached to the pad. She didn't remember ripping it off, and she didn't see any paper lying around.

Did Terry tear off a piece of paper for a wad of gum? she wondered.

As Kera returned to the room, she began to make small talk, but Red wasn't fooled. She knew this was an attempt to ease the tension in the air.

"Kera, what brought you over, girl?" Red asked.

"Nothing. Just checking you out." She handed Red a glass of fruit punch and sat across from her in the cream chaise longue. "What's up with you and Bacon?"

Bingo! Instantly, Red knew Kera had read her letter and was wondering how to play this. If she told Kera that she was shiesting Bacon, how would she look? If she lied, and played like everything was all good after Kera had read the letter, what would she say? What could she do?

Just as Red was about to get the shit going, her doorbell rang. She sprang from the couch and sprinted toward the wooden door.

"Who is it?" Red screamed through the door as she threw both hands up in disgust. Just when she thought she was living in the cut, it seemed as if everybody and their mama knew where her crib was. Bacon had gone out of his way to have a place where he could rest his head in peace from niggas in the hood. A place where he could go to sleep and have his family live without the threat of danger.

Obviously, Red had let one bitch too many drop by the crib and now her shit was on blast. She knew that sooner, rather than later, she would have to leave her gracious abode. It was only a matter of time before Bacon became aware of the news that his crib was Grand Central Station.

"Who is it?" Red screamed again, knowing she could easily peek through the window on the side of the door.

"Sasha," a voice answered with an edge of irritation.

Red opened the door. Sasha stood there with a smirk on her face. She turned to wave good-bye to her driver. Red looked at the driver and cursed inwardly. *Another muthafucka with my address*, she thought.

"Hey, girl," Red said as she turned to walk back to the great room.

Sasha followed and spoke to Kera as soon as she saw her. "Whud up, ho?" Her voice remained flat and her tone cold.

"You got it, bitch," Kera replied dryly.

"Red, why you actin' like you didn't know I was coming over here? Had me screaming through the door like I'm crazy and shit."

"Girl, 'cause I can do that. Y'all better recognize. Dis my house," Red reminded her. "No girl, seriously. It just feels like Grand Central Station today. If one more person rings my bell, I think I will scream."

"Well, what's good, ma?" Sasha asked.

"Shit, after that running I just did, a bitch is hungry. Let's take this meeting to the kitchen, and Sasha, I know you don't have your dirty-ass shoes on my carpet. You know better than that."

Sasha looked over at Kera, who was barefoot and smirking at her like she was a kid getting in trouble from Momma. Without even looking back, Red walked out, knowing that Sasha was taking off her shoes and that the two would follow behind her.

Red padded barefoot across the plush carpet until she reached the hardwood floors in her kitchen. She began removing pots from underneath the kitchen cabinet to prepare a meal. From where she stood she could see Sasha and Kera as they sat on the sofa in the great room adjacent to the open kitchen. They were close enough that she could tell they were talking, but far enough not to hear their actual words. Red knew that the bitches were up to something and she was going to use whatever she had to ensure her plan went as expected.

"Sistas, I got a problem," Red said slowly and softly, almost like a whisper, to no one in particular. She looked on as Sasha and Kera entered the kitchen, curiosities piqued and ears perked. Her plan was beginning to work. Bewildered, both girls looked at each other, but said nothing, taking a seat next to the counter where Red was cutting up some lettuce. "Let's not all be concerned at the same damn time," Red said sarcastically, still looking down.

Sasha shrugged. "I can't believe you got a problem that you can't solve."

Kera sat quietly on the bar stool, rubbing her stomach. She wondered what the prima donna's problem could possibly be.

Red paused for dramatic effect and heaved a deep sigh. "Okay. I know you all know that Bacon left me the house and everything."

The girls listened closely for more details. Kera was hoping for all the details, as she had never really known how Red got the house in the first damn place. As the pots came to a boil, filling the kitchen with an aroma of spices, Red knew that now was the perfect time to give the two a foolproof explanation for the letter that she suspected Kera had read.

"Well, it's really not completely paid for and . . . um . . ." Red paused for a minute after telling the lie to allow her words to sink in.

"Say what?" Kera asked in disbelief.

"I need to keep up with the mortgage or I will lose the house," Red blurted out. She couldn't help but notice the sneers of satisfaction spread over her so-called friends' faces. Realizing that she saw their smirks, they turned their mouths upside down to fake looks of concern and empathy for their girl.

The room fell silent. The two looked at Red, whose head hung low like she was holding back tears. Inside, Kera was thrilled with the thought of Red losing her home. She wondered where the bitch would stay and if she would be reduced to living in the projects, like the rest of them.

"So, what are you saying? You, the Puerto Rican Kay Chancellor, behind on the *rent*?" Sasha emphasized each word with gusto.

"Homes have mortgages," Kera corrected.

Red silently laughed as she watched Sasha fight the urge to turn around and spit in Kera's face. Sasha had told Red she thought Kera was a dumb ass for getting knocked up by Terry's man. The drama behind that rumor was the topic of discussion on every set and in every beauty salon, but Red kept that information to herself. Kera and Sasha became cordial by default on the strength of Red.

Sasha's relationship with Red was a little different than Kera's. Sasha was somewhat of a top bitch herself. Her man, Catfish, and Red's man, Bacon, were partners in the streets. During their good times, the four of them would take trips to Jamaica or Cancún and eat filet mignon and caviar. They all hated the caviar but bought it anyway because they could.

Catfish was so black that his skin looked like silk. At the same time, his mouth resembled a punch bowl. His teeth were bucked from years of sucking his thumb and his thin mustache was similar to the whiskers on a catfish. To add to the image, he had big beady eyes—and his left eye had the nerve to be lazy.

Niggas couldn't even call Sasha a gold digger. Any woman willing to endure Catfish earned every dime. Due to Catfish's reputation, Sasha had a good amount of respect from the streets. Niggas viewed her as a soldier, something that was heard of but rarely ever seen. When Bacon and Catfish were out of town for days or months at a time, from the outside looking in, Sasha never crept around.

Initially, Red looked to Sasha for direction on how to hold her man down, but Red soon got hip to the schemes that Sasha played on Catfish. Once Red went along with a secret or two for Sasha, they began cosigning for each other, one lie after another. They became close with the mutual understanding that one hand washed the other and both hands washed the face.

After three years of living the lavish life, Catfish's stash got low. To her credit, though, Sasha didn't vanish on him . . . completely. She just let the rope get a little longer, doing for him when she could and, more often than not, when she wanted to. Sasha still had her trick game going. She was pretty, no doubt. Sasha was a chocolate sister who wore a pixie cut so that she could always wear sunglasses on her head. Sun or no sun, Sasha kept some designer shades with her.

Although Sasha was older, Red was far wiser than her years revealed. There wasn't much to it; Red was in her prime fighting shape. Sasha was a contender, true enough, but she could do nothing with Red at this point in the game.

"So how far behind are you on the *mortgage*?" Sasha enunciated each word perfectly.

"Three, and next month, they start the foreclosure proceedings. If I don't do something, I can lose the house." Red turned her back to the duo. "That is, if I don't pay the past due amount and start keeping up the bills." Red sat down on the bar stool in front of the open range, put her head in her hands and began to cry.

Kera walked over to Red and attempted to embrace her. Her mouth opened wide as if to say, "Oh, my God!"

"Girl, that is awful! What happened to the stash he left?" Sasha asked, looking over at Red with fake concern.

Red couldn't believe her ears when she heard Sasha ask that. Sasha was biting the bait, because her ego wouldn't allow her to believe that Red would try to play her.

"Please, you've seen Red's lifestyle of the rich and famous." Kera smirked.

Red held her tongue. She knew that in order to pull this off, she had to allow the girls some amount of gloating. It was cool for her, though. She planned to set things up right.

"Yeah, we all know Bacon left some dough. I mean, but how long does that last? Shit, I dress to impress, no secret there. Between my car note and our"—Red pointed to each of the girls—"lifestyle, we're just about broke. Remember our cruise, and the magnums of Cristal at the clubs on Friday nights?"

Both girls nodded, recalling the cruise through the Virgin Islands. They had no choice but to feel twinges of guilt, but not for long.

"Okay, so whatchu gon' do?" Sasha asked.

"I was wondering if either of you wanted to be my roommate. You know, move in here. Live together and make it work. I mean, you could move in in what, a month?"

The idea of them living in Red's plush crib turned her misfortune into their opportunity. Kera's mind began to work. *I could take the bedroom on the left side of the hallway,* she fantasized. *I could raise my baby in a nice home.* "Girl, I'm wit' it. I can move in today. Shit, I need a place to live," Kera blurted out.

Red had hoped like hell Kera would be the last to speak, if at all. But of course, being the freeloading bum she was, Kera jumped at the offer instantly. There was no way that Sasha was going to let Kera save the day, and besides, Red knew damn well Sasha had always wanted to get up in her crib.

Red knew she had to fake excitement since she was supposed to be in desperate need of their help. She already knew that Kera wanted to be all up under her. Although she didn't show any excitement, Red also knew that Sasha wanted to be close to her, especially since Sasha could no longer afford Catfish's place, which Red thought was da bomb.

Red turned away and smiled inwardly. She'd played it just right. Red had found out from Bacon that Sasha was living pillar to post and tricking out of control. She also knew that Sasha was living on her last stacks left by Catfish before he went to prison on the same murder charge that landed Bacon in jail; through the grapevine, she heard that Sasha was trying to sell his spot to any hustling nigga she knew with big dough, all to no avail. Sasha had tried to go the land contract route, which meant someone—or a nigga on the street—had to come up with some dough to give her. The days of assumable mortgages were gone.

Catfish had pimped the crib out, spending at least $50,000 on upgrades. There was no way someone was going to cough up all that dough when the market value was much less. Sasha would have had to sell the loft for a loss. With Red's real estate background she had the solution to Sasha's problem and was about to offer it. Sasha was what was known in the industry as upside down on her loan, which meant that she owed more than what the loft was worth.

"Red, I can't move in. I got a place." Sasha turned her palms up to the ceiling in an indecisive motion.

"Yeah, I know, but what I was wondering was, if you were still selling it?" Red looked Sasha dead in the eye.

"Can't sell it." Sasha went on to explain her situation. "Been tryin', 'cause the note is kicking my ass, girl. I pay like three thousand a month. I'm tired of doing it. Catfish said he didn't really care what I did. If I could get some money, fine. My main thing is getting it out of my name and saving my credit at the same time."

"Yeah, niggas put shit in your name and then they go to jail, leaving you holding the bag," Kera added in her two cents.

"Sasha, I'm gon' help you figure it out, I promise. I think I might know someone who would be interested." Red smiled to hide her true intentions.

Red moved closer to Sasha and handed her a glass of wine. Two new roommates were more than enough. Red couldn't imagine having more than that. Besides, if her plan worked, it would be short-term rather than long-term.

"Ladies, it'll be fun living together." Red reached out for a group hug. "What we need to do is lay down the rules."

"Wait! Damn! What is the amount of the rent—I mean, mortgage?" Kera corrected herself with a nervous look at Sasha. "I mean how we gon' split it and who gon' get what room?"

"Yeah, I know. That's *this* important," Sasha added.

"The mortgage is thirty-two hundred. Because it's my house, I'll have the largest room. Also, since I'm the only one with a car, the garage will be no issue. I think it's fair that you guys pay fifteen hundred each, all utilities included."

"Bitch, please! Fifteen hundred dollars with what? My looks?" Kera flipped her hand and ricocheted her head back on her neck.

"Look," Red explained, "that includes all utilities and the fur-nishing."

"Do we get to have visitors?" Sasha asked. "Overnight guests?"

"For that price, yeah. 'Cause you paying the cost to be the boss. But you some chinky-ass bitches."

"What the fuck is chinky?" Kera asked, rolling her neck.

"Cheap and stingy," Red responded.

"I don't have that type of dough," Kera confessed.

Red had to think. She knew that Kera—rather, the non-pregnant Kera—could get money. But now Red wasn't sure how much Kera's stock was worth. However, Red knew that Kera was good for being a reliable cohort in crime and she was going to set up just for that.

"Kera, what can you pay? What can you put into the pot?" Red asked.

"I know I'll have some stamps. I mean, I juice a couple niggas here and there, but it will be work coming up with that type of money. Especially with my belly getting bigger and bigger."

"Honey, that's what this is all about," Red confirmed. "All of us doing what we gotta do to make it. You got to pay to play. Look, y'all can have overnights but don't OD, and you know I don't do traffic. Niggas comin' through, fuckin' up the shit I worked for."

"Schemed for." Kera smirked.

"What-the-fuck-ever, bitch. Look, both of you just give me a grand a month but utilities are not going to be included."

Red looked on as the wheels seemed to be spinning in Sasha's head. She could tell Sasha was considering the reduction in her monthly expenses. Sasha and Kera looked at each other and then both nodded their heads.

Kera reached out to shake Red's hand. "Deal, ho."

"Deal, bitch." Red squeezed Kera's hand in return.

"Deal, ho." Sasha shook Red's hand next.

Red finalized the agreement. "Deal, bitch! You ladies get the keys when you pay your first month's rent, plus same deposit. Sasha, don't even worry about your place. You just be packed and let me work on that problem."

Red had gone to real estate school for six weeks the summer after she graduated from high school. With her Realtor's license, she was able to make her own hours and do some really good deals that brought a nice profit. After the first year, she decided that working, whether it be for a couple of hours a week or not, was not for her.

She liked being in control, not having to depend on anyone but herself. And the way she saw it, tricking was just like selling real estate. She had a possible buyer who was interested in what she had to offer and it was her job to convince him that he had to have it— all of it. Before long, the guy signed on the dotted line and she had walked away with his cash and, in some cases, his heart. Red robbed most of her victims blind: she left her victims tricked out of whatever it was that she wanted or needed at the time. She prided herself on being ten times smarter than anyone around her. She thought five steps ahead and always had a backup plan.

Her real estate license was current so at any time, she could go back to working anywhere in the state of Michigan. She also had connections with a title company and a Realtor's office, so it always looked like she had a broker and things were right with the paperwork.

Red ordered her new roommates to set out the fine china in the formal dining room while she put the finishing touches on dinner. She lit the three-tiered candelabra and the girls sat down for a delicious meal of shrimp scampi with pasta and salad. For added pleasure, they sipped on Merlot. Red grabbed the radio remote and the sounds of Mary J. Blige filled the air. Each of the ladies loved the home's ambience, and felt good that they would have one another to lean on.

CHAPTER 4

Turned Out

Brooklyn, New York
(1995)

*F*or the longest time Red felt that she had life all figured out. But at the tender age of fifteen, who could really know anything? The Puerto Rican Day parade was something that Red always looked forward to during her summer vacations to New York. Years back, her mother, Julia, had followed Red's father to the Motor City for his chance to work on the assembly line at the General Motors plant. Her father had been stressed and unemployed. Detroit was going to be the land of milk and honey for the young couple.

Unfortunately, after the move, Julia missed her family and her roots and hated her new surroundings. The city had more Middle Easterners in its midst than Puerto Ricans, and she was always mistaken for a Mexican. People figured if she spoke Spanish, then she was a *mexicana*. This infuriated Julia greatly, which was one of the main reasons why she went to New York every chance she got.

For as long as Red could remember her parents spent most of their time arguing and fighting. Red's mother finally became fed up. Her husband never did get on at the factory plant and instead worked a series of low-paying, menial jobs. First, he started out cutting lawns and then became a short-order cook at a diner where he got fired for stealing money from the waitresses' tip jar. Then he began talk of starting his own business.

That was when Julia realized that she'd given up her life for her man and he couldn't satisfactorily provide for his family. After several months of name-calling, physical fights and numerous threats, Xanthin called it quits. Julia divorced him and took back her maiden name of Gomez and gave Red—whose real name was Raven—the same last name.

Growing up, Red loved the weekend and summer stays at her *abuela*'s. It was a chance for her to embrace her roots and freely experience a Hispanic-populated neighborhood. During the annual Puerto Rican Day parade, people of all shades and colors came out to show pride. Although Red's father was a black man, it didn't even matter. If you could speak Spanish—and Red could—and your mother was Puerto Rican, which Julia was, that was all that mattered. The different hues of the people excited Red. She felt connected to all people of color.

That summer, Red was waiting her turn for the man to add the purple syrup she loved to her Sno-Kone. Out of nowhere, this strange man appeared and, figuratively, swept her off her feet. When Red thought of Blue and how they met, it was something she couldn't share with her so-called friends. Red quickly developed a new sweet tooth, not for candy but for a man, who became her first love.

Blue stood a stocky five feet, seven inches. He was so black, you thought he was blue—that was how he got his moniker in grade school. Her first instinct was to inquire which borough he was from. However, his gold fronts were a dead giveaway—Brooklyn.

"Hola," Red said as she walked toward him, licking on her cone.

"Hey, mami." Blue fell in step with her. His tone confirmed for Red that he was not Latino but black.

"What's good?" Red stopped to allow him to come closer.

Even as a teenager, Red was not the type to approach men. They always found a way to meet her. Nonetheless, there was something profoundly special about this nigga that was different from the rest.

Red had chosen never to go past the point of fondling when it came to getting freaky. But from the looks of this man, that was soon going to change. Red felt her panties getting wet just at the sight of him. She had never felt her little na-na tingle like that before and it baffled her.

The distinct fragrance of Blue's Bulgari cologne complemented his fresh-to-death look in the latest Nike sweat suit and fresh sneakers to match. Red could tell he was older than her by a couple of years. He was a man and she was tired of playing with boys.

Red's instant attraction for him couldn't be concealed. Without her even noticing, she was smiling and nodding her head "yes" before he even spoke a word.

" 'Sup, mami? I saw you over there, posin' to be chosen. What's ya name?"

Unable to control her nervousness, Red stuttered, "R-R-Raven, but all my friends call me R-R-Red."

Red knew Blue took pleasure in her nervousness, and she was glad he didn't have a problem with her jailbait age. At fifteen, she was no match for a thoroughbred nigga who had been locked up three times and just turned twenty-four. If this were a casino, Red would have known the odds were against her.

Quite the lothario, Blue felt like the woman did all the choosing, so it was on her if she decided to stay or leave. He waited for a sign. The air held silence, the chemistry told the story—she wanted him.

After a while, the quiet between them started to feel awkward.

Secretly, Blue had a vengeance against the redbone honeys. As a boy, the light-skinned girls had always rejected him. Growing up dark-skinned with shiny white teeth seemed more like a curse than a blessing.

It was only in recent times, when dark chocolate brothers became the "in" thing, that he even got some play. Before that, the high yellow brothers dominated the set. They were the definition of handsome. Now the old adage "the darker the berry the sweeter the juice" took precedence and the sun-kissed men got their chance to shine. Blue took his newly appreciated looks as a license to maim. Maim every light-skinned woman who dared to give him a chance.

It only took two weeks for them to knock the boots. Although he liked Red, Blue was all about fulfilling his male ego. He was very pleased that he was able to obtain his goal so quickly. Blue had sex with Red and was able to detach from her early, which was part of his scheming plan. He was waiting for her to leave town so that he could move on to the next young bitch. All the romance that came after the sex was just to keep Red at bay until she left.

Although he was doggin' her out, he was smooth with it from the start. For their first date, he met Red around the block from her grandmother's building because she wasn't allowed to date. When she slid into the leather seat of his Benz, Blue's hand reached behind the seat to retrieve a bouquet of flowers for her. "These for you, baby," Blue said as he leaned over to kiss her cheek. When Red didn't resist, Blue knew his plan was working.

"Thank you," Red replied. "They're beautiful."

"Red, baby, I got a surprise for you." Blue took her to Mr. Chow for dinner, where every dish they had was foreign to her. Red thought Blue was a person off the silver screen. Billy Dee, Casanova, Rudolph Valentino, none of them had anything on Blue.

After weeks of flowers, expensive shopping trips, dinner at some of the city's finest restaurants and mind-blowing sex, Red thought she had fallen in love and that Blue felt the same. But fast money was his main squeeze. Blue was in the street gettin' it. The rock slangin' hustle had his pockets right and that was his main priority.

Over the next month, Blue took Red for weekend getaways and had her lying to her grandmother. Blue sexed Red in every position he wanted, and she took good instruction on just how he liked his dick sucked. She tried to do everything she could to please her man. Blue being older felt like a blanket to her, a shelter, a covering she never had, particularly because her father died shortly after the divorce from Red's mother, when Red was only five.

For Blue, Red was nothing more than a conquest. As a pupil, he would have given her an A+ on her oral sex game.

"Yeah, lick the head, right there," Blue would instruct.

"My jaw hurts," Red would complain.

"That's 'cause you gotta relax your mouth," Blue would advise.

Red wanted to keep him at all costs. And like her mother taught her by example, sex was the way to keep a man; especially one like Blue who had his choice of women. Red felt special because he chose her.

"When your jaws get tired, just lick the head and keep your mouth moist. Don't let it get dry. While you suckin' it, speak that Spanish shit to me. That's a turn-on."

"Okay, papi. *Estoy bien para ti.*"

"Yeah, baby, I don't know what that shit means, but it sounds good."

Red licked her lips and smiled. "It means I'm being good for you."

Blue continued to coach while Red complied. And so it went.

"If you let me suck your titties, I can make them grow," Blue promised. Red, who wanted to be more developed before her time, fell for every trick in the book.

Blue could do whatever he wanted with Red. Her body was not fully developed to the point it was today but her taut and supple flesh was something that turned Blue on.

As with all things, with time comes age and with age comes wisdom. The only problem with Blue, and ultimately for Red, was that Blue felt that the only thing better than old pussy was new pussy. After several months, Red's pussy became old pussy, so Blue bounced.

"Why you don't call me back when I leave a message?" Red screamed into the phone one night.

"Look, if you gon' talk to me like that, I'm hanging up." And hang up Blue did, over and over again. Red sank back into her pillow and turned her face to hide the tears when her grandmother came into the room to check on her.

Red had managed to spend her entire summer with Blue and hadn't spent any time with her cousins like she usually did. He consumed her every thought. Puppy love was like being caught in an anaconda's grip. Red began to mope and stay in her room, with the shades pulled down.

Eyebrows knitted together in concern, Red's *abuela* came to her bedroom one afternoon. "Red, are you ill or something? You won't eat, you won't go out. You just stay stuck up in this room."

Red hadn't responded. She only wanted to make up with Blue. Nothing else mattered to her. Not bathing, not eating. She became obsessed with Blue and getting him to love her like he once did.

Red prayed all night that something would change. *If only I could turn him out in the bedroom,* she thought. She snuck onto adult cable channels looking for clues of how to love him better.

Blue wouldn't answer her pages. She never really knew where he lived; all she knew of were some of the previous places that he had taken her to.

With only three days left in her vacation, when the evening set in, Red hit the streets looking for Blue at his hangout spots. She soon found out that Blue was not all he presented himself to be. Red searched two local bars and came up short.

Crossing over the Avenue, Red took the train to Eighty-seventh Street and stopped at the Xctasy nightclub. She roamed the parking lot trying to spot Blue's Mercedes-Benz. She spotted it parked to the far left side of the lot; the license plate of the car confirmed it was Blue's. Red walked over to the car looking cautiously over her shoulder. The night air brought a chill over her body, but the heat from her vexed feelings kept her warm.

Red scanned the pavement for a rock but came up empty. She walked over to the car and had the urge to try the door handle. The handle gave and she slid into the driver's seat and noticed that the keys were in the ignition with a valet tag on them. Sweat beaded on her upper lip as she turned the ignition.

Once the engine was on, the sound system blasted. She froze, her heart pounding, then turned it down. Red's gaze darted back and forth over the lot. People were still piling into the club and the valet began walking back across the lot. He noticed the humming of the car engine as Red spotted him. Instinctively, she smiled and rolled down the window on the driver's side.

The valet wondered if the driver in the car had grown impatient waiting for her car. He figured that if she was already in her car he'd missed out on the tip and he wasn't about to do any extra work for nothing.

"Hey, I got my car. Is that okay?" Red managed to shout.

"Uh, yeah, that's cool," the attendant answered. He remembered the car, the driver and that a woman was with him. He wanted to take a second to think but instead let it slide.

Red drove the car across the lot slowly. She didn't even have her driver's license.

"Hey, wait!" Red heard the attendant yelling as he ran behind the car. She wanted to jet out of the lot but thought twice about it. She stopped the car.

"Um, your lights. I mean you don't have your lights on." The attendant was out of breath and leaned on the car. Red's eyes darted to the dashboard. She turned a knob or two to her right and the lights on the dash lit up.

Easing into traffic, Red turned the stereo volume back up, finding a jazz station. Instead of feeling sorry for herself, something clicked inside of her. She went from the pain of being a victim to the rush of being in control. Blue had had all the control. But now, driving his prized possession, Red began to understand that if she couldn't get him one way, she'd get him another.

Red thought she could call Blue and make him talk to her. She had his car, yet the uncertainty of whether or not he would get upset made her think twice about her next move. Her inner voice told her that Blue was not coming back. He had shitted on Red. So the more she drove the less she cared about getting Blue back, and the more she thought about paying him back for her pain.

Red drove all the way to Long Island. During the forty-five-minute trip, she replayed the relationship repeatedly in her mind. The car lights began to mesmerize her as she gripped the steering wheel. As the melodic jazz music floated through the speakers, Red wondered why the men she'd encountered were so cruel.

My mother met Jerome right after my father's death. You would think he'd be like a father to me, but nah, he made it quite clear by his actions that I was not his child.

I still remember that day, when everything changed. As my mother left the drink next to the table, she turned and looked at me as if it was the last time we'd ever see each other. She grabbed her car keys and left me alone with Jerome. His caresses began to get more aggressive and his hand inched farther up my dress until it reached the lining of my panties. Then his hand moved from the front of my panties to the rear of them, massaging my young ass. His touch made me squirm. It felt unnatural. At six years old, I knew that this was wrong.

"No," I whispered to him, but it was no use. He continued to massage my young clit through my panties with his thumb. The harder I squirmed the more he rubbed as he licked the side of my face. Suddenly he inserted his finger into my vagina. That was when my mother reentered the room and he quickly pulled his finger out. However, the pain was still there. I had been violated.

"Mommy, he touched my private parts," I later explained. I had learned that word back in day care. They told us there were good touches and bad touches and no one was to touch our private parts in an inappropriate manner.

As I stood there in silence, I knew it was wrong. My mother may have been everything to me, but when she didn't take my word over Jerome's just because he was giving her a little extra ends, it really hurt me.

I learned then that bitches couldn't be trusted and that a woman would always take a man's word over another woman's. I would never trust any woman again with my secrets.

Every young girl needs her mother, and when I needed mine to listen, she wasn't there.

• • •

Blue left Red with both a blessing and a curse. She missed him dearly because of how well he treated her during their short-lived romance. But now, she wanted to see his demise. She was furious that another guy had taken advantage of her innocence. She wanted him to feel the pain she felt.

Once she hit Long Island, she found a phone booth and paged Blue. Sure enough, unlike her previous pages, the foreign number made Blue call back immediately.

"Yeah," Red said into the receiver in a disguised voice.

"What up?" Blue said.

"When was the last time you seen your car?" Red whispered. Red imagined that the mention of his car raised Blue's ears like a dog called to attention.

"What?" Blue spoke louder into the phone. Red could hear the music in the background, which meant that he was still inside the club and had no idea that his car was gone.

Blue searched frantically in his pockets for the valet claim ticket. His heart pounded but began to beat slower as his nerves calmed. He detected something familiar in the caller's voice. "What about my car?"

"I got your car and if you want it back come meet me," Red demanded.

"Red?" Blue said into the phone, his voice filled with disbelief.

"Yeah, nigga, so now you know my voice and my name, huh? And don't hang up on me. If you hang up, you can kiss your car good-bye."

"Red, hold on. I need to pay my tab and leave the club. Give me two seconds and I'll call you back. I can hardly hear you." Before she could object, Blue hung up the phone. He dug his hand into his pocket, pulling out his valet ticket, and ran to the parking lot. He handed his ticket to the attendant, who went to retrieve the car. Blue paced back and forth.

"Nigga, where is my black Mercedes?" Blue yelled across the lot—the attendant had been searching a little too long for his car.

"Mercedes?" The attendant knew immediately what Mercedes Blue was referring to: the Mercedes with the young girl in it.

"Oh, yeah." The valet ran back over to Blue. "The girl. The girl took the car. I thought—"

Blue punched him right in the mouth.

Red was getting more furious by the moment. *How dare he make me wait,* she thought. Before she allowed her emotions to get the best of her chance for revenge, she breathed deeply, inhaling, then exhaling, blowing hard to calm herself. Red knew Blue had to have gone to the parking lot. There was no way he would have gone back to partying after hearing her threat. She could do nothing but wait for the phone to ring again. She knew it would ring again.

Ring, ring . . .

"Where in the fuck is my car, bitch?" Blue yelled into the phone. "Bitch?"

"Look Red, stop fuckin' playin' and get me my damn car."

"Excuse me? It's no fun when the rabbits got the gun," Red said with an attitude.

Blue began to panic. He couldn't believe that this little bitch had gotten the upper hand on him.

Blue stood there with the phone pressed to his ear and looked up and down the street for the first cab he could find. He calmed down and spoke into the receiver.

"Okay, baby, let's talk. Where are you?" Blue tried to beat her at her own game in hopes of finding her whereabouts.

Red knew he was insincere, yet it felt good to turn the tables and have him kiss her ass. "You never loved me, did you?" Red asked into the phone, needing, wanting to be sure.

"Yeah, I loved you. It's just I knew you were leaving so I wanted to break it off before I got hurt."

Red didn't know which rule of the dating game this was, but she knew bullshit when she heard it. Blue's words soothed her aching heart, but her love for him was too sincere for her to accept the bold lies.

She silently held the phone.

"Come see me," Red finally said, as if reading his thoughts through the phone.

"Of course, baby. Where you at?" Blue asked.

"Long Island."

"That's kinda far. Check this out, drive back into the city and meet me at Junior's," Blue instructed.

Red was determined to keep things on her terms so she said, "No. You need to come out here and meet me at the North Randall Mall."

"Whatever, I can be there in an hour," Blue said, "I'm hailing a cab now."

"I'll meet you in the parking lot on the south side of the mall."

The phone went dead and Red began to think of her next move. *What can I do now?*

She reached in the glove box of Blue's car, searching for something to take. She found various photos of Blue and other bitches. Nothing surprising there. She also found about forty dollars in loose bills and change, which she pocketed.

She drove to a nearby convenience store and purchased two five-pound bags of sugar, a box of matches and charcoal lighter fluid. She hadn't picked her weapon yet, but she wanted to be prepared. Walking out the door of the store, she had to fight back the tears. What in the world was this about? Her sweet sixteen was a month away and she was planning a caper that could land her in jail—or worse, get her beat the fuck up by Blue.

Walking to the car Red noticed the time and figured she had about twenty minutes before Blue arrived. She drove near the airport to find a ride. Red approached the cabstand and saw a cab taking a break at the nearby Burger King. She walked over and tapped the glass. The old, gray-haired cabbie smiled and rolled down his window.

"Hey, daddy." Red spoke as if she were a woman older than her years.

"Yeah, honey. What can I do for you?"

"I need a ride back to the city and I was wondering if I could get a fare?"

"Sure, honey. Jump in."

"Well, I need to get picked up at the mall. Could you follow me there?"

"What?" the cabdriver asked suspiciously.

"I have to drop off my sister's car for her. She works night security at the mall." Red pointed to Blue's car. The Mercedes was tricked out, tinted glass, lots of chrome detailing—the works—and Red sensed the cabbie's hesitation so she pulled two twenties from her pockets.

"Oh, don't worry. I got money. I just don't want to wait for her to get off. I came over here," she said, pointing to the Burger King, "to get something to eat. Kill time before my sister gets off. Then I saw you, so I wondered if I could cab it back and meet her back at home. I got work in the morning," Red added, yawning.

"I don't go back into the city," the cabbie explained, suddenly changing his mind.

"Well, get me to the train station and I'll hop the train," Red suggested. Red faked a shiver to let the cabbie know that he needed to make a decision. "Oh, it's getting nippy." She flashed a smile.

The cabbie hesitated before he finally said, "Okay. I'll follow you over to the mall."

Red led the driver to the mall. She knew which exit to have him park at, which was opposite the one where Blue was coming to meet her. She wanted to position the cabbie in a discreet spot so that when Blue pulled up, the cab would be undetected.

Red pulled into the North Randall mall parking lot. There were a few cars there, which probably belonged to people working late, and overnight security. The security jeep cruising past them made Red think twice of torching Blue's ride.

The cabbie parked where Red indicated.

"I'll be back in about twenty minutes. Please don't leave me. I have to find my sister and give her the keys." Red handed the cabbie twenty dollars. "I'll have more. I just want to let you know that I'm serious."

Red drove to the other side of the mall. She grabbed the bag of sugar and ripped it open, making a spout. Then she removed the cap to the gas tank and poured the sugar inside. When the first bag was completely empty, she poured in the second one.

Red replaced the cap on the gas tank and checked the fuel gauge. She turned the car off, started it again and revved the engine, then drove the car around in a circle until she felt the car drag a bit. Then she parked it. Satisfied with her revenge, she felt good. Although still hurting, she wouldn't be the only one walking away bleeding.

Red took one of the keys and cut up the leather interior seats. She carved the letters R-E-D into the dashboard. She turned and slashed the headrests. Rearing back in the seat, Red kicked and kicked with all her might until she broke the knobs off the stereo. She ran to the trunk of the car, where Blue kept his extra speakers, and bashed those in with a set of dumbbells he also had in the car. Finally she left a note on the steering wheel of the car.

Blue,
 The next time I see you, you're dead!
                                                              Red

Satisfied with her work, Red headed for the rear of the mall, where she came up on two Dumpsters. Something moved in the shadows, making her heart beat fast. She wondered if she was alone. If Blue had gotten there, he'd been watching her and was probably planning to kick her ass for her actions.

Suddenly a small figure darted out in front of her. Red jumped, then let out a small sigh of relief. It was just a small cat that had been looking for something to eat in the Dumpster. Red felt no remorse, not even the least iota of guilt.

Red continued visiting New York every summer. From afar she watched Blue and heard of the rumors of his success through the grapevine. She vowed to one day take her revenge on him. Every good wasn't gone. Every shut eye wasn't sleep.

CHAPTER 5

What Goes on in the Dark

Q was puttin' in extra work. After he had time to get used to the idea, he was so excited about having a child. A month had passed since he first found out that Red was expecting and he vowed to be out of the game by the time his child came into this world. Q was determined to be legit, save enough money and go back to school for a degree so that he could maintain a legal way of life.

This was perfect for Red because she was able to avoid seeing him a lot. When she couldn't avoid him, she wore loose-fitting clothes and created excuses for not having sex with him. When Q and Red were able to spend time together, it was all hearts, flowers and candy.

Q pulled his car into one of the spots in the three-car garage attached to Red's home.

"Hey, baby," Red greeted him as he walked toward her smiling. His arms were filled with gifts. "You need to stop this," she said, indicating the gifts. Q had been spoiling Red rotten. It was to the point that she didn't even have to ask for shit, or even scheme. Red noticed the less she asked, the more she got out of him.

Red began to tear the packages open; inside one she found a set of toddler's clothes. *Oh shit, he starting to buy baby clothes,* she thought.

"Red, when am I going to the doctor's office with you?" Q asked.

"Um, you can go next month." Red walked into the great room, faking admiration over the baby clothing. She was trippin' because all of them were top-notch brand names like Guess? and OshKosh. "You hungry?" Red tried to change the subject.

"Nah, I'm good, but really, when was your last appointment? You don't have to go through this alone." Q pulled Red closer to him. With his arms around her he began to caress her stomach and kiss her gently on her cheek.

"Damn, you still small." Q was referring to her stomach still being flat. Red did her best to poke it out and consciously rubbed it the way pregnant women subconsciously do.

"I went to the doctor Tuesday."

"Damn," Q said, obviously disappointed he missed the appointment by one day.

"I promise, you can go next month. It's really no big deal. Look. It's getting there." Red smiled and placed his hand on her stomach again.

Q smiled back at her. "Come here, baby. Let me hold you."

Red squirmed, trying to get away from his embrace. The truth was, she was on her period and all she needed was for him to feel her up and discover the ultra-thin sanitary napkin in the crotch of her panties. She walked over to the kitchen, Q following, and began to pull all sorts of food out of the fridge.

"I'm so hungry," she said, eating a pickle and digging in a bag of chips. Q seemed happy to see her eating.

"I want a fat little baby. Don't do that skinny Hollywood shit, Red. I mean it. Be sure to eat. Don't be so vain about this." He paused, then asked, "How far along are you?"

Oh shit, think, Red, think! "Why are you picking on me, Q?" She began to cry.

"Picking on you? How you figure that?"

"You asking all sorts of questions and I . . . I . . . waaaaa!"

Red had to do something to divert him from probing into her fake pregnancy.

"Red, I just want to—"

"You always in the streets! You don't want me. You don't want this baby!" Red slumped over, crying hysterically but laughing inside because he was falling for her shit, hook, line and sinker.

Red knew this would back him up. He felt guilty about how he made his money and whenever Red wanted to put him on the defensive, she used this against him. In the next breath she would ask for something that put his mind back on him doing what he was doing and what he had to do. It went back and forth like this over and over again, yet he fell for it every single time.

"You said we were going to look for another house and you haven't even gone with meeeeee!" She wailed even more.

Red had been pressing Q for a new address for some time, which made him work even harder to get enough money. Red's current home was worth at least $1 million, and Q knew he would have to move her into something similar, if not better.

"So have you been looking for homes?" Q asked, trying to appease her.

"I don't want go by myself. I want you to go with me." Red made her lips quiver as if she were going to cry again.

"Baby, we can go soon. I promise," Q reassured her so she wouldn't have another crying spell.

"I still don't want to live in Detroit. I don't want to raise my child here."

"I hear you, but I ain't trying to go to New York. It's just as bad as Detroit, Red." Grimacing, Q shook his head.

"Look, I don't care where we go, really. I just wanna get the fuck out of here." She wiped her eyes with a tissue. "Niggas kill me, talking that 'I got loot' shit." For good measure, she grabbed another pickle and started eating it. "A muthafucka soon learns just how long his money is when he can't move where they want. I got people all day and night dropping by my crib. I got problems of my own I can't solve. I got my Jew bitch on my back to perform or get out of her office." Red staggered away, holding her stomach as if she were about to throw up.

She had already decided on her plan: to fake stress. Everyone knew that stress was the number-one cause of miscarriages. Red only had three options: produce a baby, fake an abortion or fake a miscarriage. The only reasonable alternative was a miscarriage due to the stress.

Red wondered what it would have been like just to date Q like a regular person. But she didn't have time for regrets. She was on a mission and had to stick to the plan at hand.

Once Red got inside the bathroom, she put the rest of her plan to work. She removed the bloody pad she wore and threw it into the toilet with a lot of tissue. *Fuck it, I'll deal with that later if the toilet gets clogged,* she thought. Splashing water on her face, as if she were perspiring, she knocked everything that was on the sink onto the floor. "Argghhhhh!" she screamed.

Q ran into the bathroom. "Baby, what's wrong?"

"Q, the baby! The baby!" Red doubled over as if she were in pain.

"What?!" Q asked, almost hysterical.

Red held her stomach as Q moved her off of the toilet. "Oh my God!" he said as he stared at the mess.

"Our baby, Q! I'm having a miscarriage!" Red cried into Q's chest. "Q, I'm so sorry," she wailed.

Tears formed in Q's eyes. Walking Red to her bed, he asked, "Should I call 911?"

Sitting on the edge of the bed, holding her stomach, she cried, "I know you wanted this baby. I did, too. Please don't leave me, Q."

Holding her tightly, he assured her, "I'm not going anywhere," while kissing her tears away.

In between breaths, she replied, "I'll call my doctor. This is something they told me could happen in the first trimester."

Not knowing how to help her, he asked, "Is there anything I can get you?"

"Can you get me some pads, Q? Super," she said as she picked up the phone. Dialing time and temperature, pretending it was her doctor's office, Red spoke into the phone. "Hi, this is Raven Gomez and I'm a patient of Dr. Nesbit and I believe I'm having a miscarriage."

Q listened for a moment, then left for the store to get what Red requested. Q rode in silence, as he shed tears for his unborn child.

Two weeks had passed and Red was coming around to being her normal self, from Q's point of view, that is. He stood by her side and didn't push the issue when shortly after the miscarriage she told him she was scheduled for a D & C. Although he wanted to accompany her, he opted not to because she claimed it was too painful and she wanted to forget the whole ordeal, plus she felt better with a woman around because they understood. Q didn't fight her on this because he felt that somehow he was responsible for the miscarriage. When Sasha came to pick her up for the D & C, they went to a mall on the other side of town.

Red continued to enjoy Q's undivided attention and sympathy, but it was starting to get old. Whatever Red wanted, Red got and she wasn't complaining but she wanted some time to herself.

Today she was lying with her head in his lap, beginning to doze off, when the doorbell chimed.

"Damn, can't have no peace with my man!" *Right on time*, Red thought as she stomped to the door, like she wasn't expecting Sasha. "Muthafuckas come through here like it's a casino." Red mumbled more profanities under her breath as she went to the glass door. Red opened the door, winked at Sasha and turned to walk back into the great room.

"Hey, girl. What's up? I'm all packed. When will I get my door key? We had a deal, remember?" Sasha asked.

"Q, this is my girl, Sasha," Red said by way of introduction.

"What's up?" Q sounded nonchalant.

"Hi, you look really familiar. You from around here?" Sasha

started her usual questions dance. She knew that to ask questions sometimes meant you would get answers. "Did you go to Kettering High School?" Sasha sat on the chaise to the left of Q.

"Nah, didn't go there," Q responded.

Sasha knew that all the criminals in the city ran through Kettering. She wanted to figure out if he was an East Side playa or a North Side hustler. Sasha could smell money on Q and she knew if Red knew him, he was a money-getting cash cow someway, somehow.

"What side of town you from?" Sasha asked politely.

"Red, baby, I gotta make a run." Q sipped the last of his drink, ignoring Sasha's last question.

"You coming back, right?" Red asked, trying to scope out his intentions. She walked Q back through the corridor that led to the garage. "You gonna spend the night with me?" she asked, holding his hand.

"You know how I feel about resting my head in another nigga's house. Can't do it."

"Yeah, I know. We got to get a place of our own. All this time we've been spending together has got a girl spoiled," she said as she put her chin down, feigning sadness.

Sasha tiptoed over to the hall, trying her best to listen in on the couple. It wasn't working, though; she couldn't hear a thing.

"I may ask Sasha to move in with me until we find something," Red confessed.

"What?" Q tried—and failed—to hide his irritation.

Faintly, the house phone began to ring.

"Want me to get that?" Sasha screamed from the hallway.

"Yeah, go 'head." Red turned her attention back to Q.

Sasha fumbled around for the cordless phone. "Hello," she answered.

"Collect call from Bacon?" the operator asked.

"Yes!" Sasha yelled. "Hello?"

"Who dis?" Bacon asked.

"Sasha. How's it going, love?"

"I'm hanging in there. Yo, where's Red?" Bacon asked.

Instead of placing him on hold, or putting the phone down first, Sasha walked right up to where she thought Q and Red would be. Sure enough, she caught them in an affectionate embrace. Red was sucking on the side of Q's neck while his eyes were closed in pleasure. They were so intent on grinding slowly back and forth, they didn't hear Sasha walk up to them. They did hear her whisper into the phone, "Bacon, I think you need to call back later."

The mention of Bacon's name caused Red to freeze and turn toward Sasha.

Red would have never taken the call and could have easily played Bacon to the left, as she had been doing the past three months. Instead she used it as a chance and reached for the phone. "Hey, Bacon," Red said as if nothing was wrong.

"Bitch, now you can answer the phone?" Bacon was furious and expected Red to be on the defensive, so he established his position first.

"Hold on a sec." Red placed her hand over the receiver and said, "Q, give me a call, baby. I need to take this."

Q screwed up his face and turned to leave. He didn't want to make a scene. He wanted to ask Red what the hell that was all about, but how could he when she was living in the man's house? Q pulled out of the garage and vowed to get Red out of that house by the end of the month, even if it took his last dime. Even if he had to commit murder, he wanted her out of there.

Red took the cordless phone and headed up the stairs. On the way she told Sasha, "Make yourself at home."

Red strolled into her bedroom and sat on the edge of her bed facing her vanity. She paused for a minute or two. Red knew that Bacon had about seven minutes left of his fifteen-minute phone call. She took a deep breath, looked at herself in the mirror for a long time and placed the phone to her ear.

"Hey," she said.

"Hey, my ass. Fuck you been?" Bacon asked.

Red knew he called to talk and not curse. Otherwise, why would he call? She knew to play cool. She hadn't mailed the letter to him, *yet*.

"Bacon, I got your fucked-up-ass letter and I know you're mad, but you just don't know what's going on out here."

"Where you been?"

"In the county, nigga, that's where," Red lied.

"What?" Bacon asked in disbelief.

"Oh, you ain't the only one with problems. Sasha was the only one who would help me out."

"What happened?" Bacon asked.

"You know, I ain't even trying to talk on this phone. I'm coming to see you this weekend," Red announced. *Damn, I got to go visit the nigga.*

"Don't lie to me, Red. A nigga need to see you."

"Not as bad as I need to see you." She knew how to make Bacon feel much better. No one wanted to be left for dead behind bars, let alone believe that someone they looked out for would screw them. "You need anything?"

That closed his mouth for certain.

"No, just you, baby." Bacon went all the way soft on her.

"I can't tell by your letter," Red said, throwing salt in his face.

"Don't even go there. Just be sure to be here Saturday." The phone beeped, signaling the end of the phone call.

"I will." Red hung up the phone, sucking her teeth in disgust.

CHAPTER 6

The Crisscross

*M*uthafucka!" Red said aloud, as she thought about her conversation with Bacon. She marched into the hallway and paused. It was getting late and she was tired. Sasha had come by, alone, and she was glad because it would give them a chance to talk and decide what would happen next.

" 'Sup, sis."

"Hey, girl." Red took the chair opposite the couch.

"Dat nigga was fine. Who was that?" Sasha asked.

"Bacon's ass." Red knew that Sasha meant Q.

"Not him. The nigga you let out the rear?"

"Oh, a friend." Red smiled and fanned her hand in dismissal.

"What? Shit, he's fine. Q, right?" Sasha waited for the 411.

"Girl, don't even go there."

"Do he got a friend?" Sasha asked.

"Just met him a couple of weeks ago."

"Mmnh? Where?"

"Girl, why all the questions?"

" 'Cause his ass is fine."

"What I'm trying to do is have him buy your loft," Red explained.

"I'd love to show him my . . . uh . . . loft," Sasha said.

"Ho, you trippin.' This is strictly business."

"I'm sorry," Sasha lied. "Do you think he really would be interested in my place? How could you do it?"

"What I want to do with him is a land contract or an assumable loan, but I need you to give me all your paperwork. Did you bring it with you?"

"Yeah, I got all my papers right here." Sasha pulled out a folder and laid it in front of her.

"Whose name is the loft in?" Red asked.

"Mine, and I have power of attorney for all of Catfish's stuff."

"Cool. This is how we gon' do it. You know the loft is overpriced; I did some comps of other lofts in the building. I also found that you owe two hundred eighty-seven thousand dollars. Now, you need to decide what's more important and you got two options: getting it out of your name or getting some money out of it."

"Ho, you know I need some dough," Sasha said, laughing.

"I think I can get you three hundred thousand dollars, but there's title, tax and all sorts of other issues to go with the closing. The other option is to refinance for about three hundred fifty thousand dollars, pull the equity and then rent it out. As long as the note is being paid, the property will pay for itself. I can manage the property through the real estate office."

"Option two sounds good as far as the equity line. Who can you get to rent it?" Sasha asked.

"Don't you worry, just know that I will take care of the lease. Out of the money we get, we will take out your rent and then you will have a little left over for yourself."

"How soon can you do this?" Sasha was eager to get started.

"In no time," Red reassured her.

"Let's do it."

CHAPTER 7

Flip Side of da Game

Red knew that she had to work her hand in selling the loft so she immediately thought of Gloria Schottenstein.

Raven Gomez had approached Gloria last year. Gloria hesitated to even talk to the young girl. Whoever said timing was everything must have seen Red stop by the afternoon she did. It was the anniversary of the death of Gloria's husband, Sherman, and Gloria's spirits were low.

"Hello," Red had said as she walked slowly into the real estate office. She strolled across the hardwood floor and stopped at the receptionist desk.

"Can I help you?" the receptionist had asked, sliding her black-rimmed glasses toward the tip of her nose.

Red was so nervous that she wanted to turn around. She gripped her résumé tightly in her hands.

"Can I help you?" the woman repeated with obvious contempt.

"I-I'm here to talk with Ms. Schottenstein."

"Do you have an appointment?"

"Yes," Red had lied.

"One moment." The woman lifted the receiver and spoke into

the phone in a whisper. She had looked up at Red and continued talking. Red had learned long ago how to ear hustle. She could tell that Gloria Schottenstein wasn't sure if she had an appointment or not. It was clear that the receptionist was searching frantically for a note or paper with the appointment penciled in.

After a short moment, the receptionist sighed deeply. "You can go in." She pointed toward the rear of the hallway.

Red had taken quick steps down the hall and noticed several unoccupied offices.

At the end of the hall was a glass door with the initials "GS" etched in the center. She had walked up to the door, paused for a moment, taken a deep breath and then knocked.

A woman's voice had said, "Come in."

The first thing Red noticed when she entered the office was that Gloria was even prettier in person than her publicity photos revealed. She smiled warmly at Red and indicated that she take a seat. Red quickly went from nervousness to admiration. Gloria's office held trophies from years past, when she was at the height of her game. She had soft leather furniture, exquisite artwork hanging on the walls and a nicely framed picture of her and her husband that sat on the corner of her desk. "I'm sorry, dear. Did I forget an appointment with you?"

"No, I wanted to come by and apply for a position with you. I lied about having an appointment. I just said that to get in to see you."

Gloria smiled. "Nice approach." She walked over to the fridge and removed two bottles of Evian water. She extended one to Red, who graciously accepted.

"Thank you." Red handed her the résumé.

Gloria looked it over. When she was done, she simply said, "So you want to become a Realtor?"

"Yes, ma'am."

"Don't 'yes, ma'am' me. You make me feel old, sweetie. Call me Gloria."

"Gloria, I want to be a Realtor."

"Why?"

The real answer was so she could make a lot of money but Red knew that Gloria didn't want to hear this.

"I enjoy working with people and helping them make their dreams come true by finding the perfect home." Red wasn't surprised when Gloria smiled at this response. She knew it was what Gloria wanted to hear.

"This is very hard work and the hours are extremely long. I built my company with one client. That client later referred me to another client, and then another."

Red absorbed every word that she was saying. This was the flip side of the illegal game. She was learning a legal hustle and getting game from a master of real estate.

Schottenstein Realty was not the largest real estate company in Detroit, but it was definitely one of the most prestigious. Gloria and Sherman had started the company in the '70s. They both put in all the hard work and muscle that a start-up company required.

Five years earlier, Sherman, Gloria's senior by seven years, died of an unexpected stroke. But despite Sherman's absence and the bleak Detroit economy, Gloria continued to lead a successful, highly profitable business and looked good doing it.

Though they were years apart and from different worlds, Gloria and Red were essentially the same. They possessed a similar quality—a quality of confidence, a commanding inner power and a drive to prosper at all costs that eluded most other women, including Red's mother.

Red and Gloria bonded instantly.

"Your reputation is all that you have in life, and all that you need in this industry. With your rep you can seal a deal or cause one to break. If you work on building your rep, the rest will follow. Join me for dinner tonight and we'll talk more."

"Sure, where?" Red asked. She was very excited but tried not to seem too eager.

"Meet me at the Monk Restaurant on Beaubien Street at seven o'clock. We will finish your interview there."

"See you then." Red extended her hand to shake Gloria's good-bye.

. . .

The Monk Restaurant was located in the upscale suburb of Gross Pointe Park, about thirty minutes away from Red's home.

Red made certain she arrived twenty minutes early and still didn't beat Gloria. She was already there having a glass of Cabernet, mingling with the guests and the maitre d'.

Seeing Red in her vintage strapless Emilio Pucci dress and matching jacket made Gloria smile. The girl was definitely a looker. Red managed to gain the stares of the men and envious glances of the women. Gloria placed her arm around Red and began to introduce her to prominent Detroit citizens.

Gloria introduced her to the mayor of Detroit, Kwame Kilpatrick. "This is Raven."

"Nice to meet you, sir," Red said.

"What a lovely name, Raven," he said with approval. "So you are working with Gloria?"

Red glanced at Gloria, who winked. Red smiled and answered confidently, "Yes sir. I'm her new junior Realtor."

Gloria liked Red and the way she handled the conversation.

"By the way, sir, congratulations on your reelection," Red said.

"Congratulations to you on your new job," the mayor replied as he was led away to meet and greet others.

Gloria knew the only way to really interview a person was to see them in different settings. Since real estate was primarily schmoozing, she wanted to see if Red could schmooze. They spent the beginning of dinner doing so as several people approached the table.

"Tell me about Gloria," Red said as she sipped her water. The dining room was dimly lit with crystal chandeliers while the tables were set with fine china and sterling silver utensils. A man played soft jazz on a baby grand piano in the corner of the restaurant. Gloria ordered the grilled chicken breast with coconut curry sauce and Red had grilled salmon with spicy black bean sauce.

Gloria broke off a piece of bread from the basket and shared the story of her business start-up with Red.

"You're a New Yorker, huh? Pretty cool place to visit, but not live," Gloria joked.

"The real estate market there is crazy," Red remarked.

"Oh, definitely. The real estate market is extremely different in New York. There is no more land to build new houses on, so the buildings keep getting taller and taller."

The conversation then turned to family. Where a person is from tells you in which direction they are going.

Red surprisingly told Gloria about the absence of her mother. She typically told anyone who asked that her mother was dead.

When I turned ten, my mother's live-in boyfriend, Jerome, began buying me all types of expensive gifts. One day, he bought me a pair of diamond earrings and that's when my mother got really suspicious. Licking his lips, Jerome asked me, "Do you want to keep getting those nice things?" He took me over to a mirror in the living room and told me to look at myself. I was thinking this nigga is out of his element when he started running his fingers through my hair.

"What you doing?" I asked.

He took a minute to respond and told me that I was the second most beautiful woman he had ever seen, my mom being the first. I'm thinking to myself, I ain't no woman yet.

"Don't you ever let a nigga get something from you for nothing," he said seriously. "You so pretty, you could make a nigga crawl." He laughed.

"Come on, Red," he begged. I liked the feeling of having power over him, false as it was. He sounded like a young dude my age trying to get a piece of the na-na.

"This is wrong," I said, trying to twist away.

"If you don't, I'll tell your mother you kissed me."

I wanted to scream but I knew deep down inside my mother would believe Jerome over me. He looked at me and gave the most evil smile I'd ever seen. It was almost like he knew what I was thinking. I thought that letting him touch me was something I could live with, but losing my mother wasn't, so I walked into my room and lay on the bed, scared to death.

"Stand up," he said, pulling out a Black & Mild. He unzipped my pants and they fell to the floor. Jerome began rubbing me like I was a *woman and kept commenting on how big my chest was for my age. He started kissing me and took off my panties.*

He positioned himself on top of me, kissing and touching me, being careful not to put all of his weight on my small body. I felt something on my leg before he got up and started unbuckling his pants. As Jerome stood there in his underwear, I noticed something trying to break through the fabric; he reached inside and pulled it out.

"What you doing?" I asked, confused. He showed me his dick as he stroked it and I told him it was too big to go in me. He just ignored my words. He began kissing on my neck and chest again, this time with more force. I kept saying to myself, God help me, *but help never came. A strange pleasure began to take over my body to numb my brain of the situation at hand. When I moaned, he asked if he could have sex with me. He spread my legs and tried to place his manhood between them. I yelled for him to stop because of the pain, but I couldn't move.*

"It'll be okay," he said softly. "I'll go slow. I'm gon' make it feel real good, okay," he said in a gentle tone. "I love you, Red." Then he kissed me again. I was disgusted with myself for liking his words. I always wanted to know what it felt like to have my father say, "I love you." When he finally got inside of me, he just kept giving me deep tongue kisses. "You are so pretty," he kept telling me. I hated Jerome for what he did to me, and for stealing my innocence. But I loved the attention, and gave myself to him without reserve.

Gloria and Red drank way into the evening, ignoring the waiters who were ready to close. They had emptied two bottles of wine before Red began to feel closer to Gloria. What was happening between them was magic.

When they left the restaurant, the two women embraced. Red held on a little tighter than she normally would have. She'd love to have a dinner like that with her mother, but how could she, when her mother had chosen Jerome—a man who still lived with her to this day—over her. To Red, her mother was dead.

CHAPTER 8

Starting Over

*T*he U-Haul driver backed the small truck up, trampling over the azaleas, landing smack-dab in the middle of the coleus and almost on the front steps of the house.

Kera had packed all of her belongings in large Glad garbage bags; being the pack rat she was, it was hard to say good-bye to yesterday so she brought it all with her today. Red's home was fully furnished, but Kera still wanted her favorite purple chair for her bedroom. She also needed her clothes, the computer, her high school cheerleading trophies, and the stroller and playpen for the baby. Of course, she had to bring the big fifty-inch TV that she'd gotten from Rent-A-Center. Then she had to have her bunny slippers and kitchen appliances, which included her George Foreman grill and her deep fryer. The girl's arteries were crying for a heart attack.

When Kera said this was her new home, trust and believe that she meant it from the bottom of her heart. She had copped a new leopard-print comforter set and matching curtains for her windows along with a complete pink and chocolate bathroom set.

There were lamps, posters of LL Cool J from back in the day, rollers, stand-up hair dryers, curling irons—you name it, she brought it.

Kera tapped on the door and dropped a huge plant in the entry. Red walked up to the door and knew what she had to do. Whoever said being greasy was easy was wrong.

"Damn, girl," Red said, looking at the truck after Kera knocked on the door. "Get the fuck off my shrubs!" she yelled. She ran onto the cobblestone pathway en route to the side of the truck.

The driver ignored her and continued to beat his hand on the steering wheel while singing at the top of his lungs to the beat of an oldie but goodie.

"I said, get the fuck off my plants, nigga!"

The driver looked at Red as if she had lost her mind. "Fuck you. Yo, Kera! Get yo' girl!"

"Girl? Muthafucka, pull this raggedy-ass piece of shit out of my flowers!" Red screamed. She turned to go find Kera, who was on the other side of the truck, still pulling garbage bags full of shit out of the front seat.

The toothless driver sat there like Kera and Red were going to move everything themselves. When he realized Red wasn't about to help, he jumped out the truck and began grabbing things with both arms. His thought was, *The sooner I get Kera into this house, the sooner I can get the hell out of here.*

"Oh no, you will not bring them nasty-ass feet into my house." Red looked back and forth between Kera and Toothless. He wore steel-toed work boots that had seen better days.

Toothless removed his shoes to reveal a pair of yellowish, stained socks, which emitted an odor that could kill a horse. Red pinched her nose and decided to walk back into the house to pour herself a drink. This shit was giving her a headache.

Kera and Toothless went up and down the stairs bringing in Kera's things. Kera did her best to maneuver, pushing or pulling whenever she could, considering her belly was getting bigger and bigger each day.

"Where is your help?" Red asked in disgust as she stood in the entryway and watched Kera struggle.

"Well, my so-called baby daddy said he would help, but you know niggas. No good, sorry muthafuckas."

"He probably somewhere laid up with Terry's ass."

"You think?" Kera responded.

"You think not?"

"Look, Red, I'm too far along for an abortion. I'm too big to kick his ass or hers. I've decided to move the fuck on with my life with my child and do the best I can. This is my new start. If he helps, fine. If he don't, oh fucking well, it's his loss."

How in the hell is not having the responsibility of a child any-one's loss? Red thought. "Yeah, girl, you right. Just keep doing what you do." Red turned to leave. She wasn't about to help Kera move her raggedy shit. *Damn, couldn't she at least find some luggage? The Asians sell Louis Vuitton joints all day, every day, up and down Gratiot Avenue,* she thought. There had to be a better way.

After the last garbage bag was hauled upstairs, Toothless left the premises. Red stood in the doorway and stared at her damaged plants. Julio, her gardener, had just manicured the landscape and Kera was fucking it up already.

Kera walked up behind her. "I'm so sorry. As soon as this load drops, I promise to replant every little flower."

"Forget it. You got your money?" Red inquired.

"Can a bitch put her feet the fuck up?" Kera flopped back onto the sofa to rest.

"Well?" Red sounded dead serious.

"Here. Damn!" Kera snapped. She pulled $2,000 out of her pocket. "Is this how it's going to be, come the first of the month?"

"Maybe." Red smiled and counted the twenty $100 bills.

"Where's Sasha?" Kera asked.

"She coming later tonight," Red explained.

"Glad I got here first, so I can get the room I wanted."

"So when's the baby coming?" Red asked, more out of concern for her plan rather than for her hopes to see the bundle of joy.

"Three more months and it's out, Auntie Red." Kera rubbed her stomach and gave a smug smile.

"You'll be a mommy." Red hugged Kera impulsively.

"Yep. I'll be a mom," Kera said proudly.

CHAPTER 9

What You Won't Do for Love

Terry pulled into the apartment complex and smiled at the sight of Mekel's truck. Although what they had wasn't new, she still had that new relationship excitement merely at the sight of him with his curly, jet-black short Afro. He had dimples in both cheeks and his skin was so light, he almost looked Middle Eastern. Her nerves continued to get the best of her because she really didn't know much about him, other than what she'd heard. She knew he had an ex-wife, although she wasn't sure why she was an ex. Sure, he'd come back to her after fucking Kera for months. Sure, he said he loved her, and, of course, he said the baby wasn't his. Despite all of this, she still wanted to be with him. It was more than how he laid the pipe. It was mostly the bank that he grossed from being a top dope man on the street.

Terry fought daily to shake the rumors of who he was hittin'. It didn't matter, Mekel always came back and she always took him back.

Turning the key in the lock, she heard the familiar sounds of Usher's "That's What It's Made For" through the door and her nose detected something delicious on the stove. It would be their night for romance. One more night away from home and her kids would not matter.

Terry left her kids with her mother on many occasions. It had gotten preposterous, but chasing Mekel and carting kids around was not an easy task. Terry was in between jobs, hustles and keeping one eye on Kera. It was typical of women to want Mekel so Terry kept her other eye on him, which she couldn't do with kids constantly around.

Mekel was born and raised on the East Side of Detroit. He was the nephew of the notorious Larry Chambers of the Chambers Brothers who got busted for running one of the largest crack rings Detroit had ever known, but that didn't deter Mekel from the streets. He then formed his own gang called the Best Friends. They had been a group of youngsters that grew up together before Mekel made a name for himself. The Best Friends never really reached the height in the dope game that they wanted, so they began to put the murder, duct tape and rape game into play.

Mekel ate however and wherever he could. He would have preferred not to eat off his looks, but being as fine as he was, he was much better at coming up off women than he was hustling in the streets.

"Mmm . . ." Mekel hummed as he stood, butt-booty naked, in front of the stove. Cooking in the nude was his pastime. Mekel shimmied the pan back and forth, tossing the scallops an inch above the pan.

Terry walked up behind him. "Something smells good, Daddy."

She began slowly, placing light kisses and nibbles up and down his back. Once she made her way down to his backside, she rubbed her hands together and spread his buttocks to insert her tongue close to his anus, teasing him ever so gently.

Mekel turned, placing his erect penis inches from her nose. He turned off the stove with his left hand and leaned back for her to handle her business. As Terry licked up and down on the head of his dick, Mekel grabbed the back of her head and began pumping back and forth to a rhythm, literally fucking her in the mouth.

Lapping and licking, Terry deep-throated Mekel like a champ.

Terry's mouth was so wide, her lips so full, she could fit a whole tangerine into her mouth. But it was her tongue that he loved the most.

"I'm about to come, ma."

Terry didn't move an inch. Instead she opened up her mouth and welcomed his deposit. "Umm, umm good," she said, swallowing. "Yeah, baby."

When they left the kitchen, they headed for the bedroom shower. Afterward Terry had Mekel lie down on the bed for a massage. She rubbed his shoulders and upper back until his muscles relaxed.

"Mekel, can I ask you something?" Terry whispered.

"What's up?" Mekel held his breath.

"Kera. Tell me what happened." Terry had never really known the details. She expected Red to tell her, but Red wouldn't talk about it. Terry didn't want to rock the boat, so she mostly ignored the issue. But with Kera's due date approaching and the rumors running rampant, she had to get closure. So she asked the other person who had been there: Mekel.

"Tell me about Kera, Mekel. Don't you think it's time that you told me what happened? I mean, is the baby yours or what?"

"Look, why you asking me this shit?"

Terry rubbed his back, moving her hand over a pimple. She popped it with the pads of her thumb and forefinger, inflicting pain. She continued to sit on Mekel so that he could not easily move.

"I deserve to know, nigga! I'm right here, right now. I'm still here and I want to know what happened."

"You need to drop dat shit." Mekel moved from under her and rolled over. Turning his back to her, he closed his eyes and faked sleep.

"Look, M. I love you, and you know this. You fuckin' someone close to me hit too close to home."

"Close? Fuck dat ho!"

"Obviously that's what you did." Terry was getting angry, yet she wanted to keep her composure in order to keep him talking.

Mekel turned to her and gave her a silent stare. Terry used to be drama-free, but it seems that shit just don't last in a relationship.

"I didn't mean that, M," Terry begged. "This shit is so crazy. Tell me what happened." She sat with her back against the headboard and exhaled a deep sigh, as if this was the end of her rope. Truth be told, Mekel did care a great deal for Terry. It was just that, well—he felt like taking the easy way out.

"Baby, charge it to the game, not my heart."

"The game?" Terry asked in disbelief. "What part of the game is it that you fuck my homegirl?"

"Look, Terry. We weren't even together when that happened."

"What? I don't wanna hear dat shit."

"It was during one of your dramatic-ass good-byes."

"And that gave you the right to fuck my friend?"

"No, it wasn't like that." Mekel pulled Terry close to him. "Look," he said, stroking the sides of her face, "you don't want to know the truth, 'cause you can't handle the truth." He tried to joke but it fell flat. Terry remained silent as she listened to the rhythm of his heartbeat. She loved this man more than life itself.

"Tell me. If you loved me the way you say you do, you would tell me," Terry whispered.

He knew damn well that she didn't want to know the truth. She saw the truth in Kera's bulging belly. She heard the truth on the streets through rumors. She caught the truth the time she saw Kera slipping from his crib. Yet, Terry claimed to want to hear the truth, as if it would make any difference. *Fuck it*, Mekel thought.

He took a deep breath.

"After I explain this shit to you, I don't want to hear no more about it. Cool?"

Terry nodded as if to agree. Her emotions were making her physically and mentally sick. If she didn't get the truth that night she was either going to kill Mekel and Kera or flip the fuck out on some padded room and straightjacket type shit. Terry swore that if Mekel ever lied to her, she was going to pull a Lorena Bobbitt and cut his dick off.

"It was right before Christmas. You had left and we argued about where I was. I was in Vegas at the Bellagio casino playing craps. I looked up to throw the dice and there was ole girl at the end of the box screaming my name, 'Mekel! Mekel! Slang it, baby!' She was in Vegas for an uncle's funeral, and her fam came to check out the Casino.

"I already had a ton of shit to drink since I was with my boys from Philly. Kera kept yelling, and let's face it, you know she ain't bad on the eyes when she brings it out at night. Titties hanging all out and shit. So, one thing led to another and she came over.

"She told me she wanted to blow on my dice, so, I let her. When she did that and licked my thumb, that was the beginning of the end. We headed back to my suite and ordered up some food. We talked a bit, and shit, Terry. I thought I was gon' fuck her and that would be the end of it." He paused to check out Terry's expression, but mostly because he didn't want to tell her that the sex was the bomb and he was like the cat; satisfaction kept bringing him back.

"And, so what? You disregard my feelings over what, Mekel?" Terry got smack dead in his face and screamed at the top of her lungs. "Some *pussy*?!"

Just as he suspected, Terry didn't want the truth. She wanted some lie about how he got tricked or some shit. The fact was, Kera was fine and Mekel's dick wanted her. It wasn't fair to say she forced herself on him, but from Terry's body language, Mekel knew that in order to save this dance, he had to turn the tables.

"Terry, Kera knew we were together. I even reminded her that you was my girl and shit but she didn't care. I thought that was fucked up because she was your girl and all, so I tried to put her out of the suite but I was so fucked up after that crap game, I damn near passed out. I think I did because the next thing I know, when I woke up, she had my dick in her mouth. Wasn't no turning back after that, you know."

"So . . ." Terry paused as she stared at him dead in the eyes. "You tellin' me all she did was suck your dick, right?"

"Yeah, baby, that's it." Mekel felt like he won. He was hoping she ignored his last statement of "no turning back."

"How she get pregnant if all she was doing was sucking your dick?" Terry needed to hear Mekel say he fucked Kera.

Mekel couldn't even think fast enough.

"Hello?!" Terry stared at him waiting for an answer. The silence was deafening.

Mekel had a stupid expression on his face because he'd had no idea that she was going to turn the shit back around on him.

"Unless things have changed and I ain't know about it, sucking a dick never got anyone pregnant."

"Baby, I—"

"I, I hell," she interrupted, tired of his bullshit. "How did your dick get into her pussy? How did your sperm get into her uterus?" Terry felt her blood boiling more and more by the minute.

Mekel moved away cautiously. Terry's nostrils began to flare. He'd gone against the playa's creed—never tell the truth, never confess and if that ain't work, always say it wasn't you, even if she saw you. Unfortunately for Mekel, it was too late.

"Why did you fuck her bareback? Why, Mekel? There weren't no condoms in all of Las Vegas? You don't know what she has and now you fucking me raw, too?" Terry's face was slick with tears now as she pointed to herself and then back to Mekel's forehead.

"Umm . . . she got pregnant 'cause, hell, I don't know! I didn't fuck her. All I did was let her suck my dick, I swear to God. I promise on my life and on everything that God loves, it's the truth."

Instantly, a calmness came over Terry. She put a hand to her moist eyes, then reached underneath the pillow and pulled out a butcher knife.

Mekel thought, *Oh, shit, she crazy! She is gon' slice a nigga!* It was then that he knew that Terry was insane, and he'd have to continue feeding her lies to avoid being killed. When his seed came, he would have to make a choice and take responsibility by remembering how it really went down.

CHAPTER 10

It Was All a Dream

"Red, are you sure you want to visit Bacon?" Q asked.

"I have to, Q," Red replied.

"Why you gotta go see him?" Q asked again.

"Because I need to tell him, face-to-face."

He stared at her as if to say, *You don't have to.* She returned his glare with one that said, *Nigga, don't go there.*

She began to put her clothes on and Q came up behind her, nibbling on her neck. "Damn, you taste good," he whispered in her ear. Being turned on by his touch, and the fact she hadn't had sex since her fake miscarriage, she readily accepted the affection.

"Q, I've missed you," she said as she turned to kiss him. Holding him close, she felt his erection pressing on her stomach.

"I've missed you, too," Q responded as he began to take off what little clothing she had on. Picking her up and carrying her over to the bed, Q laid her down. Propping herself up on her elbows, Red smiled at him with a devilish grin. As Q undressed, Red took in every inch of his body with her eyes.

"There's my friend," Red crooned as Q's dick sprang forward. Reaching out to him, she put the tip in her mouth.

"No. Not now," Q said as she was about to work magic on his dick. "It's been too long."

Grinning at him, she pulled him down on top of her. Kissing her passionately, Q eased in between her legs and flicked her clit with his dick. "Damn, girl, I ain't never felt you this wet."

"Quit talking and fuck me!" Red demanded and grabbed his ass.

In one swift motion, Q entered Red, causing her eyes to roll in the back of her head. They found a steady motion, enjoying and pleasing each other. Lifting Red's leg up on his shoulder, Q pounded deeper.

"Oh Q, baby, Q . . . Q," Red repeated.

"Goddamn this feels good!" Q yelled as his balls tightened up. "Ughhhhhhhhh!" he grunted as he shot his load inside of her.

Catching the feeling of her own orgasm, Red pulled him deeper into her while he was still in motion and moved feverishly to get hers. "Yes . . . yes!" she yelled as she came.

Q collapsed on top of Red, panting. "Damn, that was good."

"Wasn't it, though?"

Smiling at her, Q withdrew himself from her, realizing that he'd fucked her bareback; his expression didn't change. He got up and retreated to the bathroom to shower. Red looked down and noticed semen on the insides of her thighs, dripping from his withdrawal. She rushed into the bathroom to join him in the shower.

The refreshing wind blew across Red's face as she drove on the open road in her triple white BMW 525i, listening to Aaron Hall. The sweet smells of the fragrant flowers in the open fields engaged her nose and penetrated her mind, causing her entire body to relax. The forty-five-minute drive to Milan seemed more like twenty and she began to regret not coming to see Bacon more often. Really, what was the sacrifice when she could have a spring day like today, alone with her thoughts? The fact was that she was simply tired of faking it. First, she faked orgasms, then she faked concern, now she was supposed to fake caring now that Bacon was locked down?

Pushing seventy, Red kept her eye out for a roller giving out tickets since it was early Saturday morning. Turning off exit 74, she stopped at the light, turned left and drove another three miles down a lonely dirt road. *They sure know how to pick prison locations, out in the middle of West Bubblefuck.*

Parking her car in the visitors' lot, Red checked the clock in the dashboard. Visiting hours didn't start for another ten minutes, but she wanted to be first to avoid the lines, the hassles and all the other bullshit that came along with visiting an inmate. As she stared at the stone building behind the barbwire fence, she remembered how she and Bacon met almost a decade ago.

Red had just turned sixteen and still hadn't gotten over Blue. She had walked around with a sad face as if the world owed her something. Whoever said you could wear your heart on your sleeve must have seen Red wearing her broken heart on her face. She was whipped but that didn't discourage Bacon.

Red and Terry had walked into Home Town Buffet to get their grub on and Bacon's Maserati was parked out front, glistening in the sunlight. Now granted, Home Town was not the classiest joint in Detroit, but it was the hungry man's spot. They had biscuits that would make you want to slap your momma. Red had noticed the crown emblem on the hood of the car as they walked past, as she had never seen a car like that before.

"Terry, what type of whip is this?" Red asked, pointing to the car.

"Mm-mm-mm," Terry answered, her voice going up in the middle to indicate she didn't know.

Red eased closer to admire the beautiful car. Red later learned her proximity had signaled the silent remote car alarm that Bacon carried on his key chain. The thought of someone up on his car had made him leave his plate of fried chicken and dash to the parking lot.

Red's mind had begun to calculate as she stood at the crown-shaped hood ornament. She had always wanted to shine. She figured being a dime piece, that was her rightful position. She decided then and there that whoever drove that whip had to be a

King and she needed to be his Queen sitting next to him on a throne.

The girls didn't detect Bacon's approach and they were startled when he spoke.

"Why you putting your prints on my ride?" Bacon joked.

"Oh, I'm s-sorry," Red stammered as she stepped backward.

Admiring her backside, Bacon thought twice and said, "Nah, you good. I like that shirt."

Red had wanted to say thank you, but Bacon's presence had taken the words right out of her mouth.

Terry spoke up for her speechless friend. "She says thank you." Terry leaned to whisper in Red's ear, hoping to help snap her out of her daze. "Come on, girl. Let's get something to eat."

Bacon had seen her tense up as he walked closer. "Don't be afraid, baby. I won't bite you."

Red walked away and Terry followed. Bacon walked up behind the ladies into the restaurant and told the cashier to add their check to his bill. "Will you join me?" he asked them.

"Yes," Terry replied.

From that day forward, it was Bacon and Red against the world. Bacon took a wounded bird and gave her the confidence to fly again. Certainly it was not the *I-can't-eat-can't-sleep-without-you* love. It was companionship.

"Baby, you fucked with a busta. I'm a hustler and I know how to handle my woman. See, baby, success is a man's ego and a woman's sentiment. I need you by my side and all you got to do is be who you are. I know you're overworked and underappreciated. Bacon will appreciate you, baby," he said, trying to ease her fear that history would repeat itself.

Bacon made it so easy for Red to move on. There were times when she wanted to trust him, but he was a man, and that meant kill or be killed, so she always kept her guard up. Two years flew by and Red was Bacon's woman. It was so easy for her not to love him, though. He loved her enough for the both of them.

The screeching of a car parking beside her brought Red out of her daydream. *Fuck Bacon*, she thought. She checked her wallet to make certain her real identification was in place. Then she took out her dummy ID and placed it in the glove compartment; it was a crime to be caught with two IDs with different names.

Next, she began to rehearse the way she would handle Bacon's inquiries. She was supposed to visit him weeks ago, but she had managed to put it off. She didn't want to fuck his head up too bad and get tossed the fuck out his crib. She wanted to leave it on her terms.

" 'Bacon, I need some money,' " Red said aloud. "No, that won't work." Red placed her finger to her lips to think and then said even louder, " 'Bacon, I caught a case and need some money.' Nah, stupid him will just hire me a lawyer." Next she flipped the visor down and peered at herself in the driver's mirror.

" 'Bacon, I want to have your baby.' " Red laughed out loud on that one. She arranged her face into a sullen look and whispered, " 'Bacon, I just can't take you being away anymore.' Yeah, that's how I'll start it."

She flipped the visor back up, unlatched her seat belt, turned off the engine and exited the vehicle. Crossing the pebble-covered parking lot in her white Dolce & Gabbana pointy-toed pumps was a task. She was cautious to avoid getting them dirty. Approaching the tan brick building encircled by barbwire fencing, she could see groups of prisoners walking in the yard, looking outside, wishing they could be free. It reminded Red of being in a cage, unable to leave, like when she was a kid in her own home. Her empathy quickly turned into anger as she muttered, "This is some bullshit."

CHAPTER 11

As Soon as I Get Home

Entering the prison was like stepping into a thundercloud. The sunny sky no longer existed. Red made her way through the check-in line and her stomach began to turn as the smell of human funk became more and more potent. *How can anyone live like this?* she thought.

First, she was on the list, then when she got to the second checkpoint, she wasn't. Finally, they let her through. The whole point of coming early was to avoid all the drama, but instead it seemed like it just made her an easier target for the bullshit. Red's mood was fucked up.

Red sat at the square table, tapping her sculptured nails on the plastic top. She paused a moment and checked the time on her diamond-studded Chopard watch to make sure the visit was starting soon. *This muthafucka better come the fuck on,* she thought.

Bacon busted through the double doors all smiles. His skin glowed and his body was tight as hell. Red could see how he spent his time—working out.

He walked up to Red as she stood to embrace him. Bacon snaked his tongue in and out of Red's mouth and groped her so hard, she actually started to enjoy it. "Whew! Now that's a hello." Red smiled as she took his hand.

"Red, you look good." He took a step back to soak every inch of her in.

"You, too." She giggled, taking a seat. His gaze was making her uneasy. She could see the love he had for her in his eyes and the guilt of not loving him back and seeing him locked up like some damn animal was starting to melt her ice-cold heart.

Bacon scooted close to her. "So, what's up? You went to jail?"

"Yeah. It's bullshit."

"No, what's up?"

"I got into it with some girls at the beauty salon and they tried to jump me as I went to my car."

"What? Who?"

"Some of those bitches you fucked with. I'm up under the hair dryer and they poppin' shit about you."

Red was the master of provoking the other person into getting mad. Bacon couldn't really say shit because it was very possible.

"What salon was you at?"

"Vanities. You know, the twenty-four-hour spot over on Michigan Avenue."

"Okay, so what happened?"

"Nothing. We did our yelling back and forth and shit, and the salon owner called the cops."

"And?"

"And when they got there, they had a warrant for my arrest for an outstanding parking ticket and it didn't help I had a suspended license. Keep in mind, this was on a Friday night, so I had to stay in jail over the weekend. Then when Monday came, it was some holiday, President's Day or something, so I was out for a minute before court.

"When I did go to court, they gave me thirty days for driving with a suspended license. It was that or let the disorderly conduct stick, so they laid me down for thirty days. I couldn't write you.

But, instead of you thinking of me, you stressing me and there I was suffering over some bullshit, like you. Three hots and a fucking cot. Can I live?"

"So who be answering the phone when I call the house? I swear to God it sounds just like you."

"No, Sherlock. That's Sasha, you know, Catfish's woman."

"What the fuck she doing there?"

"Bacon, don't even start. Yeah, you busted your ass on the street, but nigga, I'm out there on my own trying to make ends meet."

"You know I left you with some dough. The house is paid for. Fuck you talkin' about? I thought you was working."

"I am, but shit, business is slow now. And you know a bitch needs to feed and clothe herself, not to mention pay the bills. Whatever." She sucked her teeth and turned away from him for dramatic effect.

"You out of money?"

"Almost," she whispered.

"Whatever, Red." It was going to take a little longer for Bacon to believe her story.

"Anyway, I'm helping Sasha out on the strength of you. I mean, Catfish is your dog and everything, so what was I supposed to do when she came to the house crying and shit about how they were losing the loft?"

"What? They losing the loft? That's bullshit! Red, don't be falling for some sucka shit."

"Look, you make the call. I'll bounce that bitch right out the door the minute I get back to the crib if you think she bullshittin'. You think I want a roommate?"

"Nah, don't do that. Let me check something out first."

"Whatever. Just let me know. Since I ain't kicked it with you, all sorts of shit is breaking loose on the streets. That's why it's taken me so long to come visit you. I'm sick of that shit. And the house? Please. The place is Grand Central Station. We once rested our heads in peace, but since you left, it seems like there is a gigantic flashing Vacancy sign pointing to the front door."

"I told you not to bring your peeps around. You ain't learned nothing from me. Red, you can't move a house that easy, that's why you don't let muthafuckas know where you rest your head in the first place."

"I know, I know. I just got lonely, missing you, and invited Terry over. But shit, she invited Kera and then they would get rides to the house. You know how them walking bitches be."

Bacon shook his head. All that he tried to make waterproof was starting to leak. He saw Red breaking before his eyes and didn't know what to do. "I know you get lonely. Shit, how you think I feel up in this muthafucka? I lay in my bunk every night thinking about us."

"Bacon, I just miss you so much you don't even know. Remember when it was just me and you? I was Bonnie to your Clyde," Red said, smiling. Her smile always killed Bacon. She managed to shed a tear.

Bacon wiped the tear as it trickled down her cheek. "It's gon' be okay, baby. My lawyer's working on my appeal."

"Appeal? What is that?" Red knew, but she was playing dumb.

"You know they got me for murder, not for doing what I do," he said, looking around for nosy ears.

Bacon had been making a routine stop by the spot of his oldest customer, Ronny Ray, an old-school businessman. He owned a barbershop that still had its original pole out front, classic barber's chairs and potted plants in the window that had been dead for about ten years. He spent most of his time talking to his clients— former pimps and hustlers—who never actually got haircuts but spent time and money there in other ways. Ronny Ray ran numbers, and threw the occasional c-lo dice game in the basement. But his biggest money-making scheme was renting out his hidden back office to young hustlers so they could sell drugs and hold meetings.

When Bacon first started up, he would frequently use Ronny Ray's services. After he outgrew the barbershop, he would stop by to chat it up with the old men, play a game of dominoes and hit Ronny Ray with his personal stash of weed. This one particular night he rolled by to drop off some food for the old man.

Just as he got there, a fight broke out between two dealers, Catfish and Landu. After the mayhem, Ronny Ray and two other men lay dead. The shooter escaped out the back just as the police arrived and Bacon was pinned with the murder weapon, which had landed by his feet. Luckily, he had no money or drugs on him, but the police didn't care. He was a black man at the scene of a crime with blood on his clothes and a weapon nearby. That was all they needed to throw him away.

"Red, I'm waiting for the results of this thing called a DNA test. That's where the rest of the money went. I had to get a new lawyer, pay him, then he suggested we hire a private investigator, and request an independent test. My lawyer said the DNA could set me free. I could be home by the end of the year."

Red's mind recalled the judge's words: *Isadore Jefferies, you are sentenced to twenty years.*

"Home . . . really? Daddy, I need you home." Red reached over and hugged him.

"I need to be home." Bacon kissed her on her forehead.

Surprisingly, the visit was going better than Red expected, not nearly the amount of stress that she had anticipated. They even managed to joke and laugh.

"So, Bacon, what's good up in there? I see you been pumpin' iron."

"I look good, don't I?" Bacon flexed his bicep.

"Yeah, Daddy, you look good."

"But check this out. I been writing."

"Yeah, I know. I got the letter." They both grinned at each other.

"No, seriously, I wrote a book and I want you to help me get it published."

"What? You wrote a book, as in a novel?"

"Yes. I had a lot of shit to get off my chest. The shit is fire."

"Can't wait to read it. Tell me about it."

"It's all about those who didn't stay true to da game. You know, in here I see and I hear everything."

"Yeah, the penal grapevine."

"Well, the penal grapevine says they heard you was pregnant?"

"Do I look pregnant?"

"Depends on how far along you are."

"No, nigga. Your grapevine is sour grapes. I'm not pregnant. Who told that lie?"

"Ain't important if it ain't true. I know you gon' fuck, and I ain't trying to hear about that, either. But be decent, Red." Bacon looked at her closely to check for a lie.

"The truth don't need no defending."

"Don't defend it then if it ain't true."

"I'm not gon' defend that, but Bacon, what am I supposed to do for the next twenty years?"

"I told you, I'm coming home. You can't hold me down until then? You can't wait until the end of the year to see how this goes, then decide what you want to do on a personal note?"

"Yeah, I'm here. I ain't going nowhere," Red lied.

"There's a publishing company, and all they do is put out street fiction. They call themselves Triple Crown Publications. I want you to have this book typed, and send it to them. Can you do that for me?"

"Yeah, just send me the pages and the information and I will handle it."

"Red, I got a feeling this book is it for me."

"What's the name of the book? What you calling it?" Red asked, uninterested.

"Bitch Nigga, Snitch Nigga."

"What?"

"Bitch Nigga, Snitch Nigga. And I don't want nobody to know I wrote it. We got to keep this between me and you, 'cause the shit I reveal in this book, I shoulda took it to my grave."

Red's ears perked up and in her mind she saw dollar signs. She knew that Bacon knew a ton of shit. If he wrote about all that dirt, then she believed the book would be a bestseller. Maybe he could pull a rabbit out of his hat again and be the cash cow he'd always been in the past.

"Go to the ladies' bathroom," Bacon ordered. He gave her a penetrating gaze as if he could see through her.

"What?" Red asked, not catching on.

"Go to the ladies' bathroom," Bacon whispered again. This time she understood.

Red was reluctant. She wasn't trying to be in a bathroom with Bacon. She wasn't sure if the nigga had turned into a homo thug or not. She didn't know if he was taking it up the ass or giving it up the ass, or who was tossing his salad or deep-throating him at night. Red was wise enough to not put anything past anyone.

Fuck, she thought as she walked to the restroom area. Red stood inside the last of the three stalls, tapping her foot and impatiently looking at her watch. She hoped like hell something would go wrong with Bacon's plan. After a minute or two, she heard the door open and footsteps enter.

"Red." Bacon's voice called to her.

Red kept quiet, hoping he would go away.

"Red," Bacon called again. He pushed open stall number one, then pushed stall number two. "Red!" He pushed on stall number three and met resistance.

Red kept silent as Bacon began to knock and push harder.

"Red!" Bacon jiggled the door handle as he peeked through the crevice to see who was in the locked stall.

"Red!" he said even louder this time.

Red slid the lock to the right and opened the door. She plastered a smile on her face, faking excitement. She knew what Bacon had come for—sex.

She had to pick the lesser of the two evils: suck his dick or let him stick it in. The thought of him having sex with men in prison made Red very, very hesitant about wanting him to put his dick inside her. She wasn't on that AIDS shit.

Bacon began tugging at Red's pants, making his choice apparent. He sensed her unwillingness. "Come on, baby. We ain't got much time."

"Bacon, what if we get caught? I'm scared."

Red hoped her words would change his mind, but what difference did it make to a man who had already been locked down for two years when he had good and familiar pussy within his grasp? He wanted some booty and was willing to go to the hole to get it.

"Don't be scared. The guard gave me some time. Stop playing."

Bacon undid the zipper of her slacks, revealing her G-string. He turned Red around, admiring her ass cheeks before spreading them apart. He groped her ass hard and Red felt his tongue penetrating her asshole. She gripped the back of the commode with both hands. Bacon rammed his thick dick into her somewhat dry pussy. He began to hump furiously, moving in and out with powerful thrusts. Bacon moaned aloud as they began to rock. For Red, there was more pain than pleasure as she was still raw from sexing Q earlier and she was not aroused. For Bacon, he was home again, in his bed, getting right.

Before Red could warn, "Don't come inside me," she felt Bacon's dick jerking inside of her pussy. A little trickle of cum ran down her leg as he disengaged from her body. Bacon quickly did up his khakis and Red began to pull herself and her clothes back together.

"Okay, you go back out first, then I'll come behind you," Bacon instructed.

Red walked over to the sink to check herself. Her left leg was sticking to her slacks as she felt the cum on the inside of her pant leg.

Bacon had involved her in the unthinkable: a private act in a public bathroom. Instead of feeling sorry for herself, Red straightened herself up, unstuck her pant leg and put on her game face. Her mind went back to the book he said he wrote, *Bitch Nigga, Snitch Nigga*.

Game was sold, not told, and she would make sure that she got paid for every single word that he wrote.

Fair exchange ain't robbery, is it?

CHAPTER 12

By Any Means Necessary

*A*s Red drove home, she couldn't believe that she had just had sex with Bacon. Her intention was just to go see him and hold him off until her schemes were fully executed. Instead, that nigga pumped her hard and left her with his cum on the inside and outside of her. She couldn't wait to get home and wash him off of her.

Ring . . . ring . . .

Red heard her cell phone ringing inside her purse. She turned down the radio and waited for the call to come through her wireless earpiece.

"Yeah."

"Hey, girl. Dis' Sasha."

"What's up?" Red replied.

"I was just checking on you and wanted to see how it was going with Bacon," Sasha quizzed.

Red didn't feel comfortable with Sasha's nosiness, especially since she had just left the visit.

"What?" Red asked.

"Bacon. What's up with him? You said you were going to visit him today."

"When did I say that?"

"Girl, so when you gon' go see the nigga?" Sasha asked as noise sounded in the background.

"I hadn't planned on it," Red said. "What's that sound?"

"I don't hear anything," Sasha said. "I heard he supposed to be coming home. That somebody had some new information about the case."

The phone developed static as Red drove past Detroit Metropolitan International Airport. Suddenly the call dropped.

Red was relieved. She took the exit near her home.

Red pulled up into her driveway, watched her garage door rise and admired her lovely home. It was a shame that she would be leaving it soon. In only six more months her plan would be in place. Her stash was at almost a million dollars—her goal was a million and a half—and then she would raise the hell up out of Detroit to start a new life somewhere, someplace, somehow. She had burned bridges before and she knew that the shit was going to hit the fan.

When she pulled into the garage, she noticed Catfish's black Infiniti already inside. She entered the house through the side door, walked through the hallway and into the kitchen. Placing her keys on the counter, she heard Kera and Sasha in what sounded like a small disagreement. Red decided not to even head that way. She didn't have time to play referee for them. She crept out of the kitchen and headed upstairs, digging her feet into the Berber carpet.

Sasha looked up suddenly and caught sight of her. "Hey, girl, we need you to come down here, 'cause Kera thinks she runs this place," Sasha yelled.

"What up, hos? Not now, I need a shower. Give me a moment and I'll be down." Red went to her room and closed the door.

"Bitch been out fucking, no doubt." Kera smirked. "You come home and run straight to the shower."

Red ignored them bitches completely. Her mind was on the sex she had just had. She ran the hot shower and watched as steam covered the glass. Nothing was hot enough to scrub the filth from her body. She stepped into the rush of water. Red lathered between her private parts and scrubbed until her flesh was raw, then she pulled a pack of Massengill Vinegar & Water douche from the medicine chest and cleaned her insides.

Strange as it was, Bacon was the closest she had ever come to a boyfriend. It was Red's power and confidence that he loved yet also resented.

She learned the best way to be with Bacon was to be an empty shell, not representing herself, but representing the image Bacon fell in love with. Sex was the only area they seemed to agree on in the beginning. He thought he was a champion and she played him like he was.

Red's first encounter with sex was with a man who told her that he loved her, so every time a man was inside her, she felt wanted, needed and desired. This temporary high was like a drug for her. She craved it. With her legs in the air and Bacon's dick sliding in and out of her, she felt wanted. That alone was sometimes enough for all the drama that she endured. Red never had a father to touch the side of her face and say those assuring words: I love you. Instead, her first memory of hearing them was a perversion; therefore, she did what human nature calls for us to do. She went back to what is familiar. For Red, familiarity was pain.

As close as she seemed to be to Bacon, he never really knew who Red was. Bacon would call her his wifey, but he didn't have a clue as to what kept her in tears at night. Aside from her confession to Gloria Schottenstein over dinner, Red never told anyone how she was molested as a child. But, no matter how hard she tried, she could never forget a man's hands in her panties or the taking of her innocence.

Red came out of the bathroom and sat at her laptop to go on the Internet to look at the website for Triple Crown Publications. She printed the submission guidelines. They seemed simple enough: submit the first four chapters, a synopsis and a cover letter.

As soon as Bacon mailed her the manuscript, Red would get it typed, then send it in. If his gift of gab was an indication of what he could write, that nigga for sure had a bestseller on his hands.

Red tied her Prada bathrobe snugly around her waist and reached for her Nextel phone. It was beeping that she had a message, so she pushed the envelope button to listen. First all she heard was silence, then some static. Then, faintly, she heard Sasha's voice talking to a man. Red pressed one ear closed and listened carefully.

"Why did you ask her like that?" the male voice demanded.

"You the one got me living in the girl's house and being a spy. I don't like this shit. Not at all," Sasha replied.

"Try to call her back."

"I don't think you got enough time and I don't want the phone to cut off in the middle of our talk."

"Look, the reason why you living with Red is to get information. I hope you ain't over there chasing niggas."

"No, Catfish. I'm doing what you asked me to. Don't worry. I'll find something on her. And when I do, I will let you know."

A wicked smile spread across Red's otherwise angelic-looking face. She had overheard an earful. Apparently, Sasha called her on a three-way, while Catfish listened. When the call dropped, they thought they were disconnected, but in fact they weren't. Fortunately for Red, her cell phone had recorded the entire thing. Red was livid. Her reason for having Sasha and Kera live with her was simply for extra money. She knew she would be rid of the house soon and didn't really care what happened. But for Sasha to be there with her own twisted agenda made her furious for a split second before she remembered her motto: Get them before they get you. *It's a dog-eat-dog world. And only the strong will survive.*

Red clambered downstairs to the great room, where Sasha and Kera were sitting opposite each other, still bickering. Both girls got up and followed Red as she walked into the kitchen.

"Red, tell this ho that the room she took was the one I wanted," Sasha complained.

"No, tell this bitch first come, first serve," Kera suggested.

Red poured herself a glass of cranberry juice and gazed from one girl to the other like they were from Mars.

"Look, it don't make no damn sense to be arguing about these rooms. Neither of you hos is special or in the Bible. Every room in the house is a good one, Sasha. You decided to move in three days after Kera did, so, you know the rules; you snooze, you lose."

"But I told you I wanted the room with the full bathroom inside. Now, I have to go down the hallway to take a bath or shower and I still pay the same amount that she does. I mean, if I don't have the same amenities, what the fuck am I paying the same amount for?" Sasha asked.

"You are not the president. You knew the deal when you took it off the table. Don't start no shit with this. What else is good?"

Kera piped up. "Well, I had my ultrasound today and guess what I'm having?"

"Let me guess. A boy!" Red said unenthusiastically.

"Yep!" Kera proudly rubbed her tummy.

"Will you name him after his father?" Sasha asked.

"As a matter of fact, I think I will. I ain't gon' let Mekel and his shit stop my flow."

"Momma's baby, Daddy's maybe," Sasha taunted.

"I think both y'all jealous 'cause y'all ain't got no kids."

"Sorry, honey. I don't need, nor do I want, any kids," Red replied.

Sasha was silent. Red knew Sasha had already had several abortions and Kera was right, she did want a child. Kera might not have been the brightest lightbulb in the box but they couldn't deny her bravery. She was pregnant by another woman's man and still found the strength to smile. There was no fear in her eyes; she was ready to have this child alone.

"Kera, tell me something I've been wanting to know. How in the world did you get pregnant by Mekel?" Sasha asked.

Sasha's question put Kera in a fucked-up mood. For one, Red had to have told Sasha who the father was, and two, they knew a baby came by way of fucking. So, three, Sasha was trying to purposely start some shit.

"Yeah, tell us. How did this happen?" Red added, being nosy as well. Kera now felt that both girls were ganging up on her, but she wanted to finally tell her side of the story. Kera plopped up on a bar stool, took a deep breath and told them how it really went down.

"I went to Vegas that one weekend and was in the Bellagio casino. Just cruising the floor, nothing big. I heard all of this commotion at the craps table and so I walked over there. I noticed Mekel's fine ass and he had a huge stack of chips. It looked like he was killing 'em. That made me start rooting for him, screaming, 'Go, Mekel.'

"He noticed me, a familiar face, and smiled back at me. This made me go over to where he was standing. He asked me to blow on his dice, and I did. When I leaned in to blow, he kissed my cheek. He asked me to give him a real kiss for good luck. Later, we went to dinner at the Prime Steakhouse, upstairs on the VIP floor.

"During dinner, we talked about Terry and how their relationship was going. He said they were no longer together and one thing led to another. He slid his hand to my leg and since I had always been attracted to him, it was all good. He said, 'I have always thought you were fine and often wondered what my life would be like had I met you first.' He also told me, 'Terry can't have no kids, she got her tubes tied.' So, next thing I know, we were upstairs in his suite, listening to music and looking out at the fountain light show. I ran a bath in the Jacuzzi, he lit the fireplace and it was the most romantic evening I've ever spent with anyone. It seemed like right then and there, that we fell someplace. I can't call it love."

"I bet you can't," Red said, huffing.

"But I can call it special, and we been homey/lover/friends ever since."

"Do you think you got pregnant that night?"

"I don't know what night it was, 'cause we spent every night together afterward. We got back to Detroit three days later and I saw him one last time. It seems that when he had gone home, Terry was there waiting for him and they made up. I never called Mekel or tried to steal his ass." Kera said the next words sternly as she looked at Red, making it crystal clear. "It was a one-night stand that turned into a few-night stands, and we just so happened to have made a friendly connection as a result."

"Were you salty that he went back to Terry? I mean, how could you fuck your homegirl's man?"

"Like he said, they weren't together, and like we know, I saw all them black hundred-dollar chips stacked in front of him and well, it was just for the moment. I thought that whatever went on in Vegas would, you know, stay there. But it seems that he brought back feelings and I brought back a child."

"Damn," Sasha said as she sipped her glass of wine.

"So what made you want to keep the fucker?" Red asked.

"The fucker?" Kera questioned.

"Yeah, the baby. I mean shit, why go into this a single momma and everything?"

"My baby ain't no fucker, Red."

"Girl, that was wrong," Sasha scolded. "How you gon' call the girl's baby a fucker? And to her face at that?"

"Girl, please. I don't give a fuck. The point is, she shouldn't have fucked Terry's man. I understand what happens in Vegas stays in Vegas, but they brought this shit all the way back to Detroit with a little something extra that will make its debut in three months. You don't have babies by everyone who runs they dick up in you, *especially* your girl's man! It's causing everyone grief. I mean, Terry is a lot of things, but does she deserve to see her girl walk around with her man's baby in her stomach? Damn, can we talk about something else now?"

Sasha and Red continued talking and didn't give Kera a second thought as the pregnant girl huffed out of the room. "She's probably going to sleep. Seems that is all that she does," Sasha suggested.

"So, when was the last time you talked to Catfish?" Red asked, trying to see if Sasha would catch herself in a lie.

"Girl, I am so glad to be living here with you. No more collect calls. I'm gon' write him tonight, though. That hold-me-down-baby shit gets stale."

"Did you love him, or his money?"

"You know, Red, believe it or not, I fell in love with him. There is no way I could have gone this long without loving him. He's a good dude who just got a long amount of time. When I was with Catfish, I was with him and I was happy. Can you say the same about Bacon?"

"Hell, no. That muthafucka was a holy terror," Red said, exaggerating.

"Holy terror?"

"Holy terror!"

"Girl, you ain't an angel yourself. You can be a hell-raiser."

"Yep, that's what these niggas like, a gangsta bitch."

"Looks like you learned well from me," Sasha said as she looked around the house and nodded her approval. "You sure in the hell made out better than I did, and with a lot less grief."

"Well, it seems like my grief is beginning with all these fucking bills."

"Girl, don't it go fast?"

"Too fast! Shit! It went like whoa!"

"So, the real estate business *is* paying you?"

"Yeah, it's doing me justice. But shit, who likes working?"

"When is the last time you seen Bacon?"

"Why? Are you investigating me?" Red asked jokingly.

"I'm not, but you were acting funny on the phone."

" 'Cause I don't talk on the phone. But, I went to see him today."

"Mmm? How did it go?"

"Fine. When's the next time you going to see Catfish?" Red quizzed.

"That two-hour hike to Jackson State Penn is no joke. At least Bacon's in a federal joint. Catfish in a stankin'-ass, dirty state joint. It gives me the heebie-jeebies."

Kera heard them talking below and her mind told her that they were laughing at and mocking her. A pregnant woman's emotions run a mile a minute. She strained to hear what they were saying, but it was no use. She wanted to run back down there and curse them out. Instead, she thought of revenge. If only she could find that letter and send it to Bacon.

While the girls chattered, Kera crept around Red's bedroom. She walked over to the laptop and moved her finger across the mouse pad. She looked at the pile of papers but there was no sign of the notepad on which Red had written the letter. Kera scanned from left to right. Where would Red keep the pad?

Kera tiptoed over to the huge closet and slid the door aside. In the center was a small vanity and some storage containers. On the floor there was a hatbox with the lid partially off. Kera opened the box and there was the notepad amidst pens and colored stationery. Kera flipped a couple of pages, and found the letter.

Dear Bacon,

Kera's hands began to sweat as she read the hurtful words.

> *Your dick is so little that I can't believe you even wear a size 12 shoe . . .*

Kera almost laughed when she read that and wondered if Bacon really had a small dick. She kept reading.

> *You hear my voice when you call your phone? After today, you'll hear "I got a block" on all my phones. Don't try that three-way shit either, 'cause I got Call Intercept. Fucker, just turn homo and die.*

Red was as hateful as they came, the devil's liveliest advocate when she wanted to be.

> *You a has-been and I ain't got time for no shoulda, woulda, coulda stories. You should have stayed free. Dumb ass . . . Certainly, nobody told you to fall in love with me . . . Wake up! You played yourself. Charge it to da game.*
>
> *Red*

Kera had suspected Red was lying about who she did the pee trick on; Kera figured that it was Bacon. Now, Red would reap what she had sowed.

Kera ripped the pages from the notepad. Her heart began to beat faster when she heard footsteps prancing down the hall. She closed herself inside the closet and held her breath. Red walked into her room and across to her computer table, then left the room again. Kera let out a loud sigh. That was too close for comfort. She had nowhere else to go, so she knew she had to lie in the cut until her child came and she could leave the house of hell.

Red felt an odd vibe in the air as she walked into her room. It was one thing for the bitches to be in her crib, but another for them to invade her personal space. Her room was off-limits. Red looked around, checking to see what was in place and what was not. She could have sworn that she smelled the knockoff Lolita Lempicka perfume that Kera wore.

Still, Red didn't notice anything wrong. She grabbed the papers she was looking for from her computer table and headed back downstairs.

When she returned to the kitchen Red handed Sasha the real estate papers that granted Red permission to represent her. Also included was a power of attorney, whereby Sasha consented to allow Red to sign legal papers and to handle decisions on Sasha's behalf.

"Why the power of attorney?" Sasha asked suspiciously as she looked over the papers.

" 'Cause, I don't know what I will need and I want to be prepared. Besides, the bottom line is getting you out of that loft deal, right?"

Sasha hesitated before nodding.

"I pulled the title on the loft. You didn't tell me that Catfish was on it, as well," Red said.

"It doesn't matter, 'cause I used my credit."

"But his name is on there also, so it does matter."

"You can forget getting him to agree to this. Just forget the whole thing."

"Just let me handle it." Red pushed the pen over to Sasha.

Sasha hesitated again as she held the papers. "Are you gonna play fair?" she finally asked.

"You my sister, girl," Red replied. Sasha picked up the pen and signed the last of her assets away.

CHAPTER 13

Real Men Do Real Things

A month later, Q continued to be a man of his word, showing Red, at every turn, he would be right there. She began to feel confused with him because Q never, ever required her to ask for anything. He would arrive at her door with groceries. He would slip money into her purse on GP—general principle—every chance he got. He wanted her to be okay. In fact he exhibited all the signs of being in love.

Yet for Red it still wasn't good enough. She had to push the envelope, and she often pushed it off the table. When Q was around she would pick fights for no particular reason. Red began to analyze her drama, and began to suspect that she cared about Q more than she wanted to admit. It was one thing to cause drama that created the method to her madness, but the things she did to Q didn't include any ends. It didn't make any sense.

Red's past insecurities started nagging at her and she began to put Q through test after test, trying and prying to see if he would leave.

One day Red found herself more tired than usual. It seemed that the stress of keeping the lies straight was taking a toll on her.

She went downstairs to the kitchen for something to drink, and she found Kera mixing a protein drink and taking her prenatal vitamins. Suddenly Red rushed to the trash can and threw up last night's dinner.

"Uh-oh. Looks like someone's pregnant," Kera said.

Wiping her mouth, Red straightened up and glared at Kera, then looked back at the trash can. "What?"

"Yeah, throwing up first thing in the morning . . . pregnancy?"

"No. Must be something I ate."

"Well, one sure way to find out is to eat something else; if you can't keep that down, then eat some crackers or drink a club soda," Kera added, like a friendly physician.

Red looked around the kitchen to put Kera's theory to the test. She pulled out four eggs. As she cracked them into a clear bowl to prepare her omelet, she felt Kera eye her with suspicion. Red got a small whiff of the eggs and the nausea came back.

"I've lost my appetite," Red announced and headed back upstairs.

"Pregnancy test kits are at the corner store for five bucks," Kera shouted after her.

"Fuck you," Red managed to shout over her shoulder.

In the privacy of her room Red sat on the toilet, feeling uneasy. She had never felt this way before. She had never been pregnant before, either. Red hopped in the shower and noticed the sensitivity in her breasts. Just the sting of the water made them ache. *What in the world is happening?* she thought. Rushing like she was in the military, she finished in two minutes. She put on her Puma jogging suit and did what Kera suggested—headed to the corner store for a pregnancy test.

When she returned, Q's Range Rover was in the driveway. Instead of being happy, Red was annoyed. *What the fuck he doing here?* she thought. Walking into the house she found Sasha preparing what appeared to be a plate of pancakes for Q. "Q, what are you doing here?" Red asked coldly.

"Don't you remember? We got some business to handle today."

Red tried to recall what she and Q were supposed to do;

then she remembered: she told him about the appointment she'd made to see Sasha and Catfish's loft, as a potential new residence for the happy little family. "Oh sure, give me a second to get dressed."

As Red walked past, she noticed that Sasha was a little too friendly and close to Q. A little too inquisitive about his recent whereabouts. For once, something inside of her felt insecure. *Does she want Q?*

Red sat on the toilet waiting for the outcome of the pregnancy test. A feeling of déjà vu spread over her. After three minutes the white stick began to take on a color of its own. The shade went from a light pink color to a strong cranberry hue. Red grabbed the box and read. Pink for yes, clear for no. *Pink. Oh, no!*

Driving down Woodward Avenue, Red had Q make a right turn at the Jefferson Avenue lofts. Q pulled the Range Rover up to the door and the valet opened Red's door for her. As she exited, she looked over at Q and smiled. Summer was just getting its start and the flowers were in bloom. The lobby's décor was very tasteful.

Red faked like it was the first time she had seen Catfish's loft. "What do you think?" she asked.

"No, baby. It's about you. What do *you* think? Can you feel safe here?" Q pulled Red close to him.

They took the elevator to the eleventh floor. Red fumbled with her paperwork, doing her real estate routine.

When they opened the door, the hardwood floors glistened. The place was nice, no doubt. Red knew that Q was a nigga from the hood and only dreamed of a place like this to call his own. It didn't matter about the real estate comps or true price; Q would pay whatever she told him it was worth.

Q walked up the platform that led to the master bedroom and admired the view of Canada on the opposite side of the Detroit River. Red walked over to the kitchen and pulled the drawers in and out. They looked at each other.

"You want it?" Q asked.

"Yes," Red replied.

"It's yours."

"Don't you wanna know how much it costs?"

"Don't matter. You want it, it's yours." He took her face into his hands. "Just tell me what you need."

Red began to melt as his face came inches from hers. Q kissed her on her lips, then he fell to one knee.

Her head began to spin. Q was taking her there. He pulled something from his pocket.

It was a pink emerald-cut diamond surrounded by clear round brilliants set in platinum. It almost looked like a sunflower. Q took Red's hand and slid the ring on her finger as he asked, "Will you?"

Q waited for a response and Red didn't know how to answer.

Sure, niggas said "wifey this" or "wifey that" but how many took it there with an official proposal?

Not believing what Q had just done, Red looked into his eyes. Instead of giving him an answer, she put her hands into his and gently pulled, letting him know he could get up off of his knee. *There's something in his eyes,* she thought, something different that she had never seen before. It made her uneasy, but it gave her a sense of comfort at the same time. Red stood on her toes and kissed Q with much more passion than she had previously. He returned the kiss, wanting to hold her, be one with her forever. Red took the time to explore Q's body as she removed his shirt. Placing feather-like kisses on his chest, she made her way down to his stomach and felt Q's dick straining against his pants. She released him and took him into her mouth, bobbing her head up and down, gently teasing the head. Q grabbed the back of Red's neck and created a rhythm of their own. Red's lips and tongue worked magic on his manhood, bringing him close to the point of no return.

Q pulled back and in one quick motion, he laid Red on the floor. Their breathing, although heavy, was in sync with each other. Q looked into Red's eyes with pure unadulterated lust as he undressed her. Once she was completely naked, he admired the perfection that lay before him. He covered her lips, neck, breasts and stomach with kisses that made Red squirm uncontrollably. Going down farther, Q buried himself in between Red's legs, searching for a new life of his own, enjoying what she had to offer.

Trying to suppress an orgasm, Red pulled Q up toward her. With his dick positioned at her opening, he gently entered her nest and found his home. Placing her legs on his shoulders, Red arched her back and grabbed his ass, welcoming him home. The two kept a steady, forceful rhythm as if their lives depended on it. Red felt a familiar tingle as Q's thrusts became deeper and more forceful. With his stroke technique, her eyes started to flutter and her pussy started to pulsate. "Goddamn!" she yelled as she held on for dear life and came all over his dick.

Q's breathing grew heavier. "Oh Red . . . shit, I'm cumming!" he yelled as he emptied himself inside of her. Her answer to his proposal was clear to Q.

"Mom, I need to you tell you something."

"What, girl? I got to get ready to leave."

I was sitting on my bed and my mother sat beside me. I had mustered the courage at ten years old to tell her. Hard as it was. You see, I was tired of having sex with Jerome in the middle of the night, when he was drunk, whenever my mother stepped out. I didn't want to do it anymore.

"Mom, it's about Jerome," I said.

"Okay, what about him?"

"Mom, he had sex with me."

"Who?"

"Jerome."

"Red, why do you keep doing this, saying this? You just don't want me to be happy, you ungrateful, self-centered little tramp!" my mother screamed as she jumped from my bed. I ran behind her hoping to catch her in an embrace, then maybe to shake some sense into her head. I had her by two inches in height and about twenty pounds in weight.

"Mom, don't do this to us. We don't need him. He hurt me."

"I don't believe you, and I wish you would stop. Red, it's time for

you to leave. You're a woman now and you need to go make a life on your own. You won't spoil this for me. I won't let you."

"But, Mom, where am I supposed to go?"

"You should have thought about that before you brought me in here with this bullshit."

"Mom, it's the truth! I need you to be there for me."

"Red, I think you should leave."

"How do you know that you love me?" Red asked.

" 'Cause my heart don't lie," Q replied.

"Q, there is so much about me that you don't know."

"Red, I know enough. I know that eventually you will be the mother of my child and that I want to spend my life with you."

"Q, but, I got shit with me."

"Who don't? So, will you?" Q asked again, reminding her of his marriage proposal.

"Yes."

CHAPTER 14

The Come-Up

Schottenstein Realty was more alive than usual. It was the end of the month and all the Realtors had closings and were excited about them. Red was proud to bring her recent deal to Gloria, the purchase of the loft and the equity line loan application. The loft was priced at $560,000. Gloria would get three percent of that amount and was glad to get it. Red had only one sale that month but for the amount it was, she'd be taking home a nice piece of change.

Red would receive her three percent and the profit from telling Sasha the loft sold for only $300,000. She'd have $260,000 to add to her stash.

In exchange for what appeared to be Red's diligence, Gloria decided to share some news. "Raven, I'm going to help you get your broker's license."

"Gloria, I don't have enough sales to qualify for my broker's license."

"I know. You are about twenty-five sales short, so what I am going to do is give you twenty of my sales. I want to retire, but I can't keep the company open without an active broker. You're young and you could manage things around here."

Red almost shed a tear. As a broker she'd have the freedom to go anywhere and start her own business. For once someone was willing to do something nice for her and she didn't have to trick them or trick on them, either. "Gloria, you would do that for me?"

"Raven, you are like a daughter to me. I keep telling you this."

Red walked out of the realty office five sales away from achieving her goal of becoming a broker. Everything seemed to be falling into place for her. Once she achieved her goal of hustling up one and a half million dollars, she was determined to bounce from Detroit and start a new life somewhere warm.

Pulling into her circular driveway she noticed that the house was starting to look like a dump. All it took was for one roach to move in and the place went to hell.

Red pressed the driver's window down and extended her arm to unlatch the mailbox. Inside she found a stack of letters and one large manila envelope.

There were four letters from the publishers to whom she'd sent Bacon's manuscript. The first one was from Random House. Red tore eagerly at the tiny envelope and read: *Thank you for your submission, however, the book is not a good fit for our list.*

She quickly tossed the letter into the empty passenger seat. Red used her fingernails to undo the second letter, from Jimmy Vines of The Vines Agency.

Dear Ms. Gomez,

I appreciate your submission, however, I do not represent this genre. I wish you luck with your pursuit of a writing career.

My best,
Jimmy Vines

"Asshole!" Red yelled as she tossed that letter in the seat next to her as well.

She sighed; landing a book deal was way too frustrating. It was making her feel like she was the author, she was the one being rejected. Red started to take the shit personally.

She pulled into the garage, grabbed her belongings and headed inside. As Red approached the door she heard the sounds of Biggie Smalls pounding through the surround-sound speakers that were placed throughout the house. Stepping into the great room, she saw that Kera was among a small gathering of her friends. In the center of the table was a blue-and-pink cake with a stork stenciled on it. She had forgotten Kera's shower.

"Where you been, girl?" Kera asked. She walked up to Red with a plate of chips, dip and celery sticks.

"Oh, girl, running around showing houses all damn day. Sorry I'm late." Red placed her Chanel bag on the sofa table behind the couch alongside her keys and the remaining mail. "What's good, ladies?" Red asked, speaking to the girls in the room.

Kera was walking around in an off-the-shoulder top with her protruding belly. She looked like she was going to pop any day. Everyone in the group was rubbing on her stomach and for once, Red saw the glow on Kera's face that many people say pregnant women carried. She wondered if people could tell that she was pregnant herself.

Kera looked happy, which threw Red off. She was so used to people being fake and miserable. Red could spot a fake a mile away; it was the gleam in a person's eyes or the way they relaxed their smile muscles that told the truth of the energy behind the person. But by golly Kera was just too damn jolly to be faking. The mommy-to-be was glad the stork would be visiting her soon.

"Let's open the gifts," Sasha said as she lowered the music.

As Red scanned the table filled with cards and gifts, it dawned on her that she hadn't bought Kera anything. Red hadn't thought twice about it. Immediately her mind went to all the shit she had in her closet that still had tags on it. All she had to do was run upstairs and drop something in a bag and run back down, without missing a beat. The problem was all she had to give was clothes and a new bottle of perfume hardly seemed appropriate for the occasion.

"Bingo!" Red yelled so loudly that someone thought they were actually in a bingo hall.

"What did you say?" an acne-ridden girl with braids asked.

"Oh, nothing. I just remembered that I left Kera's gifts downstairs," she lied. "I'll be right back."

This only made Kera get excited. Everyone knew that Red had exceptional taste and anything from her meant something expensive.

Red walked swiftly toward the basement door, thinking of all of the items she had stashed away, the items that Q had bought for her when she faked her pregnancy. *Hell, I don't need them*, she thought as she stood looking at the goods.

There was a stroller, a high chair, a tabletop baby seat, cases of diapers, OshKosh B'Gosh clothing, small baby sleepers, T-shirts and cases of Enfamil. It looked like Santa Claus had stopped by. At first Red was just going to grab one thing but thought, why save them? At one point she'd thought of returning everything. That was one of her old hustles when she would get clothes from the boosters: going back to the stores and trying to get as much money as she could off the merchandise. Red knew the value of kids' items was high, but she just didn't want to bother with the Toys "R" Us and Babies "R" Us stores. What better way to further wrap Kera around her finger than to give her a gang of shit for her bastard child?

Red climbed back upstairs and gained the attention of everyone. She walked over to Kera. "Close your eyes."

Kera quickly did as she was asked, and Red guided her to the lower level of the house, motioning with her other hand for the women to follow her.

"Don't peek, Kera," Red warned. She carefully led Kera down the wooden steps to the basement. Each stair creaked since they weren't carpeted. Red never had a chance to finish the basement. It wasn't on her list of priorities because it was the one place nobody ever really saw when they came to the house.

When the girls got to the basement they were shocked that it was plain. They looked at Red, and she gave them the *I know you ain't goin' there* look. When they saw all the items partially hidden by the furnace, Red gestured for them to pull the gifts out in full view. The ladies began to slide and scoot the things across the concrete floor as Red kept her hands over Kera's eyes. Kera began to wring her fingers in excitement.

"Oh, please, Red, let me see."

"No, you have to wait," Red said in a low voice.

"You don't want to spoil it, girl, trust and believe," another friend said.

"On the count of three you can open your eyes. Okay?" Red finally said when everything was arranged.

"Okay." Kera sounded like a kid.

"One . . ." The room began to count together. "Two . . ." In unison they paused. *THREE!*"

Kera opened her eyes and saw all the gifts for her child. Her eyes immediately welled with tears. Kera's aunt began to take photos. Kera reached for Red and embraced her so tightly she smeared mascara all over Red's favorite DKNY T-shirt.

"Wait, girl! You all emotional and shit," Red snapped.

"That's a pregnant woman for you," someone said.

"Red, I can't tell you . . ." Kera started but began crying again. Kera never had it so nice. A nice plush crib, surrounded by friends and family. A baby daddy, who in private claimed the child, and now nice gifts. It seemed that things were looking up for her. As everyone began to grab a gift and take it upstairs, Kera's tears went from joy to regret. Red had proven she was her friend. How could she have done what she did?

She excused herself, rushed to the mailbox and looked inside. Red noticed her actions and asked her what she was doing.

"I was wondering if the mail came." Kera played it off, walking back up the driveway.

"Oh, yeah, it's on the table next to my purse."

Kera looked through the mail and saw it was all for Red. She had left the letter addressed to Bacon for the mailman to pick up as he delivered the mail. She knew he picked up early and would do it, she had hoped, while Red was gone. And he had. However, now she was regretting her sneaky decision. How could she do this to someone who thought so much of her to get her all of those gifts?

Kera began to cry more and the tears began to spark suspicions. Red knew those were no longer tears of joy, but she just didn't know what the bitch had done. Red's eyes met Kera's and Kera assumed it was to say "our friendship is true."

She knew only time would reveal. Red grabbed her items and headed upstairs, faking fatigue.

When she got to the top of the stairs, Kera's tearful eyes were still on her back. Red managed to smile and blow a kiss at Kera. Only Kera didn't know that the kiss had sealed her fate.

Red sat in her chaise longue and removed her shoes and massaged her toes. One day she would have to give up her heels. She decided to sort through the remaining mail. The large manila envelope was from Triple Crown Publications. She decided to read that one next. Inside she found a press kit with a cover letter. Red read the letter with great interest.

Dear Ms. Gomez,

    We received your submission of Bitch Nigga, Snitch Nigga *and loved it! We want to discuss making you a Triple Crown author. Please give me a call at your earliest convenience.*

             Sincerely,
             Kammi Johnson
             Office Manager

"What?" Red said, talking to herself. She looked at her watch; it was after business hours, so she would have to call the next morning. She sat at her desk and wrote Bacon a short note telling him that Triple Crown Publications had, in fact, contacted him and that he needed to call her collect as soon as possible.

That news put a smile on her face. Red didn't bother to read the other letter from St. Martin's Press. She didn't want any bad news. Besides, Bacon wanted Triple Crown Publications and it seemed as if some of his prayers had been answered.

               •   •   •

Every day Red waited anxiously for Bacon's call. It normally took the mail about two days to get to him. On the third day she got a call from him early in the morning.

"Collect call from a federal institution. Will you accept?"

"Yes," Red said groggily into the receiver.

"Bitch, get yo' shit and get the fuck out my crib. If you ain't out by noon today, my niggas gon' come by and put yo' ass out."

"Excuse me?" Red sat upright, wide awake now.

"You heard me. I got your tight-ass letter and—"

"Wait, nigga. What letter?" Red asked, jumping from the bed, rushing to her closet and discovering the pages torn from her notepad. *Oh, so that's what Kera's tears were for.*

Red knew she had to do something—and quick.

"Wait, Bacon. I wrote that letter after I got your letter." The phone went silent. "Remember that foul-ass letter I got before I came to visit you?"

"That was months ago, Red."

"Yeah, and I wrote you back and had it addressed to be mailed to you, but then I came to see you to see if it was still good, you know . . ." Red softened her voice. "And it was," she continued, "so I was going to toss the letter when I got home and didn't. The housekeeper must have mailed it for me out of courtesy or something. I don't know how it got mailed, but I plan to find out. Anyway, baby, that letter is old. Look at the date."

Bacon pulled the letter out of his khaki pants. Red *had* dated the letter, a month ago.

Red could hear him breathe a sigh of relief. She breathed one herself. His niggas putting a bitch on the street? That caught her attention real quick. She hadn't thought of him doing it, but it certainly was an option. After all, it was still his house.

"Anyway, you calling me with all this beef and I got good news for you."

"What news you got for me?" Bacon asked suspiciously.

"I heard from Triple Crown." She paused.

"And?"

"And they want to offer you a book deal!" Red screamed into the phone.

"Word?"

"Bond, nigga."

"They gon' put a nigga on?"

"Yep!"

"How much money they talking, 'cause that book don't come cheap."

"No money yet; they want me to call, but I wanted to talk to you before I did that."

"Cool. Look, call them and spit it at them. Let them know I need at least ten thousand. But shit. Do the damn thing. Handle it."

"I got you."

"That is good news. A nigga needed that. I ain't heard from the lawyer and I needed somethin' to brighten my day." Bacon paused. "How you doing, otherwise?"

"Well, I hope you come home, 'cause you going to be a father." Red hadn't planned on telling Bacon she was pregnant. She wanted to let her fingers do the walking for the first abortion clinic. She needed, for once and for all, to stop him from thinking about putting her out again. "Yeah, and you trying to put me out in the streets after you done knocked a bitch up." Red threw it back at him.

"Naw, baby, it ain't like that. It's just that you be fucking with a nigga's head."

"How? I'm right here, right now."

"So I knocked you up? Finally you got a baby to slow that ass down."

"No, I need a family, and with you away, I don't know about this baby. I can't have no baby alone."

"I keep telling you that this lawyer supposed to make it happen with the DNA."

"Okay. When is that gon' happen?"

"Let's not get into that. I'm about to be a published author."

"Yeah, baby, you are."

•   •   •

"Triple Crown Publications. How can I help you?"

"Ummm, can I speak to Kammi Johnson?"

"May I ask who's calling?"

"Raven Gomez regarding the manuscript *Bitch Nigga, Snitch Nigga.*"

"One moment." Red was put on hold before the call was answered again.

"Hi, this is Kammi."

"Hi. This is Raven Gomez."

"Nice to speak with you, Raven. I'm the office manager and we want to make you an offer for the book you wrote."

"That I wrote? Um, well, I didn't write it," Red stammered.

"Well, then I need to speak with the author. I can only make the offer to the author or an agent. Are you the agent?"

"No, I'm . . . the author. I mean I want to write under an alias. I don't want anyone to know that I wrote it."

"That's understandable. It's a hot and spicy book."

"Thank you," Red answered, nervously.

"What's your pseudonym, then?"

"Lisa Lennox," Red said, using her club name.

"Lisa Lennox . . . nice. We work with a lot of pseudonyms in this industry. From now on, when you call the office just refer to yourself as Lisa. This way you stay anonymous."

"Okay."

"We want to offer you a twenty-five-thousand-dollar contract for a one-book deal for the title *Bitch Nigga, Snitch Nigga.*"

Red could not believe her ears.

"Yes!" she screamed into the phone, balling her fist and pulling her elbow down.

Kammi was used to excited authors. It was one of the pleasures of her job at Triple Crown Publications. "Well, I will get the contract in the mail and overnight it to you today," she said, smiling.

"Thank you!"

Red exchanged all pertinent information with the office manager. Within seconds, she began to calculate how she would doctor the contract to make it look like Triple Crown only offered $10,000, and how she could pocket the remaining $15,000. This was working out just fine.

Red wrote a letter to Bacon detailing the terms of the deal and asking him to call her ASAP!

Bacon had a book deal. Or better yet, Red aka Lisa Lennox had a book deal.

CHAPTER 15

Cheaper to Keep Her

*H*ello?" Kera answered the phone.

"What's up?" Mekel asked.

"Nothing."

"I want to see you."

"When?"

Kera had played her hand well. She didn't push Mekel to accept responsibility. This was the one thing that was most attractive to him. The average woman would have brought the drama, yet Kera played it cool. The way she accepted her responsibility and took care of her own problems became enticing to him.

"Meet me at the House of Pancakes on Seven Mile," Mekel instructed.

"I—I don't have a ride that can get me there anytime soon. I'm too big to be on the bus. I'm due any day now," Kera replied honestly. She knew that at nearly nine months, bed rest was the best she was going to get. She didn't have time to run the streets.

"Besides, Mekel, what you need to say to me that you haven't in the last nine months?" Kera was suspicious. Her thoughts were, *Don't start no shit, won't be none.*

"Naw, it ain't even like that. I need to talk to you."

"You know where I'm at." Kera paused. "Or are you afraid to be seen over here visiting me?"

Mekel knew the Seven Mile House of Pancakes was almost an hour out of the way. He was just trying to avoid conflict. He didn't have time to hear Terry's mouth. As the months went by she had become nothing but a nuisance. Anything attractive that Mekel once found in her had been erased by her bark.

In fact, he found Terry to be so insecure that it became just plain ugly. Mekel couldn't understand how Kera's pregnancy had broken her. He didn't understand that the fact that Terry couldn't have his kids ate away at her. With her tubes tied, twisted and burnt, it would take an act of God to reverse a decision that had been made three years ago.

"No, it's not that I don't want to see you. It's just . . ." Mekel paused.

"Just what, Mekel?"

"I just don't need the bullshit in my life."

"And I do? I don't need you calling me with this. I don't bother you. So why the hell you calling me now?" Kera began to get upset. "Mekel, it's too late for an abortion. So, what? You calling me to suggest that I give the baby up for adoption? Nigga, please."

Mekel knew that everything Kera said was correct. The right to life was a woman's choice, and a man had no right to make that decision for her. As a man, he knew that all he could do was be responsible for his seed and help her whenever and however he could. He wasn't going to go out of his way, but he wasn't going to dog Kera, either. He wanted her to know that.

"Look, Kera, what time can I come by? I want to see you. I'll come to you."

It didn't make Kera any difference, yet she was relieved that he was showing concern. "Stop by in an hour."

"See you then." Mekel hung up the phone and opened the door of the bathroom where he'd sought refuge to make the phone call. He looked at Terry sleeping soundly in his bed. He leaned his large frame against the door and hesitated. Mekel knew that what he was about to do just might cause him to lose the opportunity to ever see her peaceful again.

The more he tried to hide his issues, the more they continued to haunt him. Every young black man in the ghetto knows that a child needs his father. Yet there was something that was torn in him. How could he give someone what they didn't have? How could he do what he had only been shown, which was to do what was easiest?

"Terry," Mekel whispered as he nudged Terry awake.

"Yeah, baby." Terry's voice was muffled as she wiped sleep out of her eyes.

"I need to make a run."

"Where? What time is it?" Terry asked, looking at the clock on the sleek nightstand, then back at her man. She noticed that he was fully clothed.

"I need to go see Kera."

"*What?*" Terry screamed. She jumped up from the bed and searched for her clothes. "I'm going with you."

"No, that won't be necessary."

"What in the fuck you got to talk to dat bitch about?"

"Terry, here you go."

"Here I go? No, nigga! I forgave you 'cause I thought you made a mistake and was through with the ho, but I ain't gon' stand for this family gathering shit."

"Terry, I gotta be a man about this and see what's going on. As a woman—*my* woman—you shouldn't want it any other way. I mean, wouldn't you want just one of your baby daddies to handle his business? At least that's what you always bitching about, how they don't do what they supposed to do."

Mekel's words silenced Terry. That was the problem. Terry had two baby daddies who gave her three kids. Both of the men were deadbeats. That shit was what made her have her tubes tied in the first place. Not that she didn't want more kids. She just didn't want to get stuck anymore, and the pain of raising her children alone led to her decision. But now she'd found Mekel, it was too late, and she'd be goddamned if Kera got what she couldn't have.

"But, you said that you weren't the father," Terry said, sobbing.

Mekel attempted to caress her shoulders. "Still, T, there are ways to find that out."

"No! Fuck dat bitch!" Terry began to scream and throw things around the room.

When Mekel snatched his keys to leave, Terry threw the television remote at him.

"Leave. Go to your bitch then, you fucking liar."

"Terry, pack your shit and be the fuck out of my place by the time I return."

With that, Mekel turned to leave.

All Terry heard was the door closing and the sound of her heart beating louder in her chest. She had fucked up. She had sent her man out into the arms of another woman—a woman who was carrying his child.

Since Mekel told her to leave, Terry knew that she would have to beg and plead to get back in his good graces again. She knew that included her acceptance of his child, who was coming any day now. Terry began to pace the floor, becoming more and more hysterical. She was consumed with how she could change things.

"That fuckin' baby," Terry yelled to no one in particular. "If I can only get rid of that baby. If I can only get rid of that bitch."

Terry frantically dropped to her knees and started searching underneath the bed. She pulled out an Adidas shoebox and dug beneath some paper and found the solution to her problem. Mekel's problem solver, his nine millimeter.

Terry removed the clip to make sure there were bullets inside. She pulled the chamber back to check that there was one in the chamber. Next, she rushed putting her clothes on and grabbed her things to head to Red's house.

"Bitch don't even have a fucking car and he chose her over me," Terry fumed as she drove her Escalade out of the apartment complex into the morning air. If she could get there first, this would all be over.

Kera's heart began to beat fast as she saw Mekel's car pull in front of the house. She didn't want him to ring the doorbell and awaken Red and Sasha, so she'd waited for him in the foyer. Kera had showered and combed her roller wrap down. She wore a purple baby-doll shirt that flattered both her complexion and her protruding stomach.

When Kera opened the door, her smile warmed the frustrations that Mekel carried with him. Kera knew this was a hard visit and she made certain he would not regret coming.

"What's up," Kera asked, making small talk.

"You," Mekel answered, following her into the great room. "This place is nice," he complimented.

"Yeah, it's pretty. Red has good taste."

"So, how you feeling?"

"Tired a lot, and ready to drop this load." Kera rubbed her stomach. She walked over to Mekel and asked, "Wanna feel your baby move?"

"Can I?" Mekel gently held out his hand. Touching her stomach brought all the masculinity out of him. It was amazing. He had never been that close to a pregnant woman before. He had met Terry after all of her kids had been born. As he rubbed Kera's stomach, she pressed his hand harder against it. The baby began to move around.

The beautiful thing about Kera and Mekel was that nothing was planned, nothing was forced. Everything flowed easily.

"You know, Kera, at first I thought I felt comfortable with you 'cause we were in Vegas, away from everyone, a little high, but being here with you now, I feel the same way I did then. You just real cool to be near."

"You know, I feel the same," Kera responded. "But I didn't want to cause you any problems. And you know, you can't start something when you're in the middle of something else."

"Yeah, I know. That's why I didn't press the issue."

"Me, too. Besides, Mekel, I have seen so much pain in my life that I didn't want to cause any drama and don't want the drama. You know, I'm just trying to raise this baby." She patted her stomach, a look of contentment spreading over her face.

"I came here today to let you know that I'm gon' be there for you."

"What exactly does that mean?"

"It means that I'm gon' claim my child, help you financially. Hell, I might even babysit." Mekel continued to rub her stomach.

Kera wanted to bring up Terry, but she knew that would be a mistake. Mekel was there with her and that had to be for a reason.

"Okay, so we gon' have a baby together."

"What have you decided to name it, or do you know what you are having?"

"I don't know. I just want him to be a healthy baby."

"Oh. A son?"

"Yeah."

"That's what's up. Look, I want the baby to have my last name."

"Are you sure?" Kera was baffled by his change in attitude.

"Positive. I'm gon' help you."

"Thank you."

Kera and Mekel shared a small embrace. Just as they did so, Terry peered through the patio doors in the rear of the house. The sight of Kera in Mekel's arms threw her into orbit.

She raised the gun and aimed at Kera's head through teary eyes. She wanted to kill that bitch.

Tatt . . . tatt . . . tatt . . . tatt . . . tatt . . . tatt . . . tatt . . . click . . . click!

Terry fled, not knowing if she had hit anyone and not even caring. She ran to her Escalade, put the car in reverse and sped off.

Red was awakened by the gunfire, the screech of tires; she managed to peek through her drapes to see Terry's car speeding off through the neighborhood.

Red ran out of her room and bumped into Sasha. They both darted down the stairs, taking them two at a time and jumping the last one. When they entered the great room, they found Mekel hovering over Kera in a protective stance.

"What in the fuck is going on?" Red asked, looking at her rear French doors, which were riddled with bullet holes.

"Don't know, but Kera, yo, get your shit. You getting the fuck out of here," Mekel said.

"Oh, like my place is hot. The shooter followed yo' ass here," Red accused.

"Girl, please. Ain't nobody followed me here."

"Yeah? I know who the shooter was. I saw 'em from my window."

"Who? Who in the fuck wants to kill you?" Mekel asked.

"You got it all twisted. Who wants to kill you or your baby?" Red asked.

The four of them looked at one another. Kera was still shaking and in tears.

"Red, who was it?" Kera asked.

Red hesitated for a moment. She hated to betray her friend, but the bitch had lost her damn mind, shooting up her place. Before Red sold Terry out, she would make them all sweat. "Before I put salt on anyone, I need to be sure." She picked up the phone.

"Yeah, there was a shooting at my house. I need the windows repaired immediately."

"Who dat? The police?" Sasha asked.

"Hell naw, the maintenance man. I need my shit put back together."

While the foursome was still shaken by the incident, Red wasn't really as upset as she was initially. She was actually relieved that it was Terry's fool ass that snapped. Red saw every opportunity as an advantage.

"Q baby!"

"Yeah," Q said sleepily.

"Somebody shot the house up," Red said, sounding pitiful.

"What? Are you okay?"

"Yeah. I'm okay."

"Did you call five-oh?"

"What?" she said distractedly. "No, I didn't call the police yet."

"I'll be right over," Q said. Red could hear him getting dressed.

"All right. I'll stay put until you get here."

Q hung up the phone and was on the way.

Red went back to her room and called Terry's dumb ass on her cell phone.

Terry looked at the caller ID and hesitated. She didn't know if she should pick up or not, but she also wanted to know if she had indeed hit her target. So she waited until the third ring to answer Red's call. *Perhaps Red is calling me to tell me that Kera is dead,* she thought.

"Yeah," Terry said.

"Hey, girl," Red replied.

"What's good?" Terry said, playing it cool.

"Nothing. I was wondering, do you have any money?" Red inquired.

"Money? Girl, please. Why you asking me for money? You know I ain't got none."

"Looks like you got a problem, then."

"Girl, stop being silly. What are you talking about?"

"Terry. Now I normally would get mad when a muthafucka shoots up my shit. But this time, I won't."

The phone went silent. Terry already knew not to bullshit a bullshitter, and Red had her by the balls. Bitch!

"What?" Terry finally asked, trying to sound confused.

"Terry, I want a couple thousand over here today to pay for my shit you shot up and I need some hush money. That was so fucking dumb."

Terry began to cry. "Red, I'm so sorry. It's just that Kera's shit is fucking with me and we haven't been able to hang out since she's been living with you and well . . . I just lost it."

"Girl, I know. That's why you need your girlfriend to tell you when you do stupid shit. That shit was so stupid. You could have killed somebody! What good will it do you to commit murder? All you did was make Mekel fall into Kera's corner. He was hovering over her like a knight in shining armor." Red was putting salt in da game.

"Red, you shouldn't blackmail me. All the secrets I keep for you. This is part of our program, being down for whatever, right." Terry sounded desperate.

"Bitch, please. Not when you come to my crib and shoot up my shit. You don't bring shit where I lay my head at." Terry knew damn well that anything Red told her was some shit she didn't care about.

"Sorry, I can't sista-girl this one. You will pay for my windows. You will have the glass cleared from my house and you *will* sign the title of your truck over to me."

"What?" Red knew that Terry loved her truck, but Red felt like it was hers anyway since she had gotten Terry the hook-up in the first place. Red planned to sell it.

"What if we make an exchange? I won't tell Bacon about the letter you were going to send him and the other fucked-up shit you been doing since he got locked up, and—"

"Bitch, that shit is weak as hell. I don't give a fuck about that. Bacon already got the letter. Now what?"

Terry had no reply. She was out of ammo when it came to doing Red dirty.

"Have me two thousand and the title to your Escalade over to my crib in an hour, or I'll tell Mekel that you were the shooter. Look, I know you ain't thinking straight, but this is the first step back to Mekel. If he don't know, you might stand a chance at getting your man back, but you definitely owe me for shooting up my fucking house!"

"Red, I'll tell you what. I will give you the two thousand but I'm keeping my truck."

"Terry, let me tell you something. Listen . . ." Red put a tiny tape recorder to the phone and pushed rewind. Soon Terry heard her voice play back over the line. Red had recorded the conversation.

Fucking Dirty Red bitch! Terry cursed inwardly. She began to cry and said, "Oh, that shit is soooooooo fuckin' dirty. You tape-recorded me and we supposed to be friends? You got to give me that tape!"

"Sure. I will exchange it for the title and keys. See you at my place, in say what, an hour?"

"Yeah, Red. I'll see you."

The line went dead and Red put a smile on her face. *Dumb bitch! You never talk shit on the phone and you certainly never confess.*

CHAPTER 16

And Baby Makes Three

A half an hour later, Terry turned the corner on what seemed like two wheels. She was busy trying to work out an alibi. She wasn't worried about Red calling the police. Red played by the rules of the street. She kept the dirt on the low and if justice was to be served, it was handled the old-fashioned way, with revenge.

Terry's problem was trying to figure out how to get the audiotape. Blackmailers seldom lived up to their words, but she had to trust someone; unfortunately for her, it was Red.

Terry dialed Mekel on his cell phone.

He was still with Kera. Mekel glanced his phone and cursed inwardly. *Shit!*

He was through with Terry's shit and there was no getting back in for her. He knew it would be hell trying to be a father and enduring her bouts of rage. Besides, if he had to choose between an unstable jealous chick and his seed, Mekel finally had the strength to choose his child, hands down. There was no choice. She was toast.

When Terry heard the phone go into voice mail she was furious. The situation was getting worse by the second. And it hurt her heart to know that Mekel was most likely still with Kera, comforting her, while she was on the brink of losing her car, her dough and ultimately, him.

Terry hit Redial; the phone went directly into voice mail, which only pissed her off even more. *The muthafucka wants privacy,* she thought.

Terry began to wonder if it was even worth it to try and get Mekel back. It seemed to her that he was gone. She pulled into the apartment complex and stared at the entrance. Terry walked slowly, approached the door and turned the key to the apartment. Squeezing with her left hand, she hit Redial again. Terry began to feel desperate all over again. Shit was not working out the way that she had planned. Oh, if she could just turn back time. She would have handled things differently. Once inside the apartment, she began to think of her options.

She'd be damned if she let Dirty Red get in her way. Fuck it. It wasn't over.

On the other side of town, Red was looking at her watch, thinking of how she would sell Terry's truck and to whom.

The maintenance man was replacing the patio glass and his assistant was sweeping the shattered glass from the cobblestone floor.

Terry wondered whether she could have one more chance if she didn't take her things from Mekel's place. There was really no way of knowing. She could trust Red's opinion that she still had another chance and pay the ransom for the tape; or she could say, "fuck it," let them know that she was the shooter and that more was in store for them.

Terry couldn't help but remember that Red always seemed to know just what to say and what to do. She couldn't let go of the fact that Red was her oldest childhood friend. That had to mean something and she convinced herself of that much.

Terry took a seat in the tiny yet expensively furnished living room. She glanced at a photo of her and Mekel on top of the television. If Terry paid Red, and signed over the title to her car, she still could lose Mekel. Then she would be ass out, literally on left and right. If she ignored Red's threats and she was exposed, then she believed Mekel would somehow get what his hand called for.

Terry picked up the phone and called Red's house. On what seemed like the twentieth ring, Sasha answered the phone. "Hello?"

"Hey, girl." Terry faked like it was a regular chat.

"Hey," Sasha said as she caught Terry's voice.

"How's it, living in the palace?" Terry quizzed. She hoped that Sasha would give up some gossip.

"Girl, drama. A muthafucka tried to kill us today."

"What?"

"Yeah, shot the fuckin' house up and shit."

"Do you know who did it?"

"Naw, but Red claims she does. And knowing her Ms. Cleo ass, she's most likely telling the truth."

"Mmm. So who do you think did it?"

"For a minute I thought it was you," Sasha joked.

"Me?" Terry played along. "Why me?"

" 'Cause your man was downstairs with his baby momma when it happened," Sasha said, throwing salt. She still hadn't heard Terry's side of the story, but now was as good a time as any.

"What?"

"Yeah, him and Kera were downstairs when World War III was set off."

"Word? That's fucked up. You okay?"

"Girl, I'm fine, but Red is pissed. You know how immaculate she is. Her precious floors were dirty. Bitch been going the fuck off."

"Oh, so back to Mekel. Is he still there? He told me he was coming by to talk to Kera since the baby is on the way. They supposed to be doing some sort of paternity test."

"Let me peek."

After a few seconds, Terry was thrown off guard when Mekel said, "Hello?" into the phone.

"Hey."

"What the fuck you calling me over here for?" Mekel yelled.

"We need to talk. Look, how long you gon' be over there?" Terry tried to ask nicely.

"However fucking long I want to be," Mekel snapped.

"Look, this is crazy. I love you and you love me." Terry was to the point of begging when Kera walked up to Mekel with his coat and his keys.

"Maybe you need to come back when it's really over," Terry heard Kera say.

"Look, Terry, I asked you to pack your shit and get the fuck out of my crib. It don't sound like you did it yet."

Terry began to cry again. She felt like Mekel was frontin' on her in front of Kera.

"When I get home, you better be long gone. You hear me? Yeah, leave my key on the table. It's over!"

Terry felt humiliated. Mekel's words cut into her like a knife. If he just had one good thing to say or even if he had one bad thing to say in a kind way, she would have had hope. His tone and the way he was talking to her said it all. It was over. Besides, once a nigga loses respect for you, it's a wrap. Terry had been through the word wars before. Once a relationship was tarnished, the shit ain't never the same. Mekel was killing it. He spit so much venom that even Kera knew it was dead. Staying would be for Terry's affection and not his.

Terry sighed into the phone and her pride took over her sorrow and her head swelled with anger.

"Yeah, well, I'll pack my shit, but, muthafucka . . ." Terry tried to throw it back at him. She figured her exit should reflect her gangstress actions.

"Bitch, you run hot and cold. Your inconsistent ass is the main reason we couldn't make it. Dating you was like watching the weather. You never knew what you were going to get. Kick rocks and get the fuck out my crib!" Mekel clicked the phone off.

Terry held the phone in her hand in disbelief. Then she went through the apartment numbly collecting her things. She grabbed

Mekel's T-shirt that she wore the previous night and smelled it to catch the scent of his favorite cologne. Using the hem of her T-shirt, she wiped any incriminating prints from the handle of the gun and put it back in the box.

As she headed for the door, the tears came again. She began to think, *How would he feel if he came home and found me dead? Would he mourn me? Would he care?*

It was time for Terry to say "fuck it." It was time for her to go home and be a mother to her own neglected kids. And that was just what she planned to do. Start over.

Over an hour passed and Red suspected that Terry had flaked out. It didn't matter. She would still get her one way or another. She simply needed some time to figure out when and how.

Q stormed into the house, followed by his best friend, Ezekial, strapped with a nine in the waistband of his sagging jeans. Q took the stairs two at a time and headed for Red's room, where he embraced her. Next he said, "Show me where it happened." As they made their way downstairs, Red's eyes locked with Zeke's. For a second she wondered how he had gotten in her home.

When they got downstairs, you couldn't tell that three hours ago, her house was shot up. The workers had cleaned the area quite successfully.

"Red baby, this my partner Zeke," Q introduced, holding her waist.

"Hey," Red quickly replied, trying to act like she didn't know him.

She pointed her index finger and explained, "Here. The bullets came in here."

Zeke studied Red and wanted to snatch her by her ponytail and drag her face through the glass. But he held his tongue.

"That's it. You getting out of here. When is the deal gon' be final for the loft?" Q asked.

"I'm waiting on some paperwork," Red nervously replied.

"Well, start packing. You up out of this bitch. I'll put you in a hotel until the paperwork gets straight."

Zeke walked to the glass and back to Red and asked, "So, you have no idea who did this to you?"

"No, I don't and . . ." she said, turning to Q. "No, it's really not necessary."

"What? Someone shot your shit up and you want me to take it easy?"

"I know who did it."

"Who?" Q asked.

"Terry."

"Your girl Terry?"

"Yeah. She was trying to kill Mekel."

Fuckin' lyin'-ass bitch, Zeke thought. Zeke began to think of how to get his boy Q away from this triflin' ho. It would have to be over his dead body that he allowed Red to win this go-around.

"Ain't that his ride outside?" Q asked.

"Yeah, he upstairs with Kera, but I haven't told him Terry was trying to kill him yet."

"Why not?"

"I don't want to upset Kera. You know, with her being eight months and all." Red pretended that this was to be the truth. She would get Terry later for backing out on the agreement.

Meanwhile, upstairs, Kera lay in Mekel's arms and they both drifted into a late-morning nap. Just like that, Mekel had chosen Kera.

Red finally got the countersigned contract and the money from Triple Crown. Bacon was pissed about how she handled the business, but she told him, "They don't do contracts with people behind bars, and I didn't want to blow it for you. I did what you said and gave them an alias. What? You don't trust me?"

"Just send the money to the lawyer for me," Bacon requested. It was out of his hands and all he wanted to do was get back on the streets. What Triple Crown gave him was chicken feed for a free man. But to a muthafucka on lock, it was a lifeboat and he was grateful for it.

Triple Crown signed Bacon that July and planned to release the book, *Bitch Nigga, Snitch Nigga,* in late fall. The cover design was completed and the alias "Lisa Lennox" was listed all over websites and in magazine ads. Triple Crown's fan base was going wild for the book, so the publisher decided to release it early. The streets around the hood were going wild over the title.

While Bacon was thrilled that his book was being released, he still hadn't gotten over the fact that Red signed the contract.

"Look, I did what I had to do. They don't do deals with niggas in jail," she had said.

Bacon planned to handle his issues. Like he had told her. *See me when they free me.* He meant that the first chance he got.

CHAPTER 17

Every Good-bye Ain't Gone

Red stepped off the elevator and walked through the chocolate-stained door of the loft, late as usual.

Wide-eyed like a child, she smiled as she took in the work of the Roche-Bobois designer; the furniture order had arrived bright and early that Monday morning. She took in Q's relieved expression and felt a little guilty that she had managed to make money off him by selling him the loft.

"What do you think?" Q asked.

"I love it," Red replied.

Q guided Red upstairs to the bedrooms and stopped in front of the smaller of the two. The room was painted in warm yellows and browns, with hints of cool blues. The alphabet was stenciled on cornice boards around the windows.

"This nursery is for our next child," Q whispered.

Red could not believe her eyes. This man was giving her a woman's dream. Q took her into his arms and began to rub Red's stomach. His embrace overwhelmed her. Red noticed that at times when she should have had her game face on, her pregnancy made everything seem personal. Q loving her, holding her down as he was, it was sometimes too much for her to bear.

"Let's go," Q demanded, pulling her hand and heading for the door.

"Where are we going?" Red asked, still overwhelmed by the reality of her surroundings.

"They gon' be in there for the rest of the week. I want us to get away. I got someone I want you to meet."

Q and Red drove east on I-94 headed away from the city. Q took the Gross Pointe exit, driving past the water, up Jefferson Avenue. Red took in the scenery and Q hummed the words to an Usher song on the radio, all the while tapping his hand on top of Red's. *He seems so happy,* she thought.

"Where we going?" Red asked again.

"It's a surprise."

As Q drove the houses became farther and farther apart. The community seemed serene. Arriving at a small apartment complex, he parked the car in the second space available.

They walked to the door of a townhouse that had the smell of barbeque smoke.

"Quentin!" the lady opening the door screamed. She threw her arms out wide and gave him a big embrace. She stared at Red, but didn't say anything. She was waiting for a formal introduction. The woman led them to her living room, where the furniture was covered in plastic. The place was cramped but it was very homey.

"Mom, I want to introduce you to my future wife," Q announced before turning to Red. "Red, this is my mother, Patricia Carter."

Suddenly Red remembered that she didn't have her engagement ring on. She had taken it off and put it in her closet to hide it from her roommates. Q's mother looked down at her finger and so did Q. It was then that he noticed her bare finger. He played it off, though. He smiled and said, "Did you change your mind?"

"No. It's a little too large and I didn't want to lose it," Red half-truthfully explained. "It's in my room."

Red knew his mother was giving her the once-over. Red knew to play coy and so she did.

"What's your real name?" his mother asked.

"My real name is Raven Gomez."

"Like the bird?"

"Yes, like the bird."

"Okay, ladies, let's relax. Go back to your corners," Q joked, trying awkwardly to break the ice. Q had once again proven how special she was. Meeting his mother was a big thing for him.

Red waited nervously in the car as she watched Q walk into the Shrine of the Black Madonna to purchase a copy of *Bitch Nigga, Snitch Nigga*. Triple Crown was sending Red a case of "her" books, but it hadn't arrived yet. Red was a little nervous that it had hit the street before she had a chance to really see it.

As she was waiting Q's cell phone rang. Curiosity made her pick up the phone and look at the incoming caller ID number. The caller was Zeke. Red knew that nigga hated her for gankin' his dough. She thought that she had seen the last of him. Who could have imagined that her man's best friend would be a former victim. Red decided to answer the call to see what was on his mind.

"Hello."

"Speak to Q," Zeke demanded.

"Hey, Zeke, he not here right now," Red replied.

"Bitch, what you doing answering his cell."

"Zeke, can we start over? I mean, there is no reason for you to get nasty. I make Q happy."

"Ho, I'm not gon' let you rob him blind like you did me."

Men always think with their emotions. What can I do? Think . . . think . . . "Zeke, let me make this right. Is there any way I can say I'm sorry by paying you back the money you lost? I'm not admitting anything, I just don't want five thousand to stand in between me, you and Q."

Zeke began to think that he could possibly get his money back, and get some dirt on Red at the same time.

"I know how you feel and I want to make it right," Red coyly said.

"Yeah, when and where."

"Give me a couple weeks to get the money together. I'll call you then. 'Kay?" Red meekly asked.

"Tell Q I called and I'll get with you later."

After Zeke hung up Red began think of how to silence him, for good. There was no way she was letting anyone mess up what she had with Q. He was worth fighting for. Worth doing anything for.

Q came back to the car cursing.

"Can you believe they sold out?" Q looked perplexed. "I gotta get this book." He busted a U-turn in the middle of the street and headed to another bookstore.

"Damn, it must be good. What's it about?" Red asked, playing naïve.

"Do you remember that murder at the nightclub Reason Why?"

"I remember the club but not the murder."

"Your girl's man, Catfish, used to own that club or so they say. And he was with your dude Bacon. The rumor is Catfish, Bacon and his woman was up in the club. Some shit jumped off over a drug deal gone bad and they say Catfish had this nigga, Scooney, shot in the middle of the dance floor while he was dancing with Catfish's woman who was a decoy. It was a setup and it's supposed to be depicted in this book.

"That's why it's called *Bitch Nigga, Snitch Nigga*. The person who did the hit was the drug dealer's enforcer, and he, the guy, told on his enforcer. That's why I want to read it 'cause it could only have been written by one of two people, the shooter or the girl."

"Sounds interesting."

"Yeah, and that ain't all. It got all types of shit in it. It tells about every single person who ever snitched but thought they was on the low. It's a hood tell-all book. It already got shit going."

Red listened with great interest as she heard the effects of the book on the street. Still, she wasn't worried. She was more thrilled with the number of book sales than anything. Red wanted to call Triple Crown and get in their shit about the release date. They hadn't given her any heads-up that the book was coming out early. *But still, pay me,* she thought.

Q stopped in front of Northland Mall and jogged inside to Truth Book Store. He returned to the car, out of breath, and tossed one of two copies into Red's lap. The other he snatched open and began to scan.

"I want to see who this whore acknowledged." He read aloud:

> *Shouts out to the Chamber Brothers, Y.B.I.s, Best Friends Organization, East Side BK's, White Boy Rick, and the Earl Flynns. To all the Bitch Niggas, Snitch Niggas in these organizations, it is because of your mouths that we didn't survive.*

Q gripped that book and became obsessed with reading it. "Trust me, when I finish this book, I will tell you who wrote it."

Q was more involved than he let on. Scooney was his uncle—he never told anyone that. He also knew the leaders of each of these organizations, and he wanted the truth about his uncle's murder. And *Bitch Nigga, Snitch Nigga* was gonna give it to him.

Q anxiously dropped Red off in her driveway and sped off.

"Damn nigga played me for a book," she cursed out loud. *Book must be good,* she thought.

Red hadn't taken the time to read the entire manuscript, but she knew anything Bacon had to say was worth listening to. She clutched her copy of the book and pushed the remote keypad on the side of the garage. Slowly, the door rose and she walked through to her side door. She could smell food being cooked and the sound of light chatter.

Mekel and Kera were sitting in the kitchen, enjoying each other's company.

"Awww . . . look at Mommy and Daddy," Red said in a mocking tone.

"Hey, Red. How's it hangin'?" Mekel asked.

"Just fine, nigga," Red replied.

"Oh Red, you got a message to call someone named Blue." Kera's words made Red's knees get weak.

"Who?"

"Blue."

"Did he leave a number?" She got quickly back on her toes.

"No. He sounded like you had it."

"No. If he calls back, please get it."

"He said he was coming to see you."

Red decided to not even get upset with Kera. She knew she wasn't the sharpest knife in the drawer, so she just let it pass. *What the fuck does he want?*

Red poured a glass of juice and went upstairs to her room. Inside her room there was a box with a UPS label sitting beside her bed. On one side it read "Triple Crown Publications" and she instantly knew it was copies of the book. Suddenly Red remembered that she'd left the copy Q had given her on the counter next to the refrigerator. She dashed back downstairs to the kitchen. This time it wasn't on the counter. It was in the hands of Mekel, who was reading it intently.

"Hey, give up the book," she said.

"Oh naw. You gotta let me hold this. This book came for you today by the case. I carried it upstairs and put it in your room. You know Kera can't lift anything." He rubbed her stomach. "What you doing with a case of these books?" he asked.

"Selling them," Red lied.

"Cool, here you go. Your first sale." Mekel dropped a twenty on the counter for her.

Red hesitated about taking the money, until she realized she had no other reason to have a case of the books in her possession.

Suddenly the phone rang, interrupting the silence. Kera grabbed the cordless phone.

"Hello. Yeah . . . that's right . . . okay. 'Bye."

"Who was that?" Red asked.

"Oh, Blue again. He said he was on his way over."

"Why didn't you give me the phone?"

"He didn't ask. He verified your address. He asked me if you were home and said he would be right over. Then he said 'bye."

"So, he's on his way?"

"Yeah, ten minutes, he said."

Red looked at Kera and knew she didn't have time to argue. Her mind was on what she could wear for her meeting with Blue.

Kera and Mekel finished their meals and shared laughter as they cleaned the kitchen. They planned to go shopping for the baby. In the meantime, Red ran upstairs and turned on the shower, testing the water to see if the temperature was right. She removed the hair tie from her neat ponytail. Seeing Blue would be painful, yet it was still exciting.

Gazing in the mirror, Red mustered her strength. She knew that she couldn't let herself get weak. Red had waited for the day when Blue came to her. It would have been a cold day in hell before she went back to him.

Red stepped into the shower and allowed the water to cover her hair. She lathered honeysuckle-scented shampoo into her red mane and her eyes began to sting. That was when she realized that she was crying. Blue had hurt her and started all of this drama. If only Blue could have been decent to her. If only his love was as true as hers. He used to tell her, "I'm true blue, baby. You'll never find another." For many years Red believed this—she still hadn't loved a man like she had him. Yes, he would pay for his betrayal. Red, true to form, would seek revenge.

Red applied styling mousse to her hair to accentuate her curls. She applied MAC bronze-gold eye shadow and black mascara to accent her eyes, put on her lip gloss and applied lotion all over her body. She slipped on her favorite pair of ripped-up jeans and silver tank top. *Damn, I look good,* she thought, examining herself in the mirror.

Red went to the kitchen to prepare something simple. The best way to a man's heart was through his stomach. Red started to sauté some onions in the skillet. Looking at her watch she began to wonder if Blue was still coming. It was going on thirty minutes. Red prepared the ground beef, as she chopped vegetables and grated cheese. Red continued to cook to calm her nerves and kill time.

The chimes from the door caused butterflies to move into her stomach. Red counted to twenty to ease her breathing. Then she walked down the hall to the door.

Red began to breathe deeper and deeper to calm her nerves. She couldn't stand the fact that the closer she got to the door, the more upset her stomach became. Several times she felt as though she was going to throw up. The pregnancy was getting on her nerves. The day couldn't come quick enough for her appointment to get this thing sucked out of her.

Red pulled the door open slowly, cautiously peeking through the crack. She looked him dead in the eye, revealing a level of confidence that was missing in the old Red. She had more seriousness about her face, not the wide-eyed, naive glances they once shared. Blue's eyes met hers, and Red knew he couldn't get over how lovely she looked.

CHAPTER 18

Vengeance Is Mine

Blue stood in front of Red's 6,000-square-foot home with his tongue hanging out.

"Look what the cat drug in," she said as she opened her front door in order to get a better view. Blue had left her in tears years earlier. But at the moment, she was riding high, feeling good and flowing in her element.

Red noticed that Blue was shaggy, like an old wet goat. Time had not been kind to his looks or his midsection.

Red walked Blue toward the kitchen to the aroma of chopped onion, cilantro, tomatoes and homemade guacamole.

She looked on as Blue's nostrils flared in appreciation as he found his way to a retro-shaped stool at the counter. She could see he was making himself at home.

Red was glad she was wearing her engagement ring. The pink diamond sparkled under the ceiling lights.

"Yo, you married?" Blue inquired.

"Gonna be soon," Red said, liking the idea.

"Oh, it's like this? This yo' nigga's crib?"

"Nah, he got his own place." Red examined her fingernails in a nonchalant manner. "He lives downtown in a loft."

"Oh, so this you? This your crib?"

"Yes, Blue. I do have a job."

"So what you into these days?"

"I'm a Realtor."

"That's righteous. I always wanted to get into real estate."

"So, what you doing?"

"Same shit, different city. That's why I wanted to look you up. I'm gonna be in town for a minute."

"Oh, so that's the only reason you holla'd at me?"

"You know that ain't the only reason. I missed you."

"Yeah, whatever. Blue, I ain't heard from you in years."

"I tried to contact you b-but—" Blue stammered.

"But what?" The sternness in Red's voice caught him off guard and her stare unnerved him. His hands and eyes twitched and he looked away.

"But shit, fuck the past, and besides, you went and got married on me and shit."

"Nigga, tricks are for kids," Red said.

"Yeah, I see you got game."

"Not game, just survival techniques."

"Oh, so it's about survival."

"Yeah, Blue. Look, let's not play games. You know it took a minute for me to get over you, and now I have. So let's just keep it moving."

"Cool. I can do that."

"So, you got a wifey? You know, with all the women you had."

"Had? Shit, I still get mines."

"Oh, so you ain't changed." Red tried with all her might to keep her cool, but she felt her nails digging into the palms of her hands.

Maybe she wasn't completely over him. It wasn't that she still wanted to be his woman, she just wanted to get more revenge on him. She knew she couldn't make his heart ache. He would have to care for her to do that. Niggas like Blue didn't fall in love. They had been there and done that.

Red could hear his stomach rumble as he sauntered over to the fridge and took the liberty to pull a Corona from the shelf. She wondered if Blue had been smoking weed and had the munchies. When he knew her at fifteen, she couldn't cook. She wanted to show off and put out a Pyrex dish of enchiladas. *Eat your heart out,* she thought.

Suddenly they heard someone enter through the front door.

"Hellooooo . . . Sasha's home!" she sang.

Sasha glided into the kitchen, hips swiveling in a circular motion. The first thing her eyes beelined upon was Blue's backside. In her mind, he was prey. It had been some time since Catfish had left, and quite frankly, that hold-you-down-nigga shit was getting old. Lately, her clit had started to itch and she wanted to scratch it. It didn't help that Catfish's stash wasn't as long as everyone thought it was and she hadn't gotten as much as she hoped from the sale of the loft.

Sasha's eyes caught Red's and then trailed back to Blue. "Who is that?" Sasha mouthed.

Red didn't reply.

In one smooth move, Sasha sat on the stool next to Blue, who looked over and saw the short-haired sassy woman, and he was on to the next episode. Shit, the way he felt, Red had been playing too much. What the fuck did she think he wanted? A reunion? They should have been upstairs buck wild by now, but she wanted to play forty questions.

Blue turned his attention to Sasha. Red turned to her, too.

"Hey girl," Red said, setting it up.

"What's up?" Sasha replied, a twinge of attitude in her voice, showing off for Blue.

Sasha didn't think anything of pushing up on him.

"Red, who this lovely dime?" Blue rubbed his forehead, feigning the removal of sweat.

"Oh yeah, this my roommate, Sasha."

"Sasha. I like that name." Blue rubbed the sides of his low faded beard.

Same shit he said to me, Red thought. *Next he gon' start bragging.*

Blue did just that and Red stifled a laugh.

"Yeah, I'm just in town on business and shit. You know, came by to see an old friend." Blue winked at Red.

"Oh, so you remember your friends, huh?" Sasha flirted.

"Sasha, you hungry?" Red asked, switching gears.

"Yeah, smells good. I think I'll join you." Sasha flashed a big smile.

"Do that," Blue said.

"Let's get a drink and go into the dining room, while Red hooks us up with her mamacita shit," Sasha replied.

"Yeah, let's do that," Blue said.

"Blue, make yourself at home." Red shooed with her hands for them to go into the other room.

When they left the kitchen, a wicked thought popped into Red's head. *What if I got the last laugh on a nigga?* She was too old to be petty and fuck up his ride again. So she simply chilled. No, she had to come up with a different strategy.

As Red stirred the ground beef and mixed in the onions and tomatoes to stuff the enchiladas, an idea came to mind.

Red left the towel on the counter and walked into the half bath off the kitchen, grabbing a small saucer on the way. Inside the bathroom, she slipped her pants down and sat on the toilet. Red began to strain with all her might, trying to relieve her intestines of the fecal matter it contained. She grunted once, and then she grunted again. Suddenly her anus opened and she felt her bowels moving. A tiny plunk was heard in the toilet as shit hit water.

Soon another turd followed the first. Red wiped herself with the Charmin and turned to look at the two turds floating in the toilet.

She placed her hand in the chilly water and removed the longest piece of the two. She placed the turd on the saucer and covered it with several pieces of toilet paper.

When Red peeked into the dining room, Sasha and Blue were sitting in there, waiting.

Muthafucka think he gon' come visit me and shit on me? Well, he can eat shit.

With that thought, Red proceeded to mash and mix the dookey into the ground beef. The somewhat soft turd folded quite nicely as she flipped and smashed it with the spatula. The more she turned, the more the meat blended into the bowl.

Red continued to stuff the tortillas until she had folded the enchiladas nicely. She placed two of them on the plate and walked over to the table. Blue couldn't wait to grab his fork and commence to get his grub on.

"This shit . . ." Blue said with a full mouth of food, "is the B-O-M-B!" He slapped Red on her backside. "You definitely can cook, girl."

Red suppressed a smirk, then smiled like a modest chef.

"Where's my plate?" Sasha asked.

"In the kitchen." Red motioned for Sasha to follow her into the kitchen where she could talk to her. "Girl, you don't want to eat that."

"What's up? Shit, I'm hungry."

"No, it's really spicy." Red knew that Sasha hated hot foods.

"Damn, girl, you know how I love Mexican food."

"Better try Taco Bell. I didn't know you would be here, so I didn't think to make any for you," Red replied.

"Anyway girl, I was talking to that nigga and he said he wanted to do a threesome with us for some money," Sasha said. "You with it or what?"

"Nah, I ain't with it," Red said.

Red watched the back of Blue's neck bob up and down. She felt no remorse. With the information that Sasha had just given her, she was more than happy she made the nigga eat her shit.

"Look, Red, you know I need money," Sasha pleaded. "And if the nigga want to trick off, why not let him."

"Handle your business, then." Red tossed all the items she'd used to mix the shit into the garbage, including the utensils.

"Don't you know I would have preferred that? I invited him up to my room, especially after the money he said he wanted to pay. But he wants to have a threesome. Me, you and him." Sasha tugged at Red's arm.

"Hell no! Fuck that nigga."

"He paying ten thousand. We can both get five slacks apiece," Sasha coaxed.

"If it's that important to you, then give me six thousand and I'll do it."

"That's fucked up. You know I need that money."

"Exactly. *You* need it. I don't need it that bad that I can't come out on top. And I'm fucking, not sucking his dick or kissing him."

Sasha thought about the money again, then thought about the fact she ain't had no dick in a long time. "Damn, bitch, I'm horny as hell, too," she whined in a tone that really pissed Red off.

"So what the fuck you gon' do?"

Sasha had to back off, because she didn't want to fuck it up. For four thousand, she was willing to do all the above.

"Fuck it. I'm gon' tell him that we with it," Sasha said.

"Nah, let me tell him. I want to verify what you're saying."

"Verify?" Sasha said with an attitude.

"Verify. I don't know where that nigga dick done been, and I just want to make sure we getting paid."

"Whatever. While you playing select over some dough, I'm headed upstairs for a shower. We can do it in my room."

"I know you didn't think it was going down in my room," Red snapped.

Sasha waved her off. "Bitch, whatever. Don't get brand-new."

She walked off as Blue walked up with an empty plate. "Any more food?"

"Nah, nigga, you ate your share today," Red replied.

"So, what's up? You ready to go upstairs and handle your business?" Blue asked Red.

Red ignored him. She had her plan in motion so she side-stepped the question. They went up to Sasha's room and waited for her to finish her shower.

"You still remember how to suck it like I like it?" Blue asked. His eyes locked on Red's expression.

Before she could respond, Sasha came from the hall bathroom

wearing a purple thong panty set. Red stood, still fully dressed. Blue began to unbutton his clothing, piece by piece, layer by layer.

Blue positioned himself comfortably on the queen-size bed, enjoying the satin sheets.

"Don't lay your funky ass on my sheets, nigga," Sasha said.

Blue didn't pay her no attention. He didn't care. He noticed the lavender color scheme and his mind told him this was his scene, fit for a king. He couldn't believe how easy this had gone down.

Red began to undress slowly. She took her time and watched the two of them go at each other. Blue looked at Red and took her into his arms as Sasha rubbed on Red's back and placed fake play kisses along the sides of her arms.

Red whispered into Blue's ear, "Make her eat me."

"What?" Blue asked.

"I want my pussy ate," Red explained in his ear.

Their eyes met and Blue understood.

"Sasha, I want to watch you eat Red out."

Sasha looked shocked but began to obey as Red lay on her back, waiting to be served, enjoying every minute.

Red grabbed pieces of Sasha's hair, pulling tighter and watching as Blue looked on.

"I want you to fuck me, Blue," Red said to excite him.

"Get it wet for me, Sasha . . . Suck that pussy and get it right for me," Blue said.

The deeper Red pushed Sasha into her pussy, the more Sasha gyrated her face. Blue was egging her on as Red spread her vaginal lips apart.

When Red reached her climax, Sasha's chin was left dripping and Red noticed tears in her eyes. She didn't give a fuck. It was time to let the hammer fall.

Blue climbed on top of Red and penetrated her. Moaning and groaning, Blue came after just a short while. Every attempt he made to kiss her, Red dodged his lips. There was no way she was going to kiss his shit mouth. She pretended she was not interested in catching feelings. Every time Blue tried to kiss her, she replied, "This is business, remember?"

That was enough to throw him off guard.

Yeah, you gon' make me think you want me again, Red thought as he finished up his last groan.

As Blue lay in bed, the girls went into the bathroom to clean up. Standing before the mirror, Sasha saw Red enter the bathroom and close the door behind her.

"Bitch, how in the fuck you gon' have me eat your stankin' ass pussy?"

"Oh, did it stink?" Red replied, her arms folded.

"Yeah, you funky bitch. You know that shit was wrong. We were supposed to be fake fuckin', but you grabbed my head like you was my nigga or something."

"Look, you wanted to do this. Besides, the next time you call me on the three-way, bitch, clear your other line."

Sasha was motionless for a moment, trying to play it off. "Clear my line? What are you talking about?"

"Sasha, when you called me to ask about Bacon and the loft, you had Catfish on the three-way."

"I don't know what you're talking about," Sasha protested, feigning innocence.

"Let me explain it to you, then. When you called me, there was background noise. When I asked you about it, you had no explanation.

"It was jailhouse background noise that, if I was on my toes, I would have realized what it was."

Red faced Sasha eye to eye as she snarled, "Bitch, pack your bags and I don't give a fuck where you go. Tricks are for kids."

CHAPTER 19

Droppin' the Soap

The other girls were still asleep when Red backed out of the garage into the chilly morning air. Sasha obviously hadn't taken Red's eviction order seriously because she was still in the house. The girls required way too much bed rest but Red knew that the early bird got the worm. She stopped three blocks away at Starbucks, purchased a large mocha latte, and hit the expressway, headed west on I-94.

As Red drove, she listened to the messages on her cell phone from the night before.

What up, girl? It's Terry. Hit me back, it's urgent.

Yeah, right, Red thought, waiting for the next message to chime in.

Red, this is your mom. Remember me? I need you to stop by the house. I've got something to tell you.

Red felt her foot ease up off the pedal and then press down again. The sound of her mother's voice gave rise to mixed feelings. It had been almost a year since they had spoken on the phone with each other. Red wished their relationship was Brady Bunch-ish, but it simply could not be. No matter how badly she wanted it, she could not get the fairy tale to be true. Red's mother was a piece of work, there wasn't much she could do to change that.

"What the fuck does she want?" Red asked herself. There was a time when Red would break her moms off a C-note here or there. Every time she made a come up, she would look out for her mother, but that got old. She needed to feel loved by her mother and buying her affection didn't work against her mother's need to stay with Jerome, the man who changed Red's young world.

The melodic sound of Destiny's Child's "Cater 2 U" filled the car. It seemed as though the trio was cruising with her, which made Red's cares begin to melt away. She thought of Q, who, unlike her mother, was like a blanket on a winter's night.

Red found herself having new feelings. When she was with Q, she felt peace and security. She had once loved Blue until her eyes were swollen, but that was puppy love. Blue didn't care one bit about her.

Then there was Bacon. That relationship had been so dysfunctional that she was unable to compare it to anything. And yet Bacon was all she had to consider as real. The times when she crossed him or lied to him made her wonder if she was right or wrong.

It really *was* baffling to her—this thing called love. And how could she gauge it? No one had ever loved her. She just thought that Q loved the baby and was himself getting confused with his affection.

Turning into the prison yard, she began to prepare herself for another visit with Bacon. If it were not for the book deal, she would leave his ass to rot. She had no intention of keeping the baby, whosoever it was, and was going to have an abortion as soon as she could sneak it in.

Red put the car in park and felt the gravel underneath her Carlos Santana boots as she headed toward the building. After enduring the formalities of a prison visit, she was seated at the cold plastic table and chairs to wait for him. Prison took everyone down. *Why should I reduce myself 'cause a nigga got knocked?* she wondered as she waited for Bacon.

After an hour, Bacon emerged from behind the sliding door, looking handsome in a starched khaki uniform.

He slid his chair next to Red's and gently kissed her on the cheek.

Red knew she was looking good in her white Capris and white top. She knew from nightly care her skin was so soft that it felt like a baby's ass.

The scent of Bulgari had Bacon open, even though he'd had time since her last visit to analyze their past life together.

Just when he began to want to trust and love a woman, he felt her slipping away. It seemed that every time a person got locked, he thought of the finer things in life—the things that mattered. He wondered if the streets had made him the man he was and caused him to treat Red the way he did. It was fucked up, but doing time allowed him to charge some of his transgressions to the game, instead of to his own actions.

"So, where's the next payment for the book?" Bacon asked, holding his fingers in a steeple shape as though he were the DA interrogating her.

"No hello, how are you, kiss my ass. Just, where's my dough?"

"I ain't got time to play with you. I seen that book all over every bestsellers list there is. In *Essence* magazine, *Vibe*, *Smooth*, you name it, it was there. All the niggas on the pound reading that shit. But I ain't got no more money for it."

"The next payment comes in six months."

"That's bullshit. I know you, Red. You smarter than that to negotiate such a fucked-up deal."

Red flipped it. "Nigga, I did the best I could do. You wanted a deal and I got you one. I'm the one who said don't go with Triple Crown Publications, but a major like HarperCollins or some shit, but noooooo. You wanted to be down for yo' crown. So you see, nigga, dey da ones playing you. You were the one talking that shit about how TCP was the hit maker and you wanted your book with them. So, well . . . that's how the deal went."

"I want to see a contract."

"Oh, let's make this clear. You asked me to come up here to tell me that you don't trust me?" Red tilted her head to the side, placed her arms akimbo, and rolled her eyes up in her head as if she were highly insulted.

"Something like that. Your shit has been funny."

"Here you go with your drama." Acting miffed, Red released her fists, then threw her hands up in the air.

"I'm just saying. I still can't get through on the phones and shit just don't seem right."

"Keep your mind on getting free. Don't be greedy about this book shit. You want it all—socks-and-draws type shit." After all, how could he continue to knock the only person who was trying to get him some help toward freedom?

Bacon sat there staring at her. Red stared right back with her hazel eyes. She knew she had put him in check. She paused for a moment and then kept it moving. Red wasn't about to sit up in jail and let a muthafucka insult her, even if it was the truth.

"So you want chicken or pizza from the vending machine?"

Bacon bit his tongue, momentarily. "Chicken!"

After eating with Bacon, Red left the jail with one thing on her mind—the phone call from her mother, Julia. Red drove back into town lost in thought. She didn't even cut on the radio as she drove; she reminisced on her childhood. Red hoped that she was calling to say that she'd left Jerome. This was Red's dream, and her prayer.

As Red pulled into her mother's driveway on Sheridan Street, a single tear fell from her right eye. Julia's home was a little brown brick house surrounded by tall weeds on a corner lot across the street from a run-down, unattended church.

As Red opened the car door, her mother flung open her front door. She walked out looking like a middle-aged homeless woman, with hair that looked like it hadn't been combed in weeks.

"Red," she called out, a smile on her face.

"Hey, Momma." Feeling pensive, Red heaved a deep sigh and slowly entered the house, where dark furniture filled each room. The smoke from her mother's cigarette choked Red as she stepped into the door. The aura of the house filled Red with vivid memories.

"Don't look so thrilled to be here."

"I ain't. You called, so what's up?" Red asked, flopping down on the couch.

"I just wanted to talk to you."

"About what?"

"About you."

"Momma, there ain't shit to talk about when it comes to me."

"Well, how is your life?"

"Why the hell do you care?"

"Damn it! How long you gonna hate me, Red?"

"As long as you fuckin' Jerome!"

Julia gasped and put her hand up to her heart. "Oh, you gonna let that childhood shit continue to ruin your life?"

"I don't have to let it ruin my life, it does it without my permission. It controls how I treat and see men and how I've created this bullshit of a life. Momma, why couldn't it have just been me and you?"

"Red, shit, I called you over to talk about love."

"What's love got to do with anything?"

"Look, Tina," Julia said jokingly, "love got everything to do with it."

"I don't see how—you didn't love me when you had me."

"Oh child, *mi niña*, that's what you think? Shit, I loved you the best way I knew how." Julia pulled a cigarette from the pack that lay on the end table.

"I grew up with no father and a mother that had less than a ninth-grade education. I watched my mother struggle with putting food on the table and clothes on our backs as she struggled with man after man after man. I was the subject of many beatings, called a whore before I even knew what sex was and was working at the age of twelve. So don't tell me about a mother's love."

"Yeah, but yo' momma didn't let a man fuck you."

"You don't know what my momma let happen to me. Shit, my momma sold me for sex.

"Red, I stayed with Jerome because I thought that was the best that I could do. I'm fat and uneducated so I thought he was the only man that would want me. I was lonely. He beat me but provided for us, and I'd rather have a man who provided than no man at all."

"But what about me?"

"Damnit, there was no buts. I was looking out for you. Shit, I figured you would get over the shit if he did anything to you. I got over my shit."

Julia continued to talk about her childhood and things that happened to her. As much as Red wanted to play hard and interrupt her mother with an *I don't care* attitude, it soothed her spirit that her mother was trying.

"Red, I really want to leave Jerome but don't know how."

"Why can't you just get up and walk out the fuckin' door and leave that grimy-ass nigga?"

As Julia was getting ready to answer that question, Jerome burst in the door wearing a smile as if everything was normal. Red turned and looked at her mother with confusion on her face. She wondered if her mother knew that he was coming at this time. Based on the conversation, she concluded that her mother was just as surprised as she was.

Jerome motioned toward the kitchen. "You got something in there to eat?"

"No, Jerome. You home awfully early from work."

"Don't be questioning me."

He walked into the kitchen, sat down in a chair and slammed his foot on the table, suggesting that Julia go get him something to eat. Julia looked over at Red with a grim smirk on her face. It was apparent that neither of them knew what to do.

"Maybe you should leave, Red," Julia said.

"I ain't going nowhere until we finish our conversation. He don't run nothing with me."

"You see him, Red. He's just waiting for a fight," Julia whispered.

"Then there will be a fight," Red replied.

"Damnit, just leave," Julia said a little louder, getting nervous.

"You always taking his side, putting him first. You ain't changed a bit. I ain't goin' no-muthafuckin'-where."

Red sat up on the couch as if she were making her position known.

"Julia, are you gonna come and get my fucking food or am I going to have to pull yo' ass in here? Shit, what the fuck is the troublemaker doing here, anyway?" Jerome yelled from the kitchen.

Red grew irate. "What the fuck! What the fuck are *you* doing here?"

"I live here."

Red stood up from the couch as if she were getting ready to storm into the kitchen and box with Jerome. She looked over once again to her mother, hoping that she was going to interrupt and tell him to leave but she didn't. Within a split second, Dirty Red came out. She couldn't believe after all she and her mother had just talked about she was just going to sit there and let Jerome do and say whatever he wanted. The little sympathy that Red had started to have for her mother left as fire began to spew out of her nostrils.

"How the fuck you gonna butter me up, bring me over to this damn shack, just to show me you and Jerome are still together? This is muthafuckin' bullshit. I hate you, Momma."

Jerome walked back into the living room and yelled, "Don't talk to your mom like that!"

"Nigga, don't tell me what to do. You ain't my muthafuckin' daddy."

"Now you look, heifa, I told you I ain't did shit to you. You just like to keep shit going, you earth disturber! Get yo' shit and get the fuck out."

Red's mother looked on, not saying a word.

"The hell you didn't do shit to me. I remember everything. I remember your hands up my dress and your big-ass dick in my mouth. I remember the blood that crept out of my small-ass pussy. I remember my mother not believing me and telling me that I just made it up. Fuck both of y'all."

Red grabbed her purse as if she was getting ready to pull something out of it. As she flung her purse onto her shoulder, she turned to her mother and punched the hell out of her.

"This is for not believing me," Red said, huffing.

"Oh hell, no. Ain't nobody gonna be hitting my wife but me." Jerome took two steps toward the couch and karate-kicked Red in the stomach like she was a nigga in the street. Red fell back and grabbed the lower part of her stomach. She heard something inside of her go *plop* and immediately felt something wet run inside of her panties. It felt like she was urinating on herself, but she knew instinctively it was not pee soaking her underwear.

"Oh, my baby," she groaned, doubling over, holding her lower stomach. Wave after wave of cramps hit her and sweat beads formed on her upper lip.

It was just a matter of seconds before blood began to gush out of her vagina, all over the plastic on the couch. In shock, Red stared at the blood running down her legs, staining her white pants, and the plastic on the couch. Her eyes bulged with fear; she'd never seen that much blood. Was she dying? She'd heard miscarriages could be more dangerous than childbirth. The pains sure hurt.

Meantime, her mother gasped for air, and Jerome just mumbled, "How is the ho gonna be bleeding from a kick?"

With a loud scream, Red cried, "I'm pregnant, bitch!"

Frantically, Julia ran to the phone to call 911. She had no intentions of hurting her daughter. She'd just wanted there to be peace as she figured out a way to escape.

When the medics finally came to the door, Red began blurting out obscenities, vowing to fuck both of them up.

Between the excruciating pains, she panted, "Y'all gon' pay for what y'all did. My baby's daddy gonna fuck y'all asses up."

She continued with obscenities.

"You dirty, stankin' bastard, Jerome! You ain't seen the last of me!"

The medics tried to keep her calm. A young-looking EMT glanced over to where the blood was on the couch and saw what appeared to be a thick clot. Helping to strap her onto the gurney, he looked at Red and asked her if she was pregnant. She answered yes, nodding her head. With a deep, long sigh, the medic answered, "Not anymore."

As the rickety-rockety ambulance drove swiftly to the nearest hospital, Red's mind was filled with anguish, pain, confusion, revenge and her next scheme. *Karma is a muthafucka,* she thought. She lost Q's fake baby and now the baby she really *was* carrying. Shit was gonna hit the fan because although she never told Q about the actuality of her being pregnant, she'd told Bacon he was going to be a daddy. She'd had plans to go to the nearest abortion clinic to erase her mistake, but too late now. Q was gonna find out and Bacon was gonna beat her ass.

"Watch it, watch it," the medic yelled as he pushed the gurney through the entrance of the emergency room. "The patient has lost a lot of blood."

"Put the patient in room two," a nurse yelled out.

"Room two," the medic said to his partner.

Red's heart began to beat very fast, partly because she had lost a lot of blood and she was becoming faint. She was also scared as hell. A nurse came into the room and asked her if she needed for them to call anyone for her.

"Yes, my baby's father, Q. His number is 555-6667." The nurse put a light sedative in Red's IV to help calm her down and allow her to get some rest. As the sedative began to work, Red adjusted her head on the pillow and fell asleep.

When Red awakened, Q was right above her bed, rubbing his fingers through her hair.

"Hey, sleepyhead. You okay?" Q asked.

"I'm all right. When did you get here?"

" 'Bout an hour ago. Just been here waiting for you to wake up. What the hell happened?"

With a rush of tears running down Red's face, she sobbed, "I lost the baby."

"Fuck, I know that. The nurse told me. Why didn't you tell me you were pregnant?"

"I didn't tell you because I wanted to make sure by going to the doctor and getting things done right this time."

Looking at her, not sure if he should believe what she was saying, he repeated, "What happened?"

"I went to visit my momma."

"This happened at your momma's? I thought you and yo' momma wasn't even cool like that to be visiting and shit."

"Q, shh . . . let me explain. When I was a kid, her boyfriend, Jerome, sexually abused me. She didn't believe me and stayed with him. She called me to come over and I thought she was gonna tell me that she had left him but that didn't happen. He ended up walking in on our conversation.

"I got mad because he was saying some fucked-up shit to me and my mother stood there not saying anything, so I punched her and he karate-kicked me in my stomach."

"What? You were what when you were a kid? That fucker did what?" Q was pissed. Red couldn't tell if he was madder at her losing the baby or Jerome abusing her. "What is that nigga's name?"

"His name is Jerome."

"Jerome, huh?" Q repeated. "Oh, that nigga gon' be dealt with. And my baby, he killed my baby!" Q was so loud that a nurse had to come in and ask him to tone it down.

Red trembled because she had no clue what Q was going to do and if he was going to stay with her. He had made no mention of their relationship, so with concern Red asked him, "What about us now?"

"What? Red, shit, I don't know about us. I want to stay with you, but then again I just don't know. Anyway, how the hell could you be thinking about that shit after losing another child? I got other shit on my mind—like finding this Jerome muthafucka."

Red knew she had lost Q by keeping secrets. There was no need for him to stay around even after fucking up Jerome. She watched as Q paced the floor. He kept rubbing his head, mumbling under his breath. There was nothing that Red could do or say at that point.

The doctor entered the room and told her that she appeared to be okay. Although there was a little scarring she would be able to have more children in the future. He was going to keep her overnight for observation, but she could be released the next day; she needed to rest and stay off of her feet for at least a week. Once the doctor left the room, Q turned to Red and said, "You okay, right?"

"Yeah."

"Well, then I gotta go."

"Q, where're you going?"

"To think and handle some business," Q snapped.

"But, Q—"

"What, Red? I need to go. You fed me a lot of heavy shit. Your past, losing another baby of mine—just let me be."

Q left the room, huffing, and Red sat there looking dumb. For the first time since she'd been in da game Red had no clue what was going to happen next. She knew she was scheming on Gloria for the broker's license, but now it all seemed so unnecessary.

She clenched her pillow as tears dropped full force out of her eyes. *Why wasn't I good enough for my momma? Why did my momma hate me so? Am I worthy to live?* As the questions continued in her mind she sobbed and moaned for God. She hadn't called on God much before, but that day Red didn't have any other place to turn. She knew she had done some fucked-up shit in the past, but she couldn't help but wonder about all of the fucked-up shit that had happened to her.

Red cried herself to sleep, wondering if she was going to end up alone in her own pitiful, dreary life.

CHAPTER 20

The Shit Hits the Fan

After leaving the hospital, Q was full of emotion. He wanted to take his mind off of his situation and check in on an old friend. In the streets you were limited with ones you could trust. Yet, Q did have a friend that had been tried, tested and proven throughout the years.

Q walked across the cracked pavement of the hood. He read the sign that boasted "Poindexter Village Apartment Homes." Q felt that there was no way the government could call these places homes. They packed the disenfranchised into these run-down quarters like sardines.

His nostrils caught the familiar scent of piss, vomit and dead rodents, which caused him to cough a little. Every so often, Q would make this kind of trip to the hood to remind him of why he pursued the street life in the first place. It was necessary to get away from this life. He banged on a steel-gated door and heard a feminine voice behind it say, "One moment."

"It's Q," he replied before the double-latched lock was undone.

"Hey, Daddy!" the woman whispered as she peeked from left to right and then held the door open for him to enter.

"Ms. Foxy."

"Q." Foxy smiled softly as they held in a long embrace.

One of the things that endeared Q to Foxy was the fact that if you were Q's friend—and few people were—then he was by your side whether it be in public, behind the scenes, on the low or whatever!

Foxy and Q met in Jackson State Penitentiary in the days before they had separate holding facilities and protective custody set up for gays. Foxy was a transvestite.

Putting a homosexual in a male institution was just like putting a virgin in with these hardened men. They saw Foxy just as a woman. And since most of them hadn't been with one in years, they took the next best thing. Any hole was better than no hole was their motto.

Time in the joint can make the hardest nigga go soft. When they return to the street, they leave the "any hole" motto behind. For others that got turned out, sex with men changed them forever. Foxy was born gay, but she had class so she refused to be degraded for the sake of sex.

Foxy did a grown man's crime and didn't snitch like a bitch, so the justice system saw no reason to treat her like one. Her lawyer petitioned the courts for alternative incarceration, but she was turned down.

Her primary hustle now was for the numerous hormone pills she ingested daily, her breast implants, and most recently, her sex change operation. Foxy never had a problem getting her basic life bills paid, but she couldn't come up on the forty grand she needed to make her life complete. So she took it to the streets, hustling.

Foxy became a mule, taping dope to her body, traveling in and out of the country. She was one of Q's workers, and when she caught her case, he took care of her.

Q got out of the pen months before Foxy; and when she got out they spoke occasionally. Whenever Q needed the hood 411, he did a drive-by to satisfy his curiosity. It wasn't much that Foxy didn't hear. It wasn't many that she didn't know.

"So what's been going on in da streets, Foxy?"

"The same old bullshit. This damn ghetto got everybody on their toes. It done been 'bout three shootings in the last week and a half. The government ought to be ashamed to have people call this place a home."

"I was just thinking the same thing as I walked up to this piece."

"Daddy, Lando got shot as he slept in his own damn house over some weed bullshit."

"Lando? Damn, that nigga was cool as hell."

"Yeah, now he hot in hell."

Q chuckled. "You so silly, girl."

"Huh, and you know yo' girl Moesha?"

"Yeah."

"She got beat down in the alley back there 'cause she was caught fucking another girl's man. Her man beat her and the girl, Wanda, beat her, too. Shit, they should've killed her ass 'cause they left her face all fucked up."

"Shit, these bitches are scandalous."

"Speaking of scandalous bitches, did you hear 'bout some bitch name umm . . . name umm . . . Faqwana?"

"Naw."

"Well, that Faqwana bitch been going 'round trying to pull rank on every nigga that cross her path. She claiming to be the queen of da streets. Shit's funny tho 'cause people trying to compare her to Red and shit. Saying, Red betta watch out 'cause somebody trying to take her territory. Now, that bitch Red has been on everybody's lip. The notorious R-e-d."

"Red?" Q looked puzzled.

"Yeah, that ho that you been hanging around. She been known for doing some scandalous shit."

"Naw, not Red."

"Q, pull yo' dick from around your heart. Have I ever lied to you before?"

"No."

"Okay. That scandalous bitch been pulling game over every muthafuckin nigga who's crossed her path, and some bitches, too. She been in da streets causing all kind of havoc.

"Q, this chick name Lisa found out that Red was stealing checks from people around the way and threatened to tell if she didn't cut her in on the scheme. Red wasn't having that shit, so she set up a trap for Lisa's ass. She got her nigga, Hulla, to act like he was interested in Lisa and had him take her to this construction site as if he was gonna cut her in on the scheme.

"When Red pulled up on the scene, Hulla grabbed Lisa and tied her up with rope and put tape over her mouth. Red approached, saying, 'Bitch, don't you ever try to blackmail me.' "

"Hulla then poured cement all over Lisa's legs. It took two days before someone found her. Lisa was so scared that she refused to tell the authorities who did that shit to her. All she said was that she accidentally fell in the cement."

"*What!* Red did that shit to Lisa? She can't even walk no more."

"That shit ain't all. Red poured gasoline in that nigga Stiny's brand-new Lexus 450 'cause he was kissing on another girl in the club when he was supposed to be with her. She watched that shit burn completely up as she smoked a cigarette, laughing.

"She got pissed at one of her girls, Candy, so she decided to use her real estate skills to sell that bitch's home while posing as her. That bitch came back from vacation to another family living in her home. Red kicked her ass and dared her to go to the authorities. Candy was homeless on the streets with only her luggage from her trip."

"Damn, that is dirty," Q said as he put his hand on his forehead. He dry-washed his face as if he couldn't believe what he was hearing.

"You hear about that shooting at her house?"

"Yeah."

"It was her friend Terry, coming after her man. Red blackmailed Terry, making her give her money in exchange for her not telling anyone that she was the one shooting. She even tried to get Terry's Escalade, but she wasn't giving that up."

"Fuck."

"Yeah, but that still ain't all. You better sit down for this one. You know that book, *Bitch Nigga, Snitch Nigga*?"

"Yeah."

"Well, that book was actually written by that nigga Bacon in the pen."

"Hell, no!" Q remembered reading the acknowledgments and thinking that they sounded like something a guy would write despite the name Lisa Lennox on the cover.

"Hell, yes. And yo' girl Red right in the middle of that shit, giving the book to the publisher and taking all the money."

"Why in the hell is she wrapped up with that nigga?"

" 'Cause the baby that she's carrying is his. They had sex when she came to visit him at jail. Right in the bathroom . . ."

As Foxy continued giving details, Q sat with his mouth wide open, not hearing anything else that she was saying. His face began to turn red. He got up and motioned good-bye, then turned to the door.

"Q, hon, what you doing? Sit down, calm down."

Q slammed the door as he walked out, breaking the glass. Foxy ran outside after him.

Q yelled out at the top of his lungs, "Another stanky bitch. She told me that the baby was mine!"

Foxy covered her mouth with her hands and looked on in dismay. Q ran off, kicking the grass as he stumbled across the yard.

CHAPTER 21

The Reason Why

Red's hemorrhaging had stopped. She was given a D & C and was out of danger, but for two days, she lay balled up in a catatonic knot. Red just couldn't get over how much Jerome still hated her and how her mother allowed him to beat her down.

As Red began to feel more and more pain associated with Jerome and her past, tears formed in her eyes. Depression made her experience something she had never felt before—vulnerability. For that moment in time, Red was not thinking about anything except her hurt. Her nurse, Karen, stepped back into the room just enough to see that Red was drowning in her tears.

"Sweetheart, is there anything I can do for you?" she asked softly.

Red looked up in surprise, not realizing that the nurse was in the room. Without words, Red looked down at the sheets.

"I'm here to listen, if you need to talk," Karen said, sitting on the edge of the bed.

Without hesitation Red looked up. "My reality stinks and every time I smell it I cringe."

The nurse gasped as she ran her hands through Red's hair.

"No, baby, no, you shouldn't feel that way about your life. It's never over until God says it's over. It'll get better."

"How? How in the hell can it get better when I was born to a father who never wanted me and a mother who stood by as her boyfriend raped me? I have a fucked-up, poor-ass life and a bunch of scandalous schemes that are unraveling right before my eyes!"

Tears began gushing out of her eyes like a faucet was turned on. Balls of hot air burned down her throat into her stomach area. Karen listened to her sobs. Finally, Red came back to herself, and revenge settled in her heart. She had to rebound from the pain and began to look at paying back all the muthafuckas that crossed her.

To her surprise, Red realized her feelings for Q were genuine. The truth was, Q had made a difference in her life. She had to scheme less and less; if she needed something, anything, Q knew it before she had to ask, even if it was something as simple as groceries.

Q understood that a bitch had to piss, shit and eat, whereas average niggas would eat your food and drive past grocery stores, not even offering you a can of juice. Most dudes thought Red already knew how to fend for herself, which made them do nothing for her.

Q had grown to know her and that was different altogether. He had the ability to see deep inside of Red. Q saw in the hard Red a young girl looking for love. There were times when Red was with him, trying to play hard to get, and she would succumb to the soft gentle kisses that he placed on her neck and her cheek. He knew that she just wanted to be loved.

Red finally pulled herself up out of her depression. She knew what she had to do and that was to go see Bacon as soon as she was discharged from the hospital. She would have Bacon carry out her plan of revenge on her stepfather. With some fresh bruises and a doctor's report, she was sure Bacon would plan to avenge his baby's premature death. Red even planned to wear her hospital bracelet for further emphasis.

When it was almost time for her to leave, Nurse Karen popped back into the room and gave Red a reassuring smile.

"Listen, sweetheart, here are three prescriptions. One is for an iron pill because you lost a lot of blood, one is for an antibiotic, to help prevent infection. If you take these properly you should be okay within the next couple of days," she said.

"Thank you," Red said.

"After speaking with you earlier I also suggested to the doctor that you take some Paxil for your depression."

Red sat straight up on her bed and said, "Hell, naw."

"I figured you would say that, but here is the prescription anyway, and I've also written down a list of therapists in your area. But if you ever need to talk, you know where I am."

Red unexpectedly smiled at the nurse's nice gesture. She knew that she may have needed someone to talk to, but she also knew that if she focused on the pain she wouldn't be able to carry out her plan.

Bacon was sure to deliver the blow of revenge. She was sure the ass-kicking she was seeking for Jerome would be forthcoming—hopefully, this would all transpire while her mother looked on. Red would never forget how her mother hadn't come to her aid when Jerome jumped on her.

In fact, Red wanted her mother to pay for all the years she allowed Jerome to do what he did. In her mind, Julia and Jerome were really one entity, joined at the hip, and both would pay in equal measures.

Red tapped her fingers nervously on the table, waiting for Bacon to arrive. It had been three days since her release from the hospital, yet she still wore the hospital band. She hadn't seen or heard from Q, which was fine since she didn't want any complications at this point.

Generally, on any day Red could go without makeup and still look good, yet today, she didn't look herself. When Bacon finally entered the room, he immediately noticed the bruises on her left cheek. Like a radar, his eyes zoomed onto her hospital band. Bacon took her to the side and began to ask questions.

"Ma, what's up?" Bacon asked, sounding concerned.

"Them muthafuckas jumped me," Red explained, wiping a tear from her eye.

"Who? What's the deal, yo?" Bacon asked.

"I was out, trying to hustle a bit on the east side near Gratiot Avenue, right?"

Bacon nodded, as if he were there.

"And this nigga named Jerome got jiggy wit' me 'cause I didn't want to holler back. Right?"

Bacon nodded again. "Right."

"So, I tried to walk away and he started getting fly."

"And?" Bacon quizzed.

"So when I walked to my car, his girl saw me and she started accusing me of trying to talk to her man, and it really was the other way around. Right?"

Bacon again nodded, and replied, "Right."

"So, the girl jumped me, but I got the best of her. So this nigga, Jerome, grabbed me. Right?"

Bacon again nodded. "Right."

"And he grabbed me from behind. His girl was sneaking me, slapping me in my face and shit. I mean this dude was big, I couldn't break free from him. And the next thing I knew"—Red placed her head on Bacon's shoulder—"the next thing I knew she kicked me in the stomach."

"What?" Bacon exclaimed.

"That's how I lost our baby."

Bacon looked at Red and shook his head back and forth in disbelief. He had thought things were looking up. Yet there was a part of Bacon that didn't believe her, and then there was the part of him that *wanted* to believe her.

Bacon had softened during his bid. He hadn't turned bitter; in fact, he wanted more out of life and he wanted out of jail. Bacon had hoped that his appeal would go through and he lived for the thought of coming home to his wifey, Red, raising his seed and starting all over again. This had given him something to look forward to. Unfortunately, knowing that Red was a free agent, he began to doubt his options, yet he had to concentrate on gaining his freedom.

Bacon was no slouch by far. So the muthafuckas who killed his child had to be handled. There were no ifs, ands or buts about it. He had to let Jerome know that he was still serious about his, even if he was behind bars.

"So whatchu gon' do to dat muthafucka?" Red asked, calling him on his rep.

"Don't worry. I got it. What's the address?"

"It's 5432 Sheridan." Red dropped her eyes, trying to look pitiful. "Ain't you gon' write it down?"

"Like I said, I got this."

Red looked up and she understood. Bacon needed neither pen nor pad. He had etched the address in his mind like the answer to one plus one. It was easy to recall.

Red felt relieved, as she knew vengeance was Bacon's and her score would soon be settled.

"Do you need a photo or anything?" Red asked, wanting to be certain her momma got hers as well.

"Nah, I'm good. You just take care of you."

Red rose to say her good-byes. She had turned his stash into hers, gotten the money for his book deal and had the house illegally titled into her name. She no longer needed Bacon for anything.

As she went out the front gate, Bacon watched her walk away. She looked as good going as she did coming. God had blessed the earth with her. Indeed she was fine. He had wanted to hit that juicy ass one more time in the bathroom, but how hard could he push a woman who had just lost a baby? He decided to pass and hoped the next time he hit Red, it would be in the privacy of his home.

CHAPTER 22

Don't Go

*T*erry was hitting a string of clubs to try and come up on the next man. Getting over Mekel was simply not easy and definitely not working. Terry went to every party, concert, cookout, church play and pool hall in town. You name it, she was there checking for the nigga who was poppin' bottles or pulling out a fat knot. She figured there was more than one way to catch a baller, and she was pulling out all the stops.

In the clubs, she made sure she wore the sleaziest and most revealing of clothes to bring attention her way. She would get pissy drunk and dance on the tabletops, hoping that the men would flock to her. Terry just wanted a man, and she reduced herself to shit to get one.

To most on the outside looking in, it appeared that Terry had much love for Red, but that simply wasn't the case. She was jealous of her friend. For one, Red always caught the big fish and Terry didn't understand why. Terry's hook was no longer sharp. What had happened to her appeal? She used to be second only to Red when it came to getting a man's attention, but nothing she did worked anymore.

In her journal, Terry chronicled her growing envy of Red. Before, she felt like she was her competition, but now Terry's low self-esteem made her feel like she was living in Red's shadow. Her liking for Red had long turned into hate. In fact, the only person she loved was Mekel. She wanted him. She needed him. He was the only thing that made her feel like she was worthy. In her mind he was the only one who loved her.

When he met her three years ago she was working part-time as a receptionist at a doctor's office, had just broken up with her last baby daddy and was struggling. With open arms, Mekel welcomed her into his life and promised to right all her wrongs. From the beginning he saw something special in her. Even Terry wasn't sure what he saw but she didn't argue.

What she loved the most about him was the way he adored her body. Sure, Terry looked stellar in her clothes, but underneath it all was a stomach marred with stretch marks, deflated breasts and dimpled thighs. Naked, she couldn't stand up to the light. These days niggas were big freaks—she had to undress in front of them. They wanted to see what they were running up in.

She couldn't forget how her body had been perfect to the love of her life, which endeared Mekel more and more to her. He was the one man that took her as she came. Mekel realized the true beauty of a woman was her inner beauty, and that was what had made their union special.

After finding someone in the club to go home with, Terry would get dressed right after the sex and leave with a couple hundred bucks. Hell, on the real, she had turned into a low-priced whore. The bubbly numbed the pain long enough to get through the deed, but once she came to, Terry realized that more than likely they would not call, and if they did, it would be for more sex, not a relationship.

Terry was in a deep depression. She had spent days holed up in the house, leaving her kids with her mother. Her mind and her house were a mess. Finally she decided to go for a spin in her car. As she drove down the windy road in the middle of the night, Terry cried profusely, blinded by her tears to the point where she could barely see the road. Without thinking, she began driving in the direction of Mekel's house.

Terry parked outside of Mekel's apartment. The familiar flicker of the television subtly shining through the blinds made her think of the times they lay together in each other's arms. Terry began to think about how she fucked up. Glancing out of the car window, she thought, *If only I hadn't blown the fuck up about Kera's child.*

She understood, too late, the worst thing that could have come of Mekel accepting his child was that he would have to support it and have occasional visits. At least they could have still been together. Now, looking back, Terry realized it really wasn't worth her losing Mekel over her insecurities. She had no idea how she could explain that to him now.

On one hand, Terry's sensible mind told her this was true. Yes, she'd played a part in their breakup, but boy, what control ego had over her emotions. Her ego would not allow her to admit any wrong on her part—*Mekel* was wrong to fuck Kera in the first damn place. Anger replaced her sensibleness, and she began to think of how she could manipulate him back into her graces.

Before she knew it, Terry was knocking on the apartment door. She was hoping and praying he was alone. After several minutes, Terry was going to knock again, then decided to turn and leave. As she was walking away, she heard a voice call to the back of her head.

"Terry?" Mekel wiped sleep from his eyes with his balled-up fist.

"Yeah, it's me," she said, turning to face him. This was the first time they were not screaming at each other, and his gentleness allowed her not to be on the defensive.

"What time is it?" Mekel yawned, looking back into his apartment as if he was searching for a clock of some sort for the time.

Terry glanced down at her Cartier watch; it read one o'clock. Fear struck her—she didn't have an explanation for being there so late. "It's . . . um, one o'clock, M," Terry said, dropping her eyes to the floor. She braced herself for the tongue-lashing, but instead, Mekel opened the door and let her in. Apparently, he had enough of dogging her.

"Terry, come in. It's late and it's cold." His tone was indifferent and offhand, but not brusque.

Terry couldn't believe her ears. Her M had come back to her, and it wasn't just a dream.

Once inside, Mekel went to his kitchen and offered her a drink. "Can I get you something? You okay?"

"Yeah, I was just . . . out driving. Clearing my head. Thinking of you." Terry edged in closer to Mekel.

"Well, you shouldn't be doing that. Think about you and them kids and get yourself together. Terry, I hate seeing you like this. You a shell of the woman I was once in love with."

What most men didn't understand about women was that the mere mention of the "L" word gave them hope. And in Terry's case the word did just that and healed her broken heart. And when a woman still believes her man loves her, then nothing but death could keep her from fighting for it.

Terry sat on the couch and realized for the first time that she was somewhere even Mekel swore she would never be—back in his fucking face, if you cared to quote him. As Mekel sipped on a freshly opened Heineken, Terry sat silently, listening to the TV in the background.

"Where your kids at?" Mekel asked.

"With my mom," Terry replied.

"Well, I got a long day ahead of me and I'm not gonna send you out in the street." Mekel walked into the bedroom, grabbed the extra pillow from his bed and tossed it to Terry.

"Hit the sack, buddy," Mekel replied as he locked the front door and headed back into his room. Terry was so happy to be back in Mekel's apartment that she kicked off her shoes and fell into the first restful sleep she'd had in a long, long time. The familiar scent of her former second home rested in her nostrils. Mekel's cologne lingered on the pillow and before she knew it, she was off into la-la-land, fast asleep.

• • •

When it rains, it pours, Red thought. She had decided to try to lay low after her visit to Bacon. Even the thought of saving the money on the now-unnecessary abortion couldn't be celebrated. The way her mother treated her continued to replay in her mind. There was something to be said about the bond between mother and child. Red's mother was one of the worst on the planet, yet Red still wanted to be loved by her. If Red couldn't get her love, then revenge was going to be her salvation.

Once her wounds began to heal, Red started to miss Q. All of a sudden, she realized she hadn't heard from him. She knew this wasn't like him. What was going on?

Red called Q several times, yet he wouldn't return her calls. Suddenly it dawned on her. She had to be careful, because for the first time in their relationship, she was losing control. She hated to admit it, but she was losing her influence over Q. She blamed it all on the miscarriage.

There was no other way, though. In one way, her miscarriage had worked out for the best. Bacon and Q were as opposite as they could be. Even with her Latino genes, she couldn't justify claiming Bacon's child as Q's. Bacon was a tall, dark-skinned, grimy nigga. His skin was ashy black and very smooth. He wore a goatee and had coarse hair that he trained to have waves. Q was a pretty nigga. He was a clean-cut guy with curly hair and dark brown eyes. Red knew deep down that her plan wasn't going to work. With her luck, the child would probably have come out looking just like Bacon's grimy ass.

Red couldn't think of a way to continue her relationship with Q. Of course, his deciding to be with her was a result of the pregnancy. Red had gotten what she wanted out of Q—some ends. Yet she found herself, in the end, wanting him. She wanted a normal relationship. Q made it all seem so unconditional. Red had sampled his generous love and wanted it to last. Could it be that she had fallen in love?

Again and again, she mulled over that question. She was trying to finish out her plot without getting too emotionally involved.

During her time in the cut, Red started a mental game to make sure she had all her ducks in a row. It was like she was playing chess and her opponents were Q, Bacon, Terry, her mom and Jerome.

Shit, she was the Queen. As time continued to pass, her plot became even more intricate. Everyone was about to get what was coming to them and the Queen was going to prevail in the end.

The sun shining through the window awoke her from her sleep. Terry didn't want the moment to end. Her ego began to talk to her.

Terry heard Mekel in the shower and decided to make her move. Removing everything except her shirt, Terry walked into the bathroom. As Mekel stepped from the shower, Terry, ass exposed, greeted him. Instead of handing him the towel that lay on top of the toilet she hugged him, drying his torso off with her shirt.

"Terry, look. This is not why I let you stay. Let's just keep it decent."

Although the words sounded like rejection, Terry knew just what he liked. And whether Mekel wanted to admit it or not, he liked how freaky Terry was.

In Mekel's mind, he planned to make a family with Kera. At least that was what his head told him. But when all his blood left his brain and went to his other head, well, the rest, as they say, is history.

The sight of Terry deep throating his dick in the mirror turned him on. It was better than watching a porn flick. Morning sex was something that men loved, and Terry knew this, particularly about Mekel. It was no secret that he started off his day by masturbating. He told himself it prevented prostate cancer. Whatever made him feel better.

Terry was a pro with her head game. Literally, she had the glide just right, the rhythm down pat and she made it all seem effortless. Terry knew when to go slow, speed up and take him to the climax.

Mekel wanted a woman in the daytime, but Terry was all the freak he needed at night. It had been several weeks since he had gotten his nut off, and he was horny as hell. During Kera's pregnancy, Mekel hadn't touched her. Before Terry knew anything, he was fucking her mouth like it was a pussy.

Mekel nutted in her mouth, pulling slightly back to continue nutting on the side of her face, all while he watched himself in the mirror. The shit turned him on. Mekel had never seen himself in action. He definitely didn't want to make a video, so the chance to see himself surrounded by mirrors did something to his self-esteem. He turned into stud man.

Mekel ripped Terry's shirt from her body and the passion electrified the room. Mekel bent Terry over the sink, facedown, and proceeded to bang her back out, looking for nut number two.

Mekel kept looking at himself and Terry's pussy felt real good to him. He didn't have a care in the world. He knew Terry couldn't get pregnant. He knew that Terry knew it was over, and he was with Kera. Plus, he knew that he could get away with fucking Terry however he wanted. Too much power wasn't always a good thing. As far as men were concerned, carefree sex was next to new pussy.

Collapsing on top of her, Mekel let out one final grunt, and then he stepped back into the shower. As he exited, Terry took a shower, wanting to clean up as well. As the water trickled down her body, she noticed her pussy was somewhat sore. *It was all worth it, though,* she thought. She smiled as she remembered the pleasure that Mekel was experiencing. She just knew that Kera couldn't do it like that.

As Mekel pulled his white knit sweater over his head, Terry appeared in his doorway wrapped in a towel. She didn't seem like she had anywhere to go anytime soon, so Mekel tried to politely move her along.

"Terry, shouldn't you be leaving to get your kids?"

She shook her head. "Nah, I'm straight. It's still early."

"Look, Terry. Let's not mistake a morning screw for a lifetime commitment. You already know why we won't work," Mekel continued as he patted cologne on the sides of his face and back of his neck.

Terry looked at Mekel and the room began to spin. No, he was not trying to wham-bam-thank-you-ma'am her here.

"What?" Terry screamed. She could feel herself losing control.

"Here we go," Mekel said, picking up his car keys. "You got three minutes to raise up. I ain't got time for this shit."

As tears began to fall, Terry *really* looked at Mekel. For the first time, she saw him for what he was—a nigga who took the pussy that was put in his face.

Mekel began to rush through the front room, grabbing Terry's items and nearly throwing them at her. He had seen so many of Terry's tears that the sight of them didn't faze him.

"Why? Why did you fuck me then, if you didn't want me?"

"Want you? Terry, please. You know the deal. I tried to be nice to yo' ass and this is the drama I get in return. You's a fuckin' drama queen and I don't need it. I damn sure don't need your pussy."

Mekel was hoping that the more he hurt Terry, the faster she would leave, and that this would be the last time. The pussy was good, but her emotions were weak, and he didn't need the drama. Especially with a new baby in the picture.

"How could you do this to me?" Terry pleaded. "You know that I love you."

"Love me? Love yourself and just leave me the fuck alone. I should have left your ass out in the cold. I should have known you wouldn't act right."

Tears streamed down Terry's face and her voice almost cracked. "Now this is my fault? My fault 'cause your bitch got a big belly and your dick got hard?"

Terry did not want to hear Mekel's answer. She could see by the cold look in his eye that it would not be of any benefit to her. He no longer seemed to have any guilt about getting Kera pregnant. In fact, he felt justified because of how Terry reacted.

"Get the fuck out!" Mekel yelled, looking at his watch.

"I'm not leaving until you talk to me."

Mekel slid his keys into the front pocket of his black slacks. He grabbed Terry by her wrist and held her clothing with his free hand. Next, he opened the front door and threw her clothes into the yard in front of the apartments. The morning dew was still on the blades of grass and the air was a tad bit chilly, but he didn't care. He wanted her out of his apartment and finally out of his life.

He grabbed her purse and threw it across the yard. He then continued to push her outside, wrapped only in a towel.

As he walked past her, Terry tried to attack him. Instead of landing a blow, she stumbled and fell. When she reached out both hands to catch her balance, the towel flew from around her torso, and she was exposed. For a moment, Terry simply sat there, crying, not believing she'd sunk so low. Once she saw Mekel climb into his car, Terry, too distraught to wrap the towel around her, ran to him. As she reached for the door handle to get him to stop and talk to her, Mekel put his car in reverse and glared again at Terry.

As he pulled off, Terry felt her nails breaking, so she let go of the door handle. In disgust, she sat on the damp grass, still naked as a jaybird, her buttocks stinging from the grass blades, sobbing.

Mekel looked back, shook his head and simply drove off.

CHAPTER 23

Game Over

$\mathcal{B}$acon picked up the receiver and, with some degree of nervousness, dialed. *What a muthafucka would give to be free,* he thought.

Bacon firmly believed in the adage "Never let your right hand know what your left hand is doing." Certainly, he couldn't depend on his niggas in the streets of Detroit to come through. He knew that in his home city, the streets weren't always loyal to a muthafucka in da game. Most of the time, it was when people were down that the streets kicked the hardest. Bacon had seen some of his closest confidants clamor for pieces of his fortune, and he was cool with this. What he had was a confidante he kept to himself. He gave her a call.

"Hello?" the woman answered.

"You have a collect call from a federal prison. Caller, please identify yourself after the tone . . . *Beep* . . . Bacon." The recording spoke into the voice machine.

"Yes." She spoke into the phone in a soft tenor voice.

"Foxy?" Bacon asked as his heart beat loudly.

"This is she," Foxy replied.

"Thank God you're home."

"What do I owe the pleasure—or displeasure—of this phone call?"

"Foxy, I need your help."

"So, how are you?" she asked.

"It's been rough," Bacon confessed. "Damn, sorry like hell I didn't listen to you, though. You know about my partner and everything."

"Bacon, no need to go into spilled milk, especially over this phone. How can Foxy help you?"

"Foxy, my girl done flipped on me, and she ain't been taking care of me like a nigga thought she would." Bacon paused for a reply, but Foxy didn't give him one. "And, well, I ain't got nobody looking out for me."

"Okay." Foxy continued to listen.

"I've been dealing with this lawyer. And, well, it's really too much to get into over the phone. Can you come visit me?"

"What?" Foxy asked. "Where you at?"

"I'm in the feds in Milan. It's about a three-hour drive for you. Right outside the D. Will you please come?"

"Bacon, you asking me to drive three hours, then counsel you. You taking up a day out of an old woman's life."

"How much?"

"Five thousand."

"Don't got it, but I can get it," Bacon promised.

"Your word is your bond. Let me get a pen to write down your information, and I'll be there in a week."

"Foxy, this is an emergency. I need to see you as soon as possible."

"Don't you need to put me on the list?"

"No. I can talk to my case manager and get an emergency visit. I just need your full name."

"Frank Burns. I'll be there tomorrow."

Bacon hung up the phone and commenced to dialing again.

"Triple Crown Publications. How can I help you?"

"You have a collect call from a federal prison."

"Yes, I'll accept the charges."

"Hello . . . Hello . . ." Bacon said into the receiver, relieved the call was accepted. "I need to speak to the owner or manager."

"This is Kammi. I'm the office manager. How can I help you?"

"I'm one of your authors, and I haven't been getting my money."

"Oh, okay. What's your name?"

"Bacon. I mean . . . well, the book is called *Bitch Nigga, Snitch Nigga*, and it's under the name Lisa Lennox."

"Oh, yes, our bestseller. Well, that book was written by a female, sir. Maybe you have it confused."

"Nah, bitch."

"What did you call me?"

"Excuse me. I'm just a little upset. I wrote that book, and my girl turned it in to you. She's been working with you."

"And she'll have to keep working with us. I'm looking into the file, and I don't see a Bacon or any other contact person listed. I'm sorry, but I can't discuss the book or anything with you."

"What? Wait, don't hang up. What you don't understand is that I wrote that book, and I'm not getting paid. I need to get my money sent directly to me."

"I'm sorry to hear you have issues, but we don't deviate from the contract. I'm afraid you'll have to talk to the person you were working with. It wasn't us."

"You mean to tell me you just gon' take my book and not pay me? Triple Crown done robbed me, right?"

"Sir, from the notes, the payments have been made to the author. I can't give you any other information."

"Can I get a copy of my contract?"

"Sorry. Privileged information."

"Sorry. Yeah, you is a sorry bitch, and when I get out—"

The Triple Crown office manager hung straight up on what she thought was a fool.

When he gets out . . . Kammi chuckled to herself. It was not uncommon for her to get collect calls; some of their authors were incarcerated. She did remember the terms of *Bitch Nigga* and the request by the submitter that an alias be used. Nevertheless, she definitely had nothing to do with that because TCP had handled business on their end. Her job required that she go by the folder.

She felt sorry for the guy and wondered if something shady was up, but she knew not to take it to her boss. If it didn't make dollars, it didn't make sense. Kammi stuffed the folder back into the file cabinet and proceeded to complete the daily tasks of her job.

Bacon was heated. He'd gotten nowhere with Triple Crown, and he knew that Red would lie if he asked her. He wanted to have her come for a visit so he could wring her neck. Clearly, he had gotten over her miscarriage. He decided that it was a good thing for him not to have a child with her trick ass. Bacon had one thing on his mind: getting free and seeking revenge on those who had done him wrong.

Three people—Red, the head of Triple Crown, and Jerome—had it coming, and he was going to get revenge or die trying.

Since the book's release, word was that there was a hit out on him. He knew he would soon have all of his answers.

Red's cell phone rang as she lay in bed, still trying to rest and get her health back together and get over the heartache at losing Q. There wasn't much that Red couldn't shake, but this love thing was hard.

Red looked at the ringing phone and the caller ID: it was Terry. *What this silly bitch want?* Red thought as she picked up the phone and answered. "Hello."

"Red?" Terry said, almost asking rather than knowing.

"Who else?" Red said smartly.

"I-I-I need you. I need someone to talk to."

"Look, Terry, what is the problem? Don't tell me it's Mekel and his shit."

"I love him, Red, and I need your advice on how to get him back."

"Shit, girl, I got man problems of my own. The one sure way for a man to come back is if he loves you." Red felt herself getting misty. She realized that she was talking more to herself than she was to Terry.

"I've tried everything."

"Yeah, I bet you have."

"Sex, lickin', the entire nine."

Red had thought of those options herself, but they were so temporary that they were hardly worth trying on someone she loved.

"Don't work in the long run. I mean, if you trying to get some short dough, some shoes or your hair done, then yeah, but if you trying to make a nigga love you, nah. Girl, take it from me, if he loves you, he'll come back. You don't have to trick him."

"What am I supposed to do?"

"Let go."

The phone went silent for a moment. Red knew her shit was fucked up, and there was so much of a web to untangle that it seemed impossible. Terry had had a chance with a man who did care and in his own way had loved her.

"Red, I love him. I can't let go."

"Terry, you have to. He got a family now, and it won't ever be the same. Not with that baby between y'all. That baby changed da game completely."

Terry let Red's words marinate and she knew it was the truth. That muthafuckin,' bastard-ass, stank-ass child did make it worse.

Red was getting soft, and the last thing she wanted was to bond with Terry and claim defeat.

"Look, Terry, I gotta run."

"Where you headed?"

"To Scott Memorial Hospital. Kera had her baby last night. Girl, just let it go. Mekel is a father now. They had a son."

Before Red could finish her sentence, she heard Terry bawling and wailing. Red simply hung up the phone and headed to the shower.

Terry adjusted a blond wig on her head just so, gazing into the mirror of a public restroom just three blocks from the hospital. She didn't think about a plan; she was running off desperate emotions.

When she arrived at the hospital, it was four o'clock in the afternoon.

She parked her truck a block away, hoping to avoid detection. As she sat in the truck, she focused on fucking Mekel up and leaving him in the ruin of her piss. She realized that she couldn't make a move until dark, so she paced outside, talking to herself to pass the time.

"That bastard. He fuckin' think he gon' play daddy. Shit, I'm gon' take everything he think he love, then cut his dick off so he can never fuck another bitch." For the next two hours, Terry continued to murmur obscenities about Mekel and the baby. By the time the sun went down, she was like a crazed animal.

Dazed, Terry walked up to the hospital and looked up at the front entrance as if she had forgotten why she was there. Passing through the lobby, she didn't bother to stop when the lollipop-sucking receptionist asked, "Can I help you?"

Terry stepped it up as the elevator doors almost shut in her face. Standing nervously in the rear, she spoke to the man closest to the buttons.

"The maternity ward, please."

The man obediently pushed the button marked "Maternity."

Terry walked to the nursery and joined the spectators. The newborns lay in glass bassinets in the front of the window. She found the bastard, wrapped in a blue blanket with a snug hospital cap on his head. His name tag identified him as Baby Simmons: eight pounds, two ounces. She noted how the baby's eyebrows crossed his forehead, making a fuzzy bridge over his nose in the exact same way Mekel's did. Terry was more upset than ever. There was definitely no chance that Kera had lied about the paternity.

Small beads of sweat formed on Terry's nose, and she felt tears glazing her eyes. As the reality of the child lay before her, it made her furious. Terry forgot all about being a mother herself. She saw the baby as nothing more than a mere obstacle to her road to happiness. She would be there with her man, living happily ever after, she reasoned, if it weren't for this child.

The kid has to go, she thought.

As visiting hours came to an end, and the hospital's hustle and bustle began to slow, Terry never took her eyes off the child. Her stare was so intense, an overweight grandmother asked her, "Honey, is anything wrong?"

"N-n-n-no," she lied. "Just looking at my nephew."

When another stranger noticed her and commented about her standing in front of the nursery for more than thirty minutes, Terry realized she had to hide before anyone else saw her. She didn't see Mekel, but she knew he was there, celebrating the birth of his first child. Terry stowed away in a nearby storage closet next to the nurses' station. Around seven o'clock, visiting hours ended and the nurses changed shifts. Inside the closet, Terry heard Mekel's and Red's voices floating from the hospital corridor. She had forgotten that Red was supposed to visit.

Shit, Terry thought, *that damn Red. What if she tells them I called her ranting and raving?*

Sure enough, as Mekel and Red walked down the hall, she heard Red telling Mekel to watch his back.

"Mekel, that damn Terry called me, and she was pissed."

"Red, you told her that the baby was bo—"

"Hell, yeah, nigga. I told her that y'all done had yo' baby, and I was coming to visit."

"Fuck, Red. You know she's a crazy bitch."

"Nigga, please. Just watch yo' fuckin' back."

Terry peeked out; as soon as she saw the nurse leaving the nursery and the new nurse checking the log, she swiftly made her move. She hurried out of the closet and into the nursery, lifted the baby and got away undetected. She laughed under her breath, trying to control her hysteria.

With the baby tucked under her arm, Terry picked up her pace as she made her way to the door marked "Exit."

She held Mekel's baby tightly to her bosom and tried to burst through a side door to make her escape. Without warning, blaring sirens suddenly went off, causing the child to cry and Terry to become more nervous. Sensing that she had been caught, she dropped the baby on the concrete floor and jetted for the adjoining stairs.

Fortunately, the hospital had installed alarms for this very type of situation. Lunatics tried to kidnap children every day, and at Scott Memorial, it wasn't happening. Security was on Terry before she reached the bottom step of the stairwell. Hidden cameras in the nursery had caught her running away with the infant. A silent alarm had alerted hospital staff even before she'd reached the side door.

The next thing Terry knew, she was under arrest for attempted kidnapping and was headed to jail.

CHAPTER 24

What If

With trembling fingers, Bacon dialed his lawyer's office to discuss his appeal. His heart pounded as the phone rang. Finally, when the receptionist on the other end of the line answered the phone and accepted his call, he blew a sigh of relief. Something in his gut told him he would soon be free—to handle his business in the streets and restore some order to his chaotic life.

He had to settle the shit that happened between Red and the bitches who killed his child. He also had to see what the fuck was up with his book and, more important, his money.

"Yes sir, Mr. Stein has been waiting for your call."

The receptionist actually sounded happy to hear from him. Bacon held the receiver, listening intently. He breathed deeply, keeping his anxiety to a minimum.

"Young man, I've been waiting for you to call." Stein cleared his throat before continuing. "I wanted to speak with you before I send you the paperwork."

"Yeah, what's good?" Bacon asked, trying to be nonchalant.

"Well, we've looked over the appeal and—oh, please hold for a moment."

Bacon began to get impatient as he leaned against the cold cement block wall, watching as the other inmates waiting for the phone grew annoyed.

"Sorry about that," Stein said, returning to the line as if he hadn't missed a beat. Although he was irritated, Bacon knew not to let his lawyer know.

"Cool. And what? Tell me something good."

"You're free," Stein said. "You won the appeal."

"When? What? When do I get out? My God. Man, thank you!" Bacon screamed, dropping the phone for a minute.

"I'm sending the release paperwork."

"Can you bring it to the jail? Please, man. I'll pay you whatever. I just got to get out of here."

"In that case, I can bring it tomorrow. With some signatures and processing you'll be out in a matter of days. Say, the end of the week."

"Thank you. Thank you."

"It wasn't so hard. The eyewitness was a flake, and well, they overturned your conviction. You're a free man."

"Well"—Bacon's excitement was quickly replaced with coldness—"hurry up and get yo' ass here. I better see you first thing in the morning."

Bacon couldn't believe his ears. It took him a minute to shake it off. Here he was, trying to put a hit on Red, when in a matter of days he could handle her himself. He slammed down the receiver and walked away from the phone, hoping, praying that Foxy came to visit. Now more than ever he needed a friend on the outside.

Pacing, Q knew what he had to do, and it had to be done clean. Breaking up was hard to do, and even more devastating when it was with someone he truly loved. Q had been holed up in his new loft, which he was supposed to be sharing with Red and their child, and the emptiness reminded him of how his heart ached. It pained him to think of Red, and as the days went by, he became mad as hell and even madder at himself for caring so much.

He knew he could recover from this bullshit, but he didn't know if he wanted to. During the last five days or so, he'd tried to make sense of it all. He tried to rationalize that he was really a true-blue nigga and the loss of his girl and the baby that wasn't really his had him fucked up.

Q knew that not to be totally true. He understood that a man loves the child through the mother. That was why when men didn't go near the child, most often it was based on the poor relationship that the male had with the female.

Even with the relief of not having a child to tie him to Red, he still felt connected to her. He began to think about the time when Red surprised him wearing a beautiful black lace dress with her back out as she walked down her long staircase. She'd pulled her hair into an updo with kiss curls hanging down and finished the outfit with a pair of strappy stilettos. She had flashed her bright smile, and his heart had immediately melted. He had extended his hand to her and grabbed her waist, gently kissing her on her forehead, telling her she looked gorgeous. They'd left the house to attend an R. Kelly concert.

After hearing so much about bumping and grinding, Q knew he was going to get some pussy that night. The thought of that night and how Red looked still made his dick hard. Could it be that he had, indeed, truly fallen in love with Red?

Mekel clutched Kera's hand as they watched baby Mekel through the glass of the nursery. The tiny tubes inserted in the baby's nose and the beep-beep of monitors was a sick sight to the first-time parents. They had no idea how their baby was doing. He lay still and lifeless, and Kera's knees began to buckle underneath her.

There was a fifty-fifty chance of the baby coming out of the coma induced by the fall. Even if he survived, the chance of brain damage was great.

"The good thing is that the baby was healthy and of good birth weight," the doctor said to them in the hallway.

Mekel tried his best to calm Kera and to keep himself from crying as well.

Red stood by in shock, more at the fact that Mekel really cared about his child and how he was all over Kera than at what Terry had done. Red watched as Mekel held Kera and kept her close to him. He even grasped her hands with his. He spoke sweet affirmations, giving them both something to hold on to.

Red tried her best to comfort them, but she was sinking into her own private depression. She had a good man but fucked it up. Her scheming went too far, her farce was uncovered too early and ultimately she had nothing to show for it.

Q wouldn't take Red's phone calls, and his silence was killing her. Calling to curse her out would have been better than saying nothing at all. That way she'd hear his voice and get a chance to say the three words to him that she had never said.

"I love you," Red said out loud to herself more than to anyone else.

When Red left the hospital, all she could think of was Q and how she wished she could turn back the hands of time. She would love Q with all her heart. She would trust him.

Then her mind turned to Bacon. She could no longer take satisfaction in knowing that he had no idea about Q or the money she had stolen from him. As far as she knew, he was falling into her plan and had no idea how much of a pawn he really was in Red's life game of chess.

Leaving through the hospital's front door, Red saw that the police still had Terry outside as a spectacle for all to see. She looked pitiful.

Dumb bitch, Red thought.

From the police car, Terry glanced over at Red and her face lit up with hope until Red met her eyes with a cold glare and turned away.

Without looking back, Red climbed into her car and headed east on I-94. The radio was turned to an old-school station and "Ooo Baby Baby" by Smokey Robinson & the Miracles played. As Smokey crooned the words, "I did you wrong," a tear streamed down her face.

She thought of the quote, *The saddest words of tongue and pen are the words, it might have been.*

As Terry was driven away, handcuffed in the back of the police car like a common criminal, she thought of the fate of her own children for the first time in days. *What will they do without me?* she thought. Terry buried her face in the vinyl seat and sobbed.

The two cops in the front seat just shook their heads. They had seen desperate people; every day, in fact. But baby thieves were the most pitiful.

In the backseat, Terry continued to cry. She couldn't stop. In her heart, she knew she had thrown her life away, all over a man.

Q showered and stepped into his Egyptian-cotton robe. The first thing he was going to do was sell the loft. After all the hustling he did to buy it, it was time to let it go. There was no longer a need for the place. Q passed the baby's room, and once again his heart ached, seeing how the nursery was all decked out. In his mind, he kept hearing words like *scandalous bitch* echo over and over. Once again he had gotten got by another trick-ass, triflin' ho.

At first Q wanted to make Red suffer for the rest of her life by taking away everything she thought she'd gained. He even considered ruining her name in the streets so no other muthafucka would go near her, yet he knew she wasn't worth it. With age came wisdom, and he wanted to get revenge on Red in a way that would last her a lifetime. He wasn't going to yell and scream or beat her ass. He simply planned to walk away.

Q had gotten out of da game with money to burn, thanks to the encouragement of a "wifey" and "family," and he planned to stay free.

At the same time, he knew there was no way he was going to escape the jaws of prison after all his years of hustling if he stayed in da game, and he wasn't going to turn around and go to jail for murdering or maiming a bitch. No, he was simply going to give her a playa's revenge.

No words, no drama. He was going to cut her off from what he knew to be her life supply. He was going to let her go. Just as the invention of the wheel changed the world, Q knew he had been the best thing in Red's life.

Q had come into Red's life to bless her. He knew she was foul, but he just never credited her with being triflin'.

Bacon watched as Foxy, dressed in a Gucci dress with matching shoes, settled in to visit him.

"What can I do for you? You got ten minutes. I hate this place." Foxy glanced over her shoulder.

"Foxy, can you keep a secret?" Bacon asked.

"A secret? Of course I can. You wanna tell me one?"

"I need somebody I can trust."

"Okay."

"I'm coming home earlier than everyone expects, and I need a place to crash. Can I stay with you?"

Foxy looked Bacon's buffed body up and down and smiled. "Of course, Daddy. When you coming?"

Foxy drove home, anticipating her next move to prepare for Bacon. As soon as she dropped her keys on the kitchen table, she reached for *Bitch Nigga, Snitch Nigga* and began to read where she'd left off. It was something about that book and Bacon coming home that left her feeling creepy.

Foxy felt like the only person who could have written it was Catfish or Bacon.

She was itching to talk to someone to see if anyone else knew how Bacon beat a murder rap and was coming home, but she didn't want to blow up her spot by spreading gossip. As tempting as it was, Foxy was going to keep Bacon's secret. Instead, she put on her pajamas, got into bed and read the rest of the book that just might have the answers she was searching for.

One week and a day after Foxy's visit, Bacon stepped up to her front door. She took him in and caught him up on all the latest street gossip. She mentioned every dirty little thing that Red was involved in except the baby. She also advised him on the street game and who was hot and who wasn't.

A week after that, Foxy put the moves on Bacon. She knew he was going crazy with no pussy, and Foxy was the closest thing to pussy he could get.

She put on some soft music and began by rubbing his shoulders to loosen him up. She then began gently trailing her tongue down his back to the crack of his ass. She licked his asshole, stroking it back and forth before moving her tongue toward his dick.

At first, she teased him, only stroking his head, then she began to swallow his dick like it was a lollipop. After several minutes of her giving him head, Bacon turned her over and fucked her in her ass with the speed and power of a jackhammer. His breath was heavy and constant, and Foxy was screaming like a cat. As they climaxed, Bacon's body shook like an earthquake, and he moaned before flopping on the bed.

Driving Foxy's Cutlass, Bacon pulled into the parking lot of Triple Crown Publications. The building was impressive. The outer walls were made of reflective glass, and it sat on thirty acres of land with a pond in the front, near the entrance. A lion sat on either side of the door and the letters "TCP" and three crowns gleamed at the top of the building.

Even though the building was nice, it was not as impressive as the checks Bacon was supposed to receive. Bacon thought of the office manager and her smart-ass comments. He thought of the owner and how she was never available to take his calls.

Stank-ass bitch.

He also thought of how millions had been made off his books while he sat rotting in a jail cell.

Stealthily, Bacon scaled the rear fire escape to the second floor window. Looking twice over his shoulder, he shattered the nearest window with the butt of his nine millimeter and tossed the Molotov cocktail he'd brought with him inside.

As soon as it hit the floor, the crude bomb exploded into flames. Bacon leaped down the fire escape and jumped back into his ride. As he drove off, the building erupted into flames.

On the nightly news, the reporter said, "The only thing left standing of the Triple Crown Publications office is the three-tiered crown on top of the building." The reporter pointed to the rubble; the crown now stood on top of a heap of ashes. Bacon had burned down TCP.

Tears streaming down her face, the owner, Jennifer Nicholas, stood in front of the camera, near the rubble. The reporter wondered who would do such a horrible thing to such a fantastic urban publishing house, and why.

Ms. Nicholas shook her head. "I have no idea. If anyone has any information, please call the police department."

Bacon stared at the TV screen, thinking, *They know why.*

CHAPTER 25

Amazing Grace

Mekel bowed his head and before he knew it he was praying. For the first time in his life, he took control as a man and went before God for his family. Squeezing Kera's limp hand, he pressed his forehead against the back of her hand. Although his lips hardly moved, he prayed out loud.

"Dear Lord, I know I haven't been much of a man, but you have blessed me with a son to rear into a man in this world. God, if you would please let my son live, I promise to serve You all the days of my life."

Kera raised Mekel's head to hers and they embraced. They held each other without speaking.

Soon after, the nurse came into the room, reminding Mekel that visiting hours were over. When Mekel left, Kera lay back on her upright hospital bed. In spite of the sedative, she couldn't sleep. Her thoughts wandered and took her to a point she didn't want to face. Why should she be worthy of God's forgiveness?

Kera had a lot of guilt from her past and couldn't believe that God would come through for her. The truth was she had little faith in a forgiving God. She believed more in a God of retribution and that she was being punished through her baby for her past sins.

She felt a mixture of anger and guilt for Terry. In the first place, Kera knew that Mekel was Terry's man. But looking back, she'd been on that cash chase and nothing mattered but her own desires. A string of all the men she'd lied to and tricked as well as all the conniving she had done through the years paraded across her conscience.

However, Kera thought of all the blessings and grace she had received with her baby—in spite of the way he was conceived. Kera felt tears splash down her face. Inwardly, she asked the Lord to forgive her for her sins.

She hoped that God gave her some credit for having her child instead of aborting it. A sense of peace washed over her. Perhaps there was redemption after all.

Feeling encouraged, Kera picked up the phone beside her bed and dialed Red's number. Something was on her mind and she had to get it off her chest. She hoped that if she told the truth, then God would honor her prayers and save her son.

"Hello?" Red's voice sounded as if she'd been in a deep sleep.

"Red, it's me, Kera," she whispered into the phone.

"Is everything okay?"

"Yeah, I-I just wanted to thank you for all that you did for me and my son. And well, Red, you've been so good to me that I felt, that . . . umm . . . I owed you an explanation."

"Explanation? For what? Kera, what are you talking about?" Red's antennae went up.

"When I first moved into your place, I didn't really think that you were my friend. And well, I didn't like you, Red. In fact, I hated you. I hated everything you had and I was jealous. One day I found a letter you had written to Bacon in your closet," Kera explained, getting teary.

"And, go ahead . . ." Red prodded. Red had more on her plate right now than she could say grace over. And every time she wanted to be on the up-and-up, the reality of shiesty muthafuckas in her face was the truth she lived with daily. It didn't pay to play fair, when no one else was.

"Well, I mailed the letter to Bacon with hopes of getting you in trouble. I'm just glad that nothing really bad happened. The reason why I'm telling you this is that I don't want to live like that anymore and I consider you one of my closest and dearest friends. So I just wanted to let you know that I did you wrong and I'm asking for your forgiveness. Red, will you, can you please forgive me?"

Kera began wiping the tears from her eyes. She'd never been more sincere in her life. She was prepared to move out or whatever. All she wanted was for her baby to live and be normal again.

Red, on the other hand, was heated. Sure, she was sorry about the baby. And she'd had her suspicions of Kera, but for girlfriend to confirm that her betrayal was a reality was just too much.

When she thought of the different paths Terry and Kera took, she realized that she might have sided with the wrong person. For all she knew Terry was the true friend and, through a twist of fate, she had gotten the hand that Kera deserved. At this point in her life when nothing was going right, Red didn't have room in her heart for understanding. *Hell no, I can't forgive you,* Red thought. Why should she get forgiveness when no one was giving her any understanding?

"Sure Kera, I forgive you. Now get some sleep." Red hung up the phone and stared at the ceiling.

Red rolled over to drift back to sleep, thinking of a way to repay Kera for her treacherous deed.

Meantime, Kera rolled over thanking God for His mercy and feeling so happy that Red had forgiven her. Perhaps God would answer her prayers after all.

After the initial high that torching Triple Crown brought, Bacon came down to reality and realized that he still didn't have the money from his book. Rumor had it that the owner had filed for more insurance money than the damages actually were worth. Instead of taking money from the company, Bacon had put money into its pocket.

There had to be a better way. Bacon was getting cabin fever. Foxy was doing all she could to make him feel at home, but it just wasn't happening. Bacon knew that sooner, rather than later, he had to leave the comforts of Foxy to get back out on the streets.

Absently, he shook his head. It's something when a man escapes the jaws of a bid. It made him think twice and then three times. Bacon was not nearly the hothead that he used to be. He was trying to be way smarter than who he was when he got caught up in the bullshit. Bacon knew damn well that Catfish was behind his demise, and that Catfish, who came in the place later, was the one kicked the gun near his feet after the murder. Bacon knew it wasn't much he could do to make Catfish's life worse. Even so, Bacon wanted that nigga to rot.

He kept thinking about Red and how she thought that she would get away with her shit. He just couldn't let that happen. Sure, he wanted to stay free, but he wanted revenge against Red equally, if not more. Could he rest free without revenge? He had tried and the answer was no. Bacon was willing to risk it all. Red's ass was grass and he was the lawn mower.

Later that afternoon, while Foxy relaxed to the soothing rhythm of a massage chair in the pedi spa, her cell phone vibrated in her lap. Careful not to smudge her freshly applied French manicure, Foxy answered.

"Hello?"

"Foxy. What's good?" Q asked.

"Q, it's good to hear your voice."

"Yeah, just checking on you," he said, knowing she would fill him on all the latest gossip before long. Q didn't need eyes in the back of his head, when he had Foxy's nose to the street.

"I'm good. How are you?" Foxy asked.

"I was gon' stop by to check you out."

"Umm . . . Q, I don't think that would be a good idea."

"Oh, it's like that. You got a man, now." Q's voice took on a playful note.

"Yeah, something like that."

"No problem. I don't want to fuck up your happy home. I'll get up with you later." Q cleared his throat and continued, "Hey, have you heard anything about Red? She still in the same place? I wonder what trick she got up her sleeve for the next nigga."

"I'd stay clear of her, Q. Between you and me, her man is home."

"Who, Bacon? That nigga got twenty years."

"No, he's home and he's looking for Red. I hate to know what he gon' do when he finds her."

Before Foxy could complete her sentence, Q hung up the phone in shock, anger and disbelief. One thing he knew about Foxy, she didn't lie. True enough, she couldn't hold water, but she'd add to a story before she took away from it. If Foxy said that Bacon was home, by some miracle, he was indeed home.

Kera rang the doorbell before inserting her key at Red's house, but before anyone could answer, she walked in, followed by Mekel, holding their bundle of joy, who had pulled through his medical crisis.

As they stepped into the room, they noticed movers packing boxes and dismantling the once plushed-out crib. Kera intently eyed the situation and thought, *I guess she couldn't forgive me.* Kera caught herself and turned her thoughts to the positive. God would handle the situation just as He had with her son. She put a smile on her face despite what she thought was going on.

"What's the deal?" Kera whispered to Mekel, looking around the room in dismay.

"Knowing Red, who knows?" Mekel stepped over a box.

Red came down the stairs to meet the couple and their baby. As soon as she laid eyes on Kera, suddenly the hostility she felt inside for the new mother's betrayal melted away. Kera walked up to Red first and embraced her friend.

For a moment Red hesitated, then hugged Kera back equally. Inside though, Red's emotions were mixed. For one, she felt so lonely without Q in her life. Lately, she'd wondered what all that scheming and conniving was for. Was it for the money that she had stashed? Because when it was all said and done, in the end, Red realized that success was nothing without someone to share it with. She wanted so badly to share it with Q. And, although she was happy for the new couple and their baby, she felt a little bit jealous. Who did she have in *her* corner? Plus, she'd lost her baby and now—in a way—she wished she hadn't.

Mekel followed Kera to her room and laid the baby in the bassinet to continue his restful sleep. Sitting on the edge of her bed, he patted the mattress, motioning for Kera to come beside him.

"Kera, it looks like Red is moving. What you gon' do?"

"I dunno," Kera replied, gazing around her room. Kera didn't have anywhere to go, and yet she didn't really care.

"Mekel, God miraculously saved our son. And, well . . . I'm just so happy that he's alive nothing really matters. I just want a place for me and my son."

"Our son," Mekel corrected her, taking her hand into his.

"Even if I have to go to the welfare department to find something, I will."

"No, I don't want you to do that."

"I gotta do something. Who knows what's on Red's mind? I can't depend on her anymore. Maybe it's time to move on." Kera looked around the room she had fixed up to be her baby's nursery.

"You can depend on me," Mekel said with all seriousness as he knelt before Kera.

Kera was speechless. For the first time in her life, she had more than she'd ever wanted. Mekel's eyes looked so sincere.

"I want to spend the rest of my life with you, Kera." Mekel took both her hands into his and she noticed that his were trembling.

Kera's eyes filled with tears.

"How . . . what? Why? Why are you saying this? Is it because of the baby? What about Terry?"

"No. First, understand it is because I find peace with you. When I prayed for our child, I prayed for you also. Next, Terry is history and if the police meant what they said, she will be gone for years."

"M, I know your history with Terry, but she still has to pay for what she did to my son."

"That is *our* son, and I agree; she has to pay for that shit."

"Really, I mean, I don't wish jail on nobody, but my . . . *our son* had nothing to do with that. He almost died."

"Enough said. I want you to be as happy as you have made me. Kera, you know we vibe. That's how we got here. And I was afraid of your peace. I love you and everything about you. It's time for me to be a man. I want my family."

Mekel took Kera in his arms and they embraced for what seemed like hours. Afterward, Mekel helped Kera pack her belongings and took his family home.

Q tossed *Bitch Nigga, Snitch Nigga* to the side of the bed. He folded his arms behind his head and stared at the ceiling. His thoughts roamed over and over to the final chapter of the book. He wanted to know who had murdered his uncle. He grabbed the book again, flipped to page 306 and read the passage aloud.

> *In the hood he was known as a stand-up nigga, but, in fact, he was a snitch bitch nigga. He had beady eyes that were unforgettable and resembled one of God's creatures. In the Bible, it said Jesus used this creature to feed a multitude of men. But in reality, there was no way God would use this creature, for it was the foulest in the land. It was a known scavenger. It would eat anything and live in the dirtiest conditions. It was even sacrilegious to Muslims to touch or eat. This Bitch Nigga, Snitch Nigga was named appropriately on the streets.*

210 Vickie M. Stringer

Q sat still for a moment as this information filtered into his psyche. "What Muslims won't touch or eat?" he mused. "This book was written about Catfish.

"Oh, my God. Catfish's girl, Sasha, is staying at Red's house—the house that Bacon bought her. Red's been living with the enemy. She's in danger!"

Sasha couldn't explain how or why she'd been thrown out of Red's crib. Sure, Red had asked her to move. She credited it to their heated argument and the obvious interest she'd shown in Blue. With the drag on the loan processing, Sasha just counted it as a loss. When the movers showed up, Sasha packed up, no questions asked.

Although Sasha would do anything for Catfish, he'd gone too far when he wanted her to kill Red. She just couldn't do it. Sasha knew that no one else knew about the hit but her and Catfish so she couldn't figure out why Red was putting her shit out. Moving in with Red to spy on her was Catfish's plan, but Sasha, as scandalous as she was, didn't have the heart to commit murder.

Sasha noticed that Red was packing her shit up also. *Shit, Red must be leaving this shit behind,* Sasha thought. Her mind began to race as she wondered again if Red had figured the shit out.

As Sasha packed her last suitcase, she peeked out of the curtain, waiting for her ride to pull up. Sasha didn't care about Catfish and his agenda with Bacon. The beef was all over the streets where Bacon was telling niggas from his bid that Catfish put the murder on him.

Sasha paced back and forth, and on the last spin, she peeked out and saw Blue's car outside. For a split second Sasha felt a hint of guilt. She had refused Catfish's latest collect calls, and had spent the remaining money. She plotted on moving on to the next opportunity; after all, it only knocks once.

Yeah, it was wrong to man share, but with the shortage of men, who gave a fuck? She picked up her bags and headed for the door. Sasha knew that if Red had found out her ass would be dead, so she looked forward to moving on and moving out. Blue had promised her a life in New York. She was gonna take it. Besides, Blue and Red were history.

When Sasha climbed into the car, Blue leaned over and kissed her on the cheek.

Finally someone to take care of me, Sasha thought as they drove off.

Blue had a different take: *If this bitch act a fool, she gon' get dropped off at the Brooklyn Bridge.*

CHAPTER 26

The Contract

Gloria Schottenstein hissed a sigh of impatience as she waited for Red to arrive at the closing for the home at 3124 Colonnade Drive in West Bloomfield. Red was due at nine o'clock, and here it was nine thirty. Annoyed, Gloria spun her pencil around and tapped it on the desk. Just when she was about to get up and pace the floor, the office door flung open and Red rushed in, out of breath.

"I'm sooooooo sorry that I'm late. The packing company ran late," Red apologized.

"No problem, Raven. Let's get started," Gloria said tightly.

Gloria and Red left the small, quaint Bloomfield office and headed toward the conference room. The buyer, NBA star Maurice Clarence, his lawyer, and the title agency representative, Kevin Perch, each greeted Red and Gloria with a smile as they entered the conference room. Everyone was prepared and finally present for the successful sale of Red's house. The documents were laid neatly in a pile, awaiting the buyer's signature. Red knew that she had to sell the house at that very moment. She couldn't afford for the process not to be completed. As many times as she had sold other people's homes, she knew she could sell the one she lived in with no problem.

"The property clearance is complete and all we need are a couple more signatures. Oh, you will love this home," Gloria assured the buyer, as she fumbled through the paperwork.

"Why are you selling it?" Maurice Clarence asked Red.

"Because I'm moving to a smaller place. But I'll need one week before you take possession. I still have last-minute items to remove from the house." Red shrugged as if it was no big deal.

As Perch looked over the papers, he noticed that a necessary signature in proxy to make the transaction complete was missing.

"There's a signature needed for one Isadore Jefferies," he advised.

Red and Gloria's eyes met. Red knew Bacon's signature was needed because he was the only one who signed for the house when he bought it. But she planned the closing specifically to occur at her office, by the title company of one of Gloria's oldest business partners. Certainly, if something were amiss—and it was—then Gloria would handle it.

Gloria gathered the papers in front of her and looked at Red again. She cleared her throat. "This is no problem. No problem at all. I have the permission of Mr. Isadore Jefferies—it's perfectly fine if Raven signs for him. They're considered common-law married, so it's no problem."

Perch sucked in his breath as though he were hesitating, and Red got a little nervous. Her palms began to sweat and her heart pounded so loudly she was afraid everyone in the room could hear it. She slowed the rhythm of her breathing in order to keep from showing her apprehension. If this didn't work, she would have to walk away empty-handed. All of her plans would go up in smoke.

"I'm not sure, Gloria," Perch said. "This is an expensive property and I would hate for there to be any problems."

Red watched Gloria raise an eyebrow, but her boss didn't say anything. Red turned her lips down and heaved a deep sigh, but threw her shoulders back as if she was sad at selling her home, yet resigned to doing so.

At that moment Gloria said just what Red knew she would.

"There is no problem. Raven works here and if there are any issues, I'll vouch for this process. Besides, I know them both."

After much confirmation the papers were signed and all the documents stamped. When the title agency issued her a check for $1.6 million, Red's head began to spin. She was so relieved. She shook hands with all parties and waited for them to leave.

After the closing, they both received their commission checks. Red nodded. "Thanks for everything. I'll miss you."

Red drove out of the parking lot and headed nowhere. As the wind blew lightly across her face, she thought of Q and how he'd once told her of a place he went to find refuge. Red went seeking that same solace.

St. Joseph's Cathedral sat off the intersection of Livernois Avenue and Green Acres. The church had been standing for more than one hundred years and was considered a landmark. Red parked the car and looked again at the envelope that contained her check. It was over, but why didn't it feel complete? It had all gone the way she planned. She was in the top position to walk away, yet still she felt incomplete.

The air turned slightly chilly; Red shivered and huddled in her jacket. Feeling a sense of surrender, Red entered the cathedral. In the atrium, she passed a basin of holy water on her left and dipped her fingers inside the bowl and anointed her forehead. She felt a sense of calm. She stepped inside the church and beheld the grandness of the entrance. The stained glass windows bounced a reflection of holiness off them.

The sound of her heels clicking on the marble floor echoed throughout the church. She was thankful to have the place to herself. When she reached the front pew, Red stepped inside the row and knelt. Folding her hands on her forehead, she found herself praying, not for anything in particular. Red prayed for what seemed like hours, when in actuality it was only several minutes.

Suddenly she felt a presence behind her. At first she dismissed it as another parishioner coming to pray, but the presence still lurked behind her—she could see the shadow on the floor in front of her. Red's heartbeat quickened. She turned to face whoever it was.

From a kneeling position the man seemed ten feet tall. Red stood slowly, believing this to be the end of her life. She was ready for the unexpected. The image before her had a hoodie covering his face.

The stranger lifted his hand to remove his hoodie and Red gasped and covered her mouth when she recognized Q.

She couldn't believe her eyes. Instinctively, she knew it was up to her to make the first move so she reached for Q's embrace. As her hazel eyes searched his face, looking for a response, he pulled her close to him. She could tell from his caress he'd missed her. There was no doubt.

Finally Red pulled away. "Q, how did you find me here?" she asked.

"I was on my way to the airport and—"

"Airport? For what?" she interrupted.

"I need to get away for a while. You know, get my shit together. Anyway, I saw your car outside and something made me curious as to why you were here. So, when I came inside, you were kneeling."

Red sat down on the wooden pew and Q sat beside her. Their voices echoed off the ceiling, so they whispered to each other.

"Q, please forgive me."

"Red, I tried, but I can't."

"So you came here to not forgive me? Look where we at, Q. You can forgive me. I'm here asking for God's forgiveness. Can't you give me yours?" Red tried to take his hand into hers, but Q pushed it away.

"Red, I just can't. You had no right to trick me like you did. That sh . . . stuff was foul."

"Q, you're right. I was foul, but I did what I thought I needed to do at the time."

"You didn't have to do that to me."

"I know." Red let her tears fall from her eyes.

"Red, there was no need for the b.s. I really cared for you and all you could think about was scheming."

"Q, you're right again. I didn't know any other way. I did what I thought I needed to do."

"What do you mean by that? Why are you repeating yourself?" Q mumbled as he heaved a deep sigh.

"Q, because my life was fucked. I went through hell living with my mother and her boyfriend. That nigga hurt me. All y'all niggas hurt me. I did what I thought I needed to do to protect myself. You have no idea what it's like, thinking you have no one to depend on."

"Yeah, I do. The streets do it to you all the time, but Red, I ain't the streets!"

"Do the streets let your mother's boyfriend fuck you and then have your mother tell you that you are lying? Do the streets allow your own mother to not even be there for you and to deny what is happening? I know I've done some crazy things, but hurt people hurt people."

Red attempted to wipe her tears but they flowed endlessly, staining her face.

Q had nothing to say. For the first time, he wanted to listen. The feelings of wanting to slap the shit out of her began to fade because he needed answers for himself. Q was wise enough to know that yelling and berating her wouldn't do him any good. The question for him was, did he fall in love with a scheming bitch or did he fall in love with what he saw in Red, a sophisticated survivor who had made bad choices?

As Red continued to pour out her past, Q placed his arm around her shoulders to comfort her until she stopped crying. Just because it was over didn't mean he couldn't be her friend. Q also worried about Bacon being free and didn't want to add another heavy burden to Red's pain. Q wanted to make sure that Red was out of town and safe before hearing about Bacon being out. He didn't want to alarm her and cause any delays.

"So, what are you gon' do?" Q asked.

"I'm moving. Just want to get out of here," Red replied.

"Okay, what about Sasha? She know you moving?"

"Sasha got put out a week ago."

To Q, Sasha being gone was a good thing—it meant Red was safe. He kept the conversation moving.

"Red, I know you got a stash. Ain't that what you girls do? Try to stack the next man's cash?"

"Yeah, Q, I got money."

"Well you need to take it and leave Detroit. Ain't nothing here for you."

"You here." Red's voice lifted in hope on the first word. She wanted to know if he still loved her.

"Yeah, but not for you," Q replied, hardening his heart, hurting internally. He wanted to take her back, but he knew she needed to leave town for her own safety. Q became afraid that if he showed any signs of affection that he would not be able to do what he needed to do, and that was let her go and convince her to leave.

"Q, I . . . I . . . I love you." She lowered her eyes.

"Red, you don't love me. You love what you thought I could give you. You love my money."

"Yeah I loved money, and I wanted what you have, but I got to know you and fell in love. I feel horrible about the way things went down. You have to believe me," Red pleaded.

"What I believe is that you played me like a mark and all for what? The love of money."

Q stood and began to walk away. Red reached for his arm, but he snatched it away, rushing out of the church. Red followed behind him, tears welling up in her eyes. She never would have believed that she would run after a man, but today she was. If she could, she would throw her arms around his feet and beg him not to leave. She wanted him to know that she was a changed woman.

"Q, wait. Please hear me out."

He stopped when they were in front of Red's car, holding up his palm in a halt sign. "Look, Red, it's too late for us. Just do you. I saw your car and I stopped to see you. I'm glad you leaving and like I know, you got enough money to bounce. So, just keep it moving."

Red looked into Q's eyes and saw that he meant what he said.

His jaw looked set, and his eyes were hard. She still decided to plead with him. "Q, the money is nothing to me."

"Tell that to someone who didn't experience you lying to them."

Red reached into her purse and pulled out the envelope with the $1.6 million check inside. She clutched it tightly, tears streaming down her face, then held it out toward Q.

"Q, I would trade all of this in for you. I realized it doesn't mean anything if I can't have you."

Red shoved the envelope into his hand. She didn't want the money without the man. She hit the lock on her car doors, jumped inside her ride and drove off before Q could protest. It was no use. She had lost Q and she had given him the check for the house. It didn't matter. She wanted the past to be just that—the past.

CHAPTER 27

The Big Payback

After mulling over his next move, Bacon decided it was time to go get what was rightfully his. He not only wanted the money that he'd stashed with Red before his incarceration, he wanted the money from the proceeds of his book sales.

As evening fell, Bacon paced back and forth, contemplating what he would say to Red. He was standing outside Foxy's door, on her stoop, wondering if it was safe to make a move. Finally he decided that it was time. Bacon put his hand on his waist, checking to make sure he had his gat.

He looked to his right and then his left. It felt reasonably safe, so he stepped into the chilly night air. *Time to pay the piper,* he thought. After a half hour wait, Bacon hopped the Number 2 bus headed out west. The bus was damn near vacant. Weekdays were always slow for this route. Besides, not many Detroiters ventured into West Bloomfield. Bacon sat at the rear of the bus and got comfortable for his forty-minute ride.

As he sat alone in the back, he began to think about going home. He was ready to move back into the home he busted his ass for. The home Red had inherited and then played foul. Just thinking of how that dirty bitch was resting her head in a house that he, himself, hadn't been able to rest in caused the heat in his nostrils to flare hotter.

Bacon rubbed his hands together. Yes, he planned to put Red's ass out and reclaim his kingdom. The King was home and he was ready to let everyone know it, especially her. Her night was going to be cold and dreary once the two of them finally came face to face. Bacon not only wanted to put her ass out, he wanted her to feel pain. He wanted retribution for Red and restoration for himself. Bacon felt that as smart as Red was, she had also become careless and stupid. She would never expect the justice system to work and for him to roll up at the crib unannounced. Living in the suburbs had given her a suburban mentality. Yes, she was slipping. She'd become careless.

Watching Red drive away, Q felt unnerved. For the longest, he stood there numbly, thinking, wondering, if he'd said all the right things. Had he done the right thing by not telling Red about Bacon being out? Q knew that Red's mind was a little off balance since the miscarriage and he couldn't judge her reaction. *Anyhow, women were always unpredictable,* he thought. Although he didn't want Red harmed, at the same time he didn't want to get twisted up in any of her bullshit, either.

For the first time, Q looked down at the wrinkled white envelope that Red had smashed into his hands. The return address on the envelope was for Schottenstein Realty. Because of the purchase of the loft, Q knew Red did business with them. *Hmmm.* He wondered what the envelope could contain.

He flipped the envelope over and, with his index finger, ripped the seal off. Inside there was a light blue-check, which was made payable to Raven Gomez for $1.6 million. The dollar amount wasn't so surprising, because large amounts of money were normal for street niggas like Q. What caught him off guard was that the check appeared to be legit. Street money with commas and legal money with commas were two different things. Legal zeros in your bank account were impressive. Q couldn't figure out why Red

had given him this check. He began to play the conversation between them over again.

"I would give all this up for you."

Red's words spun around and around in his head, just as
clearly as she had spoken them a few minutes ago. Q's ego celebrated, as he now felt redeemed, holding the check in his hand. Although it was addressed to Red, he knew with an endorsement in a
matter of days the check would be good and deposited into his ac-
count. All the money that she tricked out of him, she had just paid
him back with interest. He could cash the check, be through with
Red and be compensated for the past, all in one fell swoop. Q was
never the type of man to gain off a woman, but considering the cir-
cumstances, fair exchange wasn't robbery.

As she drove away, Red could barely see the street before her for
the blinding tears in her eyes. But like Morton salt, when it rained
it poured, and she flooded her face with salty-tasting tears. When
Red ran through the yellow light on Woodward Avenue, she didn't
give a fuck. Sure, she knew the cops laid low, waiting on a car to
speed by, but she didn't care.

She just wanted to get home as soon as possible, grab her bags
and bounce. She blanked her mind out as to the lost money. She
didn't want regret to sink in about giving the check to Q. If he
couldn't forgive her, perhaps the check would make up for the
grime she'd done against him. She had asked for forgiveness, told
the truth and offered him her heart. Yet it still wasn't good enough.
Oddly, though, she wasn't hurt by Q's rejection. She knew she had
hurt his pride. And if he was anything, Q was a proud black man
who didn't like to get played. Red knew that she'd played him and
she would have understood if he'd smacked the shit out of her
upon seeing her. The pain and agony of not being with him was
eroding her. She had hoped, like in a fairy tale, that he would be
her king and forgive her faults. Yet she knew that like in the past,
none of her childhood dreams ever came true. Red knew she had to
let him and all the other shit go.

Nevertheless, Red had found peace in her actions. She truly

meant it when she'd told Q she loved him. And, because love is what love does, and showing beats telling, Red had put her money where her mouth was. She'd given Q all that she had—and that was the money. Hell, if he really loved her, he would come back, one day.

Red raised her right hand to wipe her tears and lost control of her car, veering into the next lane, sideswiping a beige station wagon. The driver rolled down his window and cursed loudly, "You fuckin' bitch. Watch where you're going!"

The car slowed to pull over to talk to Red but instead of stopping, she ignored the driver and the collision, and kept driving. She sped up, pushing the car to seventy miles per hour as she headed toward her home. She didn't care who she harmed, even herself. For the first time in her life, she didn't care if she lived or died.

Catching the bus back to his crib was not a good feeling. Bacon shifted back and forth on the plastic blue seat. After all, he had left Puerto Rican Mami straight for years. Ruefully, Bacon shook his head, thinking about how slick Red tried to be even upon meeting him. It was always a game with her.

"Hunh," Bacon chuckled as the bus came to a stop. He couldn't help but smirk to himself because he knew that what goes around definitely comes around.

Finally Bacon hopped off the bus and jetted across the street. He turned left at the first block and walked toward the house.

His house was the third one from the corner. The carriage lights twinkled off the three-car garage. Bacon admired his home before he walked toward the back.

A neighbor's dog barked in the distance. Its small bark was hardly enough to alert anyone that someone was on the back patio of Red's house trying to get in.

Bacon immediately noticed that the French doors that once contained single panes of clear glass had been replaced with double-paned glass. For a moment he wondered what had happened. He stood on the patio, noticing the leaves, bugs and other debris floating in the kidney-shaped swimming pool. Just like a muthafucka who didn't buy it; Red was letting the place go down-hill. Bacon thought of his gardener, Julio, and how lovely he'd kept the grounds before Bacon had gone inside. All that would soon be back into effect.

Jiggling the knob, Bacon slipped into thinking of the new things he would do to the house. The door was locked; he walked to the service door of the garage and found it unlocked. Walking through the garage, he noticed that it was dark, but empty. His heart began to pound, but his familiarity with the house calmed him. Still, the uncertainty played mind games on him. Not know-ing what was about to go down, he wanted to be prepared for the worst. Bacon put one hand on his gat; with his other hand, he turned the knob to go inside the house.

As always, the door leading to the kitchen was open. Bacon walked into the home and heard the faint sounds of music. When he and Red lived together, they made it a habit of leaving the radio on. All of the lights were turned off except the basement lights. Not wanting anyone to know he was in the house, he relied on the moon's glow descending through the skylights in the great room.

Bacon paused. For a moment he stood frozen to the spot, try-ing to absorb what was going on. The room was completely filled with boxes, which were neatly labeled. The furniture was covered with white cloths, and it was apparent that someone was getting ready to move.

Finally he willed his feet to move. Nervously, his hand grabbed the banister leading upstairs. He began taking the steps two at a time. Bacon rushed to the master bedroom. The first place he looked was the walk-in closet. Empty! None of his Armani suits or athletic gear hung from the racks. All of his designer shirts and shoes were gone. Nothing was in the closet except for a few hang-ers that obviously got left behind.

Bacon then went over to the picture that hung next to the win-dow, removed it and uncovered his wall safe. He tried the combi-nation 24-36-12, hoping Red hadn't changed it. Bacon let out a sigh of relief when it clicked. Bacon then slowly opened the door to find that his guns—a .357 Magnum, a Glock nine and a small derringer—were still there.

He also discovered the Triple Crown Publications contract. The paperwork caught him by surprise. As he read over the details, he noticed that the name "Raven Gomez" was clearly signed all over the place. Bacon ruffled through some other papers but did not find the deed for the house. What he found was a statement reflecting a payment of $25,000.

"Dirty Red bitch!" he uttered.

He also noticed that his stash of money was half gone. Bacon didn't care about the missing money—he knew he could get that back. His focus now beamed in on "get back." He felt a cold fury burning inside of him. He was bent on revenge.

Clutching the Glock, Bacon slid it in his waistband, making his arsenal total two. He left the other guns inside the safe, closed it and returned the picture to the wall. Peeking out of the bedroom window, he noticed lights approaching the house. Bacon turned and ran downstairs. As he was moving through the house, he heard the garage door opening. Bacon looked around for cover, then slid behind the study door off the great room and waited.

Red pulled her dinged-up BMW into the garage. After sideswiping the station wagon, her BMW was in bad shape. Shit, she didn't care, though. She was just so relieved to be home that she grabbed the steering wheel, rested her head on it and heaved a deep sigh. At the thought of leaving her once-plush home, her eyes watered again. Soon it would all be over. She noticed that the basement light was on and started to shiver with panic.

After taking a deep breath she remembered that she had left it on while packing and became unruffled. She turned off the ignition, grabbed her purse and headed inside the house.

Red dropped her keys on the kitchen counter, turned on the lights and grabbed a glass from the cupboard to pour herself some orange juice. She had a splitting headache. Nervously, she began to flip through the kitchen's junk drawer in search of an aspirin. As Red looked around the house, a wave of nostalgia swept over her.

Perhaps it was these feelings that made her think there was a presence in the house. Feeling spooked, Red walked over to the nook in the great room and flipped on the lights there also. Still, the home felt dark and uneasy. *One more night and in the morning it's over,* she thought.

Although the radio was playing on low, the house had an eerie feel. Red looked around for the unexpected. It felt as though someone was there, but how could that be? She walked into the study and reached for the light.

Q didn't want to run behind Red like the bitch she'd treated him, yet he knew he should have at least told her of Bacon's release. When his emotions got the best of him, he didn't care what happened to Red. Her fate would be her own, he reasoned. Looking again at the check in his hand, Q's heart softened. On the other hand, when he was being the bigger person, he knew to play fair.

In the past, he'd always wanted a sign that Red cared and perhaps this was it. For her to let go of her almighty dollar was confirmation enough for his spirit. Q understood that when a man loves a woman, he will love anything that comes out of her body, whether it is his seed or the next man's. Q had had his doubts the first time Red said she was pregnant; that was the reason for the pregnancy test. Once he found out she really was pregnant, he still knew she wasn't one to be trusted. Eventually, though, after the baby was born, he would have demanded a paternity test. If Red would have turned things kosher, none of that would have come into play.

Q always knew he was playing with fire when it came to her. When he looked back on it, from day one, she was taboo. Yet, he wanted her and no one else. Red "did it" for him. Q took a long shot dating her. He was stubborn and thought that if Red realized that he was what she needed, then her sensibility would rule over her greed. Q didn't mind that she wanted the money. He had no problem providing her with the finer things in life. He wanted her to have it all, just not at his expense.

Something in his gut told Q that Red was finally telling him the truth when she said she was leaving. He wanted to let her go in the know, and not in the dark about what was going on. Q grabbed his keys, jumped in his truck and headed to West Bloomfield to warn Red that Bacon was home.

Just as Red reached over to flick the light on, she felt a grip on her upper arm, stronger than anything she'd ever felt. The force of the grip damn near broke her arm. At first, she thought it was someone breaking into her house. Startled, she let out a gasp. But when Red turned to meet the intruder, she felt as if she had seen a ghost.

"Oh, God!"

Bacon pushed all his strength into the grip on her forearm.

"B-B-B-Bacon . . ." Red managed to stutter.

"Who the fuck else?" Bacon yelled as Red dropped to her knees.

"Please . . . please don't hurt me," she begged.

"Bitch, you thought you would get away with your bullshit." Bacon continued to squeeze and Red tried to squirm from his grasp.

Red was on both knees and Bacon loved the sight of it.

"Here we are again," he mused. "Just like old times. Did you miss me, bitch?"

"Bacon, yes, I missed you." Red winced in pain and tried to talk between gasps.

This seemed to infuriate Bacon even more. He took his free hand and withdrew one of the guns in his waistband. In one swift motion, he smacked Red across her face with the butt, busting her nose wide open and sending her to the floor. He stood there, reveling in his power over her.

Red lay on the Berber carpet, unconscious. A dark pool of blood began to spread over the once champagne-colored carpet.

CHAPTER 28

Consequences

Q found it odd that all of the lights in the house seemed to be off. If Red had headed home as he assumed, then some signs of life would be visible. Could it be that he had missed her and it was too late to warn her or even say good-bye? A chill ran through him. Q thought, *Did she even come back here?* Something wasn't right.

Q reached over to the glove compartment. Opening it, his fingers searched behind some bills, feeling for his nine. It was there where he always kept it. He closed the compartment back, feeling assured that if he needed backup, he had some.

Bacon glared at Red's motionless body on the study floor. He felt no remorse. On the contrary, he felt quite vindicated. He just wished that it hadn't ended so quickly. He had envisioned more begging and groveling. But the ho went out like a light. All that bravado, but she was still a weak-ass female. As far as he was concerned, he hadn't even hit her that hard.

"Who's the tough-ass now?" Bacon whispered. As a parting gift, he undid his zipper, pulled out his dick and straddled Red. He gazed at her for a minute, and then aimed. Bacon's piss hit Red's chin so hard that speckles of the yellow urine splattered him.

"Shit!" he cursed, not wanting to get piss on himself. He emptied his bladder on the unconscious Red. Then, he carefully placed two fingers to the side of her wrist to feel for a pulse. She was still alive, yet not moving. Bacon stared at the bloodstain on the carpet and his mind began to cover his tracks. How could he get rid of the body? Bacon slipped the gun back into his waistband and then grabbed Red by the ankles, tugging to straighten her torso out. Next, he looked around the study for something to help him get rid of the body.

Bacon stepped out of the study into the great room. He walked over to the couch and nervously snatched the white sheet-like covering off the sectional. The fabric felt heavier than it looked. It would have to suffice. He moved quickly back to the study where he'd left her on the floor knocked out cold. Bacon knew he had to complete his task, but he didn't want to do it in his home. After all, he still planned to live there.

Bacon was free and wanted to stay that way. There was no way he was going to allow this bitch lying before him to spoil his freedom. This meant one thing and one thing only. She had to die and she had to be disposed of properly.

Q pulled into the driveway, looking for signs of life inside the home. There were none. Perhaps Red had fallen asleep.

Skipping over the porch's two steps, Q leaped up to the front door and peered inside before ringing the bell. As he peeked inside, he saw movement. As Q stared harder into the window, he saw a figure that looked like the shape of a man.

Suddenly Bacon felt eyes on his back, and when he turned around to where he felt the staring, he saw a man, hands squared around his eyes, looking inside. He knew he could not panic. It was simply a visitor for Red. He had to play it cool.

Q stepped back and rang the doorbell. If Red had a nigga at the crib, then so be the confrontation. Feeling more determined than ever, Q was not turning back.

Bacon waited before deciding if he would answer the door or ignore it. When Q rang the bell again, Bacon knew he couldn't ignore it. Sucking his teeth, Bacon looked down at Red's partially covered body. "Damn, who the fuck—"

In a flurry of motion, he fluffed out the sheet to completely conceal Red and the bloodstained carpet, and then wiped his sweaty hands on the sides of his jeans. Gaining his composure, he strolled toward the door.

Standing in the foyer, he yelled in a gruff voice, "Who is it?"

"Q. Is Red there?" Q's voice was firm, resolute.

Bacon paused for moment. He wanted to yell through the door, *NO!,* but he knew that wouldn't look right.

Bacon cracked the door open and both men stared at each other, eye to eye.

Who said that only women could smell another woman on her man? In a flash Bacon and Q had a perverse understanding; intuitively, they both knew that, at one time, they had both loved the same woman.

Bacon wanted to know who in the fuck was this pretty nigga calling on Red. At the same time, Q wanted to know who in the fuck was this average-looking nigga at Red's crib.

Unrelenting, Q stood confidently, waiting for a response. His confidence vexed Bacon, so he opened the door in defiance.

"She ain't here."

"You know when she coming back?" Q questioned.

"Nah, try back tomorrow," Bacon replied.

"Red asked me to meet her here," Q lied. He tried to see if he could hear any signs of Red in the background.

When Bacon didn't get the reply he expected, he slipped a bit and began to stammer his words. "D-d-don't know nothing about that. How you know Red?" Bacon's curiosity got the best of him.

Q then jumped on the defensive. He wanted to tell Bacon that Red was his woman and who the fuck was he to ask? Yet he played it cool. Looking past Bacon, and over his shoulder, Q noticed the house looked dark and in disarray.

"Red asked me to help her move," Q coolly replied. "What's up, dog? So you helping her move, too?" Q knew that he had to think quickly on his feet so he could try to figure out who this nigga was. Red never kept any photos of men in her house, but Q's gut told him that this was Bacon.

Q continued rambling, still not believing everything was as kosher as Bacon was trying to make it seem. "Was you sleep or something? I see you got the lights off like you headed to bed or something."

Feeling caught, Bacon cut on the foyer lights. This allowed Q to really see that the home was, in fact, packed up.

Q knew it was strange for the man not to open the door wider or at least invite him in. But, if Red wasn't home, then it all made sense for him not to invite Q in. Yet and still, for some reason, Q's stomach remained tied in knots. His gut never lied. Something was amiss.

He decided to try another tactic. "Okay, cuz, just let Red know that Q stopped by and that umm . . . I'll try back in an hour or so."

That bothered Bacon. He didn't want anyone coming back to his home. How could he get rid of the dude?

Closing the door, Bacon knew he had to get rid of Red's body— fast. He dashed back to the study and commenced to rolling Red up like a rug inside of the fabric.

As Q walked back to his Range Rover, his suspicions grew. Q knew that Red didn't have no other nigga and she was too professional to get a roughneck to help her move. Q backed out of the driveway slowly. He wanted Bacon to think he was leaving. He parked his car two homes down, and then doubled back through trees and bushes praying that he was undetected. He slid into the service door of the garage and noticed that Red's car was inside. He also observed the damage to the right side of the vehicle.

Q tiptoed stealthily through the garage and sidled to the door leading to the kitchen. He pressed his ear to the door and heard nothing. Just when he was about to give up, he heard what sounded like furniture being shoved and moved around. Even so, he doubted that to be true. From what he had surmised, Red's furniture was already packed up. The sound was getting closer, and Q knew he had to hide—and fast.

Meanwhile, as Bacon dragged Red's body toward the garage, he planned to stuff her inside her own car and discard her body by dropping it off the Belle Isle Bridge. He'd figure out what to do with her car later.

Bacon opened the door, walked over to Red's car and used the keys he'd found in her usual spot on the kitchen counter to open the BMW. Then he went back, lifted Red's body over his shoulder, carried her to the car and dumped her inside the trunk.

Q started to shake. As sure as he knew his own name, he knew that Red's body was inside the sheet. *This nigga killed Red!*

The thought upset him so much that his stomach began to grumble as though he was losing control of his bodily functions. Q clutched his stomach and passed a slight bit of gas. Sadness overwhelmed him and he felt like a failure for being too late to save Red. Now he felt even more responsible. He could have changed her fate. His sadness turned to anger, and his anger fueled his desire for revenge.

Before Bacon could close the trunk he sensed a presence. Q pounced and grabbed him from behind. Startled, Bacon reached for his gun. Moving swiftly, he fired three shots—*Boom! Boom! Boom!*—though he couldn't see who was on his back at this point. One shot hit the floor, one hit the wall and the third hit Red's car door.

The gunfire had startled Q, made him let Bacon go, but now he quickly jumped back on Bacon. Through the struggle, he held Bacon's arm and tried to get the gun away from his grip without getting shot in the process.

Q didn't know if he was beating him because of what he'd done to Red or if it was a territorial issue, that he had to say that Red was now his woman. He just knew he couldn't stop swinging even as he saw Bacon's blood gushing from his nose and mouth. He beat Bacon like he'd stolen something.

As the men tussled, Red's body began to react and squirm to the loud noises. She suddenly came to.

"Help, help," Red weakly cried out, startling both men.

Q heard the cries but he couldn't stop. Finally the tussling caused the gun to fall to the floor. Bacon reached for his second piece and Q wrestled it from him. As they fought, Red wiggled herself loose from the sheets and climbed out of the trunk.

For a moment the three of them stood in a Mexican standoff. Red was wiping blood from her face, Q was both startled and shocked to see Red alive and Bacon was pissed that his plan had been spoiled. Before anyone could speak, Q rushed Bacon with a football tackle, dazing him for a minute.

"Q, come with me!" Red screamed, pulling on his shoulder. She led Q to the garage door. "We got to get out of here. Bacon is trying to kill me," Red explained.

Breath ragged, Q grabbed Red by the hand and bolted through the yard, heading the two blocks to his Range Rover. Turning the key in the ignition, he pulled back in a fury and sped off.

Although dazed, Bacon was still functioning. He jumped in Red's car, determined to chase them. Bacon spotted Q's car and the chase began. Closing in, Bacon let off two more shots.

Red felt her damp T-shirt that was sticky against her breast. She lifted the shirt to her nose and got the whiff of an ammonia scent. "That motherfucker pissed on me! Where's your heat? I swear to God, I'm going to kill him."

"Not if I get to him first," Q said, reaching in his glove compartment for his cell and flooring the gas pedal at the same time.

As he held the steering wheel with one hand, Q made a phone call. He jumped on the Lodge Freeway and headed south. His Range Rover was no match for the smaller BMW.

"Where are we headed?"

"Don't worry. I got you," Q assured Red.

"I'm so sorry, I—I didn't mean to hurt you. I love you, Q."

"I know, that's why I'm here. It don't even matter."

As the couple talked, Q noticed in his rearview mirror that Bacon was gaining on them. In a swift move he changed lanes and was able to lose Bacon behind a large gas tanker truck.

The couple finally arrived at the Detroit Metro airport. Bacon followed closely, wiping his bloodied face with the sleeves of his T-shirt as he drove. Q pulled into the executive jet valet section in the rear of the airport, an area especially for private charted jets. The couple jumped out the car and ran inside.

Weaving methodically through the small crowd of VIP passengers waiting for their departure concierge, Q and Red stopped at the charter boarding area, Gate 28.

"Hello! Hello!" Q shouted, looking around.

The ticket agent appeared. She was a freckled-faced, carrot-topped young woman, who appeared to be in her early twenties.

"Mr. Carter, we've been waiting for you," she said in a bubbly tone as she looked at his boarding pass. "Do you have any luggage?"

"No, miss." He turned and looked over his left shoulder. "Can you please hurry?" He looked back at the agent, trying not to attract unnecessary attention.

"No rush. It's a private charter. We can't leave you. You're our special guest." Hesitating as she took a closer look at Red, she asked, "Is everything okay?"

"We just want to get away—fast," Q replied.

"Follow me," she said, smiling at the couple.

Looking over his right shoulder, Q saw a small commotion yards away. "Oh shit, that's that nigga," he said to himself. Red turned around and saw the same thing Q did: Bacon, walking swiftly toward them.

"Red! Red!" he yelled, drawing attention to himself.

Red clutched Q's hand and tried to look calm as they descended down the walkway to the plane, stepping quickly, not looking back. Once they were on board, the pilot introduced himself as Captain Stewart and reassured the couple they would have a pleasant flight.

Just as the jet taxied away, preparing for takeoff, Bacon arrived at the boarding gate where he had just seen Red and Q. His rage got the best of him and he grabbed the ticket agent by the neck and put his Glock to her dome. He held her face so close, her freckles almost jumped off her skin and onto his.

Bacon knew it wasn't over. Red and her nigga could run, but they couldn't hide. Not from him. Bacon was gon' get his revenge—come hell or high water.

"Bitch, where that plane going?"

"M-M-Mexico . . . Cozumel, Mexico."

Acknowledgments

First and always I'd like to acknowledge God and His mercy. Father, thank you for your favor, for to whom much is given much is required.

My mother, Star, you are my heart, always. Valen is a BIG BROTHER!!!!!!!!

My brother Michael Haggen, more than twenty years of friendship.

My godmother, Elder Vera Jackson, thank you for your prayers of protection and guidance. I'm coming to church this Sunday—promise.

To Malaika Adero, my editor, and the Simon & Schuster staff. Words can never express what a dream come true you are to me.

I've found solace in a close circle of authors whom I call friends. Tracy Brown, Danielle Santiago, Tu-Shonda Whitaker, Nancy Flowers, Victoria Christopher-Murray. Your ears and shoulders on this journey to the top of my game have meant more to me than you will ever know. One love.

To my firstborn, K'wan, they say a mother never has her favorites, but that's not always true.

To LL Cool J and his wife, Simone: you two are awesome and my brother and sister in Christ.

Brian Daugherty, aka B. You so true blue!

To the media: ABC News, *Adlib Magazine, BMR Magazine, Black Enterprise* magazine, *Black Issues Book Review, Blast Magazine, The Boston Globe, Call and Post, Can Cam* magazine, *The Columbus Dispatch, Columbus Monthly, Complex Magazine, Don Diva Magazine, Entrepreneur* magazine, *Essence* magazine, *King Magazine, Inc.* magazine, *Luire Magazine*, MTV, *Murder Dog* magazine, NBC4, *Newsweek* magazine, *Parle Magazine, Nylon* magazine, *The New York Times, Popeye Magazine*, Power 107.5, *Publishers Weekly, San Francisco Chronicle, Scwaii Magazine, Source* magazine, *Tokyo Headline, Vibe Magazine*, The Tom Joyner Morning Show, *The Washington Post, Woofin* magazine, *Woofin Girl* magazine, WOSU TV, UPN, *Upscale* magazine.

An extra extra extra extra special thanks to all of my readers, fans and supporters. Without you, Triple Crown Publications would not exist.

To my sweetheart, Steven, thank you for my precious gift.

About the Author

Vickie M. Stringer is the publisher of Triple Crown Publications, one of the most prominent African American book publishers in the country and abroad. She has been featured in magazines and newspapers such as *The New York Times, Newsweek, Essence,* and *Black Enterprise.* She lives in Columbus, Ohio, with her son and newborn baby.